Hard to Handle

Christine Warren

St. Martin's Paperbacks

This is a work of fiction. All of the characters, organizations, and events portrayed in this novel are either products of the author's imagination or are used fictitiously.

HARD TO HANDLE

Copyright © 2017 by Christine Warren.

For information address St. Martin's Press, 175 Fifth Avenue, New York, NY 10010.

ISBN: 978-1-250-07738-7

Our books may be purchased in bulk for promotional, educational, or business use. Please contact your local bookseller or the Macmillan Corporate and Premium Sales Department at 1-800-221-7945, ext. 5442, or by e-mail at MacmillanSpecialMarkets@macmillan.com.

Printed in the United States of America

St. Martin's Paperbacks edition / February 2017

St. Martin's Paperbacks are published by St. Martin's Press, 175 Fifth Avenue, New York, NY 10010.

10 9 8 7 6 5 4 3 2 1

Praise for the Gargoyle series by
New York Times bestselling author
CHRISTINE WARREN

Heart of Stone

"The opening of Warren's hot new paranormal series is a snarky, creative, and steamy success that delights new and longtime fans alike." —*RT Book Reviews* (4 stars)

"The sexual attraction . . . is palpable." —*Publishers Weekly*

"Steamy scenes, mixed with an intriguing story line and a hearty helping of snarky humor." —*Reader to Reader*

"Rousing . . . [an] engaging urban fantasy."
—*Midwest Book Review*

"Fast-paced with characters you'll love, and even some you'll love to hate, *Heart of Stone* is another winner for author Christine Warren!" —*Romance Reviews*

Stone Cold Lover

"Soars with fun, witty characters and nonstop action."
—*Publishers Weekly*

"Fascinating, complex, and so well crafted . . . perfect for keeping fans . . . coming back for more."
—*RT Book Reviews* (4 stars)

Hard as a Rock

"Fiery, fierce, and fun." —*Publishers Weekly*

"Smoldering-hot . . . the stakes are fatally high and the chemistry [is] simply blistering." —*RT Book Reviews*

Also by
Christine Warren

Hard as a Rock
Stone Cold Lover
Heart of Stone
Hungry Like a Wolf
Drive Me Wild
On the Prowl
Not Your Ordinary Faerie Tale
Black Magic Woman
Prince Charming Doesn't Live Here
Born to be Wild
Big Bad Wolf
You're So Vein
One Bite with a Stranger
Walk on the Wild Side
Howl at the Moon
The Demon You Know
She's No Faerie Princess
Wolf at the Door

Anthologies

Huntress
No Rest for the Witches

I saved the best for last.
To Josh. He won't ever read it,
but he's family, and family spreads the love.

(Don't worry, David.
Someone else has you on her dedication list.)

Chapter One

Michael Drummond was a man blessed with sisters, though there were times—much like the present—when he wished his parents had perhaps done a little less blessing and a little more sinning. Prophylactically speaking. But like the good Irish Catholics they were, Madelaine and Stephen Drummond had brought five healthy children into the world—four beautiful, independent girls and one sadly outnumbered boy, wedged smack into the middle and with no hope of escape.

What else but a sister could have Drum standing outside in the wet, unseasonable chill of a late September night with his arse turning to ice and his breath curling into a mist around his head, while all of respectable Dublin lay snug in their beds? Not a single damned thing, he acknowledged as he shoved his hands deeper into the pockets of his battered leather jacket. Nothing but a sister and the persistent tingling at the back of his neck that plagued him like an unreachable itch.

The tingling had started nearly six months ago, when the proposed peaceful events commemorating the one hundredth anniversary of the Easter Uprising had lurched off the charted course and into a chaotic nightmare of bomb shrapnel and bloodied faces. Terrorism, the government had called it, and Drum couldn't argue with the label, but he also couldn't shake the niggling certainty that the deadly attack had signaled something more.

Drum couldn't point to what he meant by that. Hell, he couldn't even wave a hand in any one, slightly indeterminate direction, but ever since the Easter riots, the air in his hometown of Dublin had felt different, sharper and thinner, like the edge of a knife poised forever at one's throat.

And imagine him spouting off such nonsense without so much as a speck of real, tangible evidence to point to and say, "Look. See how that's changed?" No, Drum had grown up differently enough to know better than that, as had the sister with a much better chance of seeing disaster looming than he did. Both of them knew better than to start shouting that the sky was falling before they had damned good evidence to back up their claims. Even the sentimentally superstitious Irish drew the line between intuition and insanity with a definite stroke of the pen. He kept his mouth shut.

He also kept up his guard, if for no better reason than to keep the dreams at bay. Ignoring his feelings had only led to fitful sleep and persistent visions of things he refused to name and would prefer not to remember. So, he took his precautions and couched them in terms of modern crime and the upswing in global terrorism. He made sure to impress on his family members that no one should take silly chances in today's world, and that family was meant to stick together and to watch each other's backs.

Which made it his own fault that the youngest of his sisters had brought him out into the unpleasant damp at such an hour. It went without saying that he'd have much preferred to be behind the bar at the Skin and Bones, his pub in the Liberties. But wandering through the streets on their own in the dark before midnight was among the things he had asked his sisters not to do, so begrudging one his company drew him a wee bit nearer the rocky shoals of hypocrisy than he liked. A year ago, he'd not have thought twice about such a schedule, but a lot had changed in Dublin town this year.

Maeve, the sister in question and the youngest of the pack of them, was late, however. As usual. She'd dragged him from the Bones less than an hour before closing, just when the Guinness flowed most freely and the music made even his toes tap behind the counter. Under circumstances like those, she might have at least put on a bit of a hurry.

But hurry wasn't in Maeve's nature, at least not in any way that had ever made sense to the rest of the world. Occasionally, she rushed here or there, most often trailing the scent of spilled, milky tea and dropping scraps of paper left and right behind her. Her goal at those times was always the book she suddenly needed but had abandoned hours earlier in the parlor, because she had relocated her scribbler's nest to the table near the kitchen, where the light was better. Or maybe it was the Internet on the computer she used no more than necessity demanded, and with the greatest reluctance, because electronic devices had never warmed to Maeve Drummond.

In either case, she would hurry for the precise amount of time needed to reach her destination, then she would burrow in like a dormouse and not stir again until the next urgent summons from a forgotten piece of knowledge only she seemed to care about. That was Maeve—twenty-four years old, doctoral candidate, and well on her way to the life of a professional academic.

This, at least, explained Drum's current odd surroundings. The Abbey of St. Ultan crouched in the shadows of Trinity College, half forgotten and sulking with it. Long abandoned by the full complement of monks, the few remaining buildings now housed a collection of ecclesiastical documents and works of art dating back past the medieval era and all the way into the heart of the Dark Ages. Scholars from the neighboring university regularly sent eager petitions to the few remaining brothers for access to the vast reserves of early printed books, illuminated manuscripts, and preserved letters and scrolls that traced their provenance back to the days of the Irish kingdoms. To Maeve, the place seemed to double for Neverland and Tír na nÓg in one shining package.

By contrast, the abbey always gave Drum the creeps. He never felt easy in the shadow of the hulking limestone buildings, the cold gray of the rock streaked with black stains he knew came from the damp Dublin weather and centuries of polluted air. But to him, they always looked like thick corruption oozing from the pores of the place. The ground beneath his feet felt a great deal less consecrated than he imagined the Church had intended. Of course, his teachers and others had always called him fanciful.

The truth was that fancy ran in his family. His grandmother had fancied away several cases of polio among family and friends well before a vaccine had been invented, and rumor had it that *her* grandmother had once fancied that the passengers aboard the unsinkable ship sailing from England to New York in 1912 might wish to get their affairs in order before the tide came in.

Drum couldn't swear to the truth of any of the family stories, but he knew for a fact that his elder sister Sorcha's poultices would cure an infection faster than any antibiotic she could prescribe, and that Maeve, for all her inattention to the world around her, always knew when the telephone was about to ring, as well as who would be on the other end of the call. She also knew when someone of her acquaintance was about to fall ill or be injured, which candidate would win an election, and who was about to have a baby of which sex, weighing how much, at which time, and on which day. It drove the family odds makers batty.

Drum had never caught so much as a glimpse of the future himself—thank heaven for small mercies—but if pressed, he would be forced to admit that he did see other things, find things. Occasionally.

At the moment, his eyes provided an adequate view of the abbey common, though the mist did obscure things at a certain distance. It wrapped around shrubs and statues, drifted among trees, and parted like whispers as Maeve's coltish figure appeared racing toward him full tilt.

Drum's mouth quirked up at the corner, and he parted his lips to tease her about imagining he had pages to wade through when a lamp from the nearby street sent a beam of light across her face. The bright glare of safety bulbs had faded by the time it cast Maeve's wide, doelike eyes and narrow pointed chin in stark relief against the clinging shadows, but it offered proof enough to show Drum that something was very, very wrong.

"Michael." The urgency in her voice rose above the clatter of sharp boot heels on the cobbled pathway and made his stomach twist hard and tight. "Hurry! We have to get away. Now."

She didn't even stop to greet him, just gripped the leather of his jacket above his elbow and spun him in the direction from which he'd come just a quarter of an hour earlier. Dragging him along like a plow behind a mule, she plunged off the path and into the shadows between the chapel and the misericord attached to the adjacent converted infirmary.

His toe caught in a rough patch of ground, and he stumbled before catching himself and hurrying after her. The blood in his veins seemed to burn with urgent energy, and the hairs at the back of his neck stood on end. He tried to reassure himself that his sister's ominous words and air of panic had just proven contagious, like a yawn, but the fist in his gut didn't ease.

"Mae, slow down," he said, pulling back against her grip. "Tell me what has you in such a state, love. What's going on?"

She shook her head, not bothering to look at him. "Just hurry. We need to get home. Something's going to happen."

His heart stumbled. "Happen to who?"

"Just *happen*, Michael. Hurry."

And so he hurried. Maeve was never wrong.

Drum let his sister lead him through the darkness beneath the chapel wall. It seemed to loom over them, canted off its foundation at a precarious angle. High above, the stone buttresses creaked like old wood, and the jeering, screaming faces of the grotesque statuary cackled down at them like fairy-tale witches.

Christ Jesus. Had he gone mad, or had tonight's beef pie contained quite another kind of mushroom altogether?

Maeve tugged harder on his hand, her much shorter legs covering the distance at a rate he had to strain to match. She ran as if the hounds themselves were chasing her, and though he couldn't see her face, he could feel the anxiety and fear billowing out of her like the steam from her breath hitting the cool air. He could almost see it, and that wasn't the sort of Sight Drum had been touched with.

"Come on, come on."

He recognized the sound of his sister's words gritted through clenched teeth, but he couldn't tell if she spoke to him or the universe at large. Maeve had never boasted much patience. She'd been the type of child who had to be reminded to let the beaters stop spinning before she stuck a finger in to scoop up the batter. It wouldn't surprise him to find her demanding that whatever she had foreseen hurry itself along and be over.

Based on her behavior and the near panic in which she had grabbed him and run, Drum on the other hand felt in no hurry at all. In fact, if the impending disaster wanted to cancel its Dublin tour date entirely, he'd not shed a tear. Maeve had begun to frighten him, and like many a man before him, when Drum got frightened, he got angry, as well.

Which meant that when the atmosphere lit up with a sudden crack of unseasonable lightning, he greeted the phenomenon with an angry shout of, "Oh, piss off!"

For better or for worse, the words were drowned out under an earsplitting crack of thunder.

Why did it feel as if the heavens had timed that specifically for him?

Drum might even have descended into melodrama and raised a shaking fist to the sky had his sister not chosen that very moment to dig her fingernails into the skin of his hand and jerk him forward. "Run!" she shouted, and hearing the terror and urgency in her voice, Drum pushed aside his own resentment and took off at a dash.

As it turned out, that first running step might have saved his life.

It was one of only three he managed, because just as he began to hit his stride, some unseen force grabbed hold of the earth's mantle and shook it like a rug on cleaning day. The ground heaved up beneath them and tossed them into the air, sending both brother and sister sprawling on their faces in the cold, wet grass. Drum had just enough time to lift his head and spit out a mouthful of soil when another crash sounded, one not at all like the sharp report of the thunderclap, barely feet away from where he had landed. On the spot where he had stood before Maeve had screamed.

Now, Drum screamed for himself.

In the retelling, he imagined he would change the scream to a hoarse, manly shout of surprise; but in the moment, the high pitch of his girlish exclamation sounded like a harmony to the unearthly shriek that shook the air around them. He half expected a *bean sidhe* to swoop down from the spire to warn them of impending death, but what he saw struck him as not half so plausible a thing.

Adrenaline picked him up like a kitten by the scruff, sending him scrambling away from that second crash in a move born of pure survival instinct. He rolled to his back and crawled across the grass like a crab, hands and feet slipping and sliding on the wet blades, wishing the continuing drizzle of misty rain would do him a mercy and obscure the sight before his eyes.

Where he had stood not a moment before, the earth gaped open in a ragged crater, clods of dark, peaty soil scattered about it like crumbs round a teacake. At least five feet wide and half as deep, the ugly gash appeared to spit out the cracked and broken remains of one of the elaborately carved statues that graced the chapel's ornate battlements.

Drum's eyes locked on the ruined hunks of stone in the same instant that another bolt of lightning sizzled through the darkness, the accompanying crash of thunder sounding almost simultaneously. The deep, echoing boom rattled the teeth in Drum's head and he winced, arms shooting up to clap over his ears as if he could protect himself from the deafening impact.

But he couldn't protect himself from the vision that appeared.

His eyes closed for an instant. He couldn't stop them, not when the lightning seemed to strike the ground just inches from his feet. Even through the shutter of his closed eyelids, the glare nearly blinded him. Perhaps it did blind him for a moment. Maybe permanently. For what else could explain the sight that greeted him when his lids lifted? Before him, the pile of stone split further and a creature from heaven or hell launched itself into the fraught night sky.

Drum had never seen anything like it. It screamed as it flew, not like a banshee but like a Valkyrie, a cry of rattling shields and bloody spears, of battle fever and furious determination. Its body arrowed through the air as if it chased the lightning back to its source. In that brief flash, its gray skin appeared silver, glistening with the rain and glowing in the blinding light. It reached its apex and spread a mantle of enormous feathered wings, casting Drum and Maeve in shadow. Then just as quickly as it had risen it dove, slicing through the atmosphere into a dense collection of shadows where the misericord backed up to the high wall of the cloister garden.

The thing let out a bloody roar, and a jagged circle of eerie red light the color of blood backlit by fire exploded. The dark light illuminated the winged creature as well as the inspiration for its battle cry—a human figure, hooded and robed all in black but for a strange sigil that marked the fabric like an insignia on the left breast.

Drum had the almost simultaneous thoughts that he should attempt to help his fellow man, and that he wanted to get no closer to the robed figure than he did to the one with the wings and tail. In fact, while the latter disturbed him because it should not have existed in his reality, the former literally made his skin crawl.

The man—well, he shouldn't assume, because it could be a woman, but it certainly looked human, at least—in black made Drum recoil on a purely visceral level. Sure, the robe thing pointed toward a certain eccentricity, but why should the simple sight of him make Drum want to take his sister and go somewhere very far away? He had no answer, but a little discomfort didn't mean he could allow himself to stand by and watch another human being be torn apart by a monster.

He had no weapon and no intention of sacrificing his own life for the sake of the stranger, but he could at least perhaps cause a distraction. Fumbling about the edge of the crater beside him, Drum closed his hand around a chunk of granite approximately the side of a cricket ball and hefted it in his right hand.

"Oi!" he shouted, following the salute with a raucous whistle. Then, not waiting to see if he'd caught either figure's attention, he hurled the stone at the monstrous creature's head.

Had Drum mentioned that he'd never played cricket? Or baseball? Or any other game except soccer, where a player never put a hand on the ball, let alone attempted to throw it with any accuracy?

The stone missed its mark entirely, instead impacting the cloister wall a good three feet behind the winged beast and even farther away from the man in the black robes. For that reason, he never expected the man to turn in his direction and send another one of those balls of red fire straight at his head.

With a shout of his own, Drum threw himself over his sister and rolled them both across the damaged earth. Maeve shouted a protest, but it cut off abruptly when the fireball hit the ground where she had lain a moment ago. For her, the close call must have come as a shock, but for Drum it was the second time tonight. Hell, it was the second time in a quarter hour!

And to think, he'd been trying to help the moldy wanker. People these days had no sense of gratitude. Perhaps this would be a good time to forget about the git and hurry their arses home?

Before Drum could collect himself to suggest as much

to his sister, the monster emitted another shrieking cry and slashed long, taloned fingers across Robe Fella's hooded face. The figure screamed and threw itself backward, raising its hands to unleash not a ball of fire, but a strike of lightning in that same disturbing shade of red.

The creature dove out of the way, and the bolt ripped past to crash into the damp earth just beyond. As it impacted, the earth shook almost as hard as it had just before the creature had appeared. A powerful beat of the thing's wings lifted it into the air high above the garden wall. Drum saw it gather itself, and the man in black must have noticed the same thing, because before the beast could strike, Robe Fella jumped up and fled through the shadows away from the abbey and out toward Dublin's rain-slicked streets.

The thunder and lightning cut off as if someone had thrown a switch, plunging the grounds into darkness. Somehow, even the lights of the nearby streets seemed shrouded, leaving Drum and Maeve helpless as newborn pups, before their eyes began to open. Drum could hear, though, and even in the blackness he heard the soft thud of feet hitting the ground and the rush of air as something moved quickly toward him.

"Who are you?" a voice demanded.

Drum was prepared for neither the question nor the sound. First, because he hadn't gotten a clear look at whatever it was soaring above his head in the white nimbus of the lightning strike and then attacking the hostile figure in the dark robes. The distance between him and his sister and the darkness had been illuminated only by occasional fireballs and lightning bolts, which hadn't provided for more than disturbing flashes caught on the fly (pardon the pun).

Secondly, Drum found himself momentarily taken aback by the question because, whatever it was that had spoken, it sounded almost like a woman. A very angry woman.

Instinctively, Drum pitched his own voice to the timbre he'd perfected over long years of living with five independent-minded females—calming without being patronizing. "Michael Drummond. And that's my sister. We're no threat to you."

The voice scoffed. "As if a human man hurling rocks and a trembling girl could threaten a Guardian. Are you *nocturnis*?"

Drum shook his head, blinking as the world slowly came back into focus. It took his eyes precious seconds to adjust to the dimness after the abrupt changes in light, but soon he found himself staring into the most unusual face he'd ever seen. A face whose curled lip and glinting fang demanded an immediate answer.

Too bad the only answer he had to offer was more like a question of its own. "I'm sorry, what?"

The face tightened, as did the fist he noticed had grasped the front of his shirt to hold him in place.

Drum was well accustomed to the nuances in the expression of an angry woman, but the creature standing before him appeared to be something else entirely. Female, he guessed, was a better word than woman, because the entity confronting him was unmistakably a she and even more unmistakably not human.

She possessed skin the color of freshly hewn limestone, first off, the pale, almost iridescent gray a common sight scattered across Ireland's green fields. That was his first clue, although he would have wagered his last euro that if he'd dared a touch, the texture would have felt silky and supple beneath his fingers. The bared fangs still in evidence discouraged such investigatory tactics.

The fangs sat firmly in the nonhuman column as well, as did the rest of her facial features. Though they were clear and angular as if sculpted by a master hand, there was something otherworldly in their shape—the cheek-bones angled a touch too sharply, the eyes a little too long. The bridge of her nose appeared somewhat flattened and her brow sliced like a knife edge above eyes so dark that no pupil showed in the blackness, but red flames seemed to flicker in the depths.

His scrutiny met with an impatient motion, and he found himself rattled by the single-handed grip she held on his shirtfront. At six feet, three inches tall and a whisker under two hundred pounds, it took some force to shake Michael Drummond, yet this female managed it one handed and as casually as lifting a teapot.

She accompanied the jouncing with a hiss that made him think perhaps he'd missed a bit of something important while he stared. His mother would be appalled by his lack of manners.

"I asked if you ally with the Order, human?" the creature repeated. "I would find it odd indeed if one loyal to the Guild chose to cast a weapon at one of the warriors they are meant to serve."

Drum shook his head. "I'm sorry, but I've no idea what you're on about. What Guild? And you're right that I'm human, but I've yet to fathom what exactly that makes you."

Somewhere behind him, Maeve let out a small squeak. He'd have called the sound a whimper, but the last time he'd done, she'd ground the heel of her shoe into his foot so hard he'd limped for three days.

Reminded of her presence, he pushed down the fascination that welled at the appearance of the female creature before him and concentrated on more important matters.

"Actually, never mind that Guild nonsense," he said, injecting some steel into his tone. "The more important question is whether you intend to harm my sister or me."

The creature made a noise like a growl and released her grip on his shirt. The unexpected move kicked at his balance, and Drum found himself bouncing onto his arse like an idiot.

"I do not harm humans. The Order and the Darkness are my enemies, not you." Rising to her feet, the gray female turned her gaze to Maeve and changed her question. "If you are not members of the Guild, then I fear things are worse than I first imagined. Some ill plan is afoot. We should all be away from here."

Another squeak came from Maeve, this one tinged with agreement, but Drum preferred not to be hasty. Actually, after getting a full picture of the strange female entity scowling down at him, he definitely felt like taking his time.

She was magnificent.

Human or not, the gray female looked like a figure straight out of his fantasies. Built like an Amazon warrior, she not only matched his height, she probably had him beat by a good two or three inches, and every single one she sported was curved in just the way to make a man's breath stick in his throat.

Drum knew that for certain, not only because of his sudden difficulty with the mundane chore of inhaling and exhaling, but because he had the privilege of seeing so much of her. Wearing only a tunic-style dress that bared both her arms and her left shoulder, and that ended halfway down the strongest, lushest, most spectacular thighs Drum had ever seen, the female appeared unconcerned with either her skimpy outfit or the chill of the night air. Rather, her attention seemed focused inward, her gaze unfocused, the tips of her wings fluttering as she stood almost as still as the Gothic Statue she resembled.

Those wings fascinated him. Huge and powerful, they must easily have spanned twelve feet or more when unfurled, but now they rested tucked against the female's back. Even so, the tips almost brushed the ground beside the end of her thick, tapering tail, and the first joints extended above her head, giving the impression of horns in the poor light. Drum could see the silhouette of feathers at the edges, but the shape appeared more batlike than avian. It made for a compelling hybrid that defied both rule and expectation.

It also made clear what she was.

Gargoyle.

Setting aside the impossibility of such a creature coming to life and wandering through the world of men, he could find no other explanation. The features, the wings, the thousand shades of gray that colored her skin and hair and clothing—it all had only one logical (highly *illogical*) explanation.

Then, of course, there were the more subtle details. She had fangs, for one—long, sharp, menacing teeth clearly made to pierce and tear into flesh. Likewise, her strong, slender fingers boasted a set of lethal-looking claws that Drum felt certain would have had no trouble reaching through his shirt and even his chest plate to rip his still-beating heart right out of his chest.

Dizziness blurred his vision for a minute while that image flashed and faded from his mind. He sent up a quick prayer of thanks he hadn't entertained the thought while she still had hold of him. He might have soiled himself, or at the very least, whimpered and cried like a little girl. Very bad for his image.

He tried distracting himself by focusing away from her hands and onto her legs—hardly a chore, given their truly spectacular appearance—but that led his gaze down to her feet, which had talons of their own. Front and back, and given the raptorlike shape of them, clearly adapted to perching high atop narrow building ledges.

Like a gargoyle.

Just what in the name of heaven itself was going on here?

Before he could voice the question, or a more diplomatic version of it, the ground beneath him heaved again. At least this time he was already down on his arse and hadn't anywhere to fall, but the sensation of solid earth rolling like the waves on the Irish Sea still sent his stomach churning. Drum considered himself a good enough sailor, never plagued by seasickness, but when the ground moved like water, human instinct rebelled against the wrongness of it.

A low rumble, similar to the earlier thunder, but deeper and more menacing, accompanied the motion. Above the noise, he could hear the gargoyle snarling and his sister crying out. Cursing under his breath at having forgotten her in his fascination with the mythical creature who sprang to life before them, Drum headed toward Maeve. He abandoned the idea of walking almost before it registered. No way could he stand with the ground bucking like an unbroken horse under his feet, so he crawled, ignoring the wet grass and mud that quickly coated his palms and trouser legs.

"Easy, Mae," he soothed, hauling her into a hug as soon as he got close enough. "It's just an earthquake. It'll be over soon."

She clung to him tight as a baby monkey. "This is Ireland. We don't have earthquakes."

Drum knew that, but what other explanation was there? The earth still quaked beneath them; therefore . . . earthquake. "Of course we do. They're simply small ones that we don't often feel. I'm certain we were due for a good rattle like this sooner or later."

"The female is correct. This is no earthquake." The gargoyle's eyes flashed with orange fire as she spoke. "Something unnatural causes this movement of earth, something beyond the power of a single agent of the Order. I can feel the magic behind it."

"Magic?"

If Drum had intended to keep the scoffing disbelief from his voice, he failed, with a show of fireworks. Sort of like the one the hooded figure had put on a short time ago. The expression on the creature's face told him that. "You saw the *nocturni* cast spells before your very eyes. You look at me right now, and yet you doubt the existence of magic, human?"

Well. She perhaps had a point.

Maeve saved him from tripping over his tongue-tied justifications. "This isn't natural, Michael. You know that. I know you do. You're not half so blind as you like to pretend."

His mouth tightened. Now was not the time to get into his female family members' favorite topic of dinner conversation—why Drum fought so hard against the set of talents that ran so strong within his family line. He had other worries more pressing, like speaking to the living statue in front of him and getting himself and his baby sister somewhere safer than the shadow of several thousand tons of potentially falling stone.

"At the moment," he answered, "I'm less concerned with what's causing it and more worried about surviving it. "

Even as he said the words, the quaking stopped, the ground going still, though Drum swore he continued to feel his bones rattling. He might even have let out a sigh of relief—a discreet one—if someone hadn't marred the moment with a wide-eyed, cryptic, and unsteady whisper.

"It's not over."

Drum glanced into his sister's blue eyes and winced. He hated it when she was right.

Chapter Two

Ash awoke in a rush of fury and confusion. Before now, her world had consisted of nothing—the literal blank of the universal nothing—for all of eternity; then, in one instant, existence had manifested itself in her being. She went from floating in the ether, just one speck among all the particles of the Light, to a fully formed individual entity in the space of one cosmic snap.

A little warning would have been nice.

She leaped into the sky because she was born to it, from it, and the rush of air against her skin helped to clear the cobwebs of nonbeing from her mind. Instinct kept her wings beating as knowledge flooded in to fill the empty space—knowledge of what she was, why she had been summoned, who her enemy was, and how she and her brothers would battle against it.

All of that came to her in a heady jolt, as if carried on the bolt of lightning that ripped through the darkness. She learned the entire history of her race in the space of a human heartbeat, and in it she saw that she stood alone.

There had never been a Guardian like her. She was the first of her kind, fierce and skilled as any other, but different in a fundamental and earth-shattering way. Because she was she.

Female.

Guardians always answered the summons as male. Ash knew it. She saw the parade of them in her mind, from the very first of her brethren to ever take wing to the ones that instinct told her walked this earth at this very moment. She saw the scope of their lineage, the story of their battles won and enemies vanquished, and she knew that her very existence had set into motion a chain of events that would alter the fabric of reality.

That was a lot to take in during one's first three seconds of consciousness. Enough to make a girl cranky. Luckily for her, fate provided an immediate outlet for her temper.

As she looked down, her keen eyesight cut through the shadows as easily as a human could see on an overcast day at noon. Hiding in the blackness at the base of a building wall, Ash spotted one of her sworn enemies—a *nocturni*—pouring his unnatural energy into the earth at his feet.

She dove straight for him, her wings swept aside and her talons outstretched like an eagle hunting a hare. Instinct must have alerted the minion of Darkness to her approach, because he spun out of reach an instant before she dug her long, curved claws into his face. She would dearly have loved to blind the evil magic user with her first strike, but it mattered not. She outclassed a single *nocturni* in combat enough to make the match almost laughable; she could afford to be patient.

The minion reacted predictably, gathering his unholy power into a ball of flaming energy and sending it shooting toward her. The sick crimson of his magic illuminated the night for an instant, which was apparently enough to allow someone else to spot them.

Ash heard someone shout from several yards away, out in the open area between the nearby buildings. An instant later, a chunk of rock came sailing through the air to shatter against the wall several feet behind where she had landed. Had it been meant for her or the *nocturni*? Either way, whoever had thrown in possessed spectacularly bad aim.

The unexpected interruption did nothing to distract Ash from her duty. She gathered herself for another attack only to witness her enemy shift his focus away from her. He gathered another ball of fire magic and cast it in the direction of the interrupting bystander. She saw it shoot toward two human figures already half lying on the wet ground, but luckily at least one of them managed to move fast enough to get them both out of harm's way. The larger human threw itself atop the other and spun them both to the right, rolling out of the way just in time for the missile to hit the earth instead of living flesh.

Furious that the vile demon worshipper would dare to attack humans in the presence of a Guardian—in *her* presence—Ash screeched and lashed out, curling her fingers into claws and slashing across the *nocturni*'s face with her deadly sharp talons. The figure jerked back and threw up a hasty counterattack in the form of a bolt of tainted electricity, like rusty red lightning. He intended it for her, Ash knew, but she leaped out of the way, and the minion was already losing his balance. The combination threw off his aim, and instead of striking her, the energy arced past above her head before crashing down into the earth.

As the magic impacted the soil, Ash felt the ground lurch beneath her feet. The very fabric of dirt and stone protested the contamination of the *nocturni*'s dark magic. It wanted him around no more than she did.

She launched herself into the air, intending to make another attack from above, but perhaps the dark mage got the message from the wounded earth. He bolted toward a nearby street, disappearing behind some sort of magical veil before she could change her direction to follow.

Cursing, she regathered her energy and turned to assess whether the human figures who remained would prove to be enemies or allies. Or perhaps no more than innocent bystanders. Who liked to throw stones.

By the time she settled her feet on the ground and half furled her wings against her back, puzzlement and shock had made her grumpy. Perhaps that explained her shortness with the human she found sprawled at her feet, the one who stared at her with wide, dark eyes, even as he attempted to shield a female of his own kind.

Even before Ash posed the question, she knew that neither of these humans belonged to the legion of demon worshippers. The taint of evil associated with the Order of Eternal Darkness left a stain on the soul that could not be concealed, especially not from one of those sworn to protect against them.

Something in the air sent her hackles rising, though, and if it hadn't come from these humans, then the current situation must be grave, indeed. She could sense a chill of darkness around them that had nothing to do with the time of year or the hour on the clock. Some evil had taken root nearby and sent its cancerous tendrils out into the atmosphere. It felt bigger than what a single *nocturni* could have managed with a few strikes of dark energy, though. Something else must be behind it. For that reason, Ash had been summoned, and for that reason, she would do the duty for which she had come into being.

She could destroy it.

First, though, she should see these humans to safety. Guardians like her existed to protect humanity; she could hardly abandon two examples of the species when they literally fell at her feet. She lived to protect them.

But how could she respond when the stupid creatures refused to heed her warnings?

Even after a second extended tremor shook them all with the violence of its intensity, the man and woman stayed in place and debated its cause rather than seeking shelter as any sensible human would.

The male, in particular, seemed determined to focus on the inconsequential instead of his own safety. Now, for example, he was gawking over the idea of magic when he should be running for his life. Luckily his sister pointed out his folly before Ash could do so—and in much gentler language than Ash had planned.

"You're not half so blind as you like to pretend," the woman said, finishing her scold.

"At the moment, I'm less concerned with what's causing it and more concerned with how to survive it," he retorted.

The quaking ceased as suddenly as it had begun, and the man—Michael Drummond, he had called himself—breathed a sigh of relief. Ash thought that might be a bit hasty. And so, as it turned out, did the human female.

"It's not over," Maeve said.

At least one of them made sense.

"Your sister is correct," Ash agreed. "The earth quakes in response to the insult done upon it. It tries to reject the contamination of the Darkness."

The human male stared at her for a moment. Then another. Then he cocked his head to the side. *"An bhfuil Gaeilge agat?"*

"What?"

The man shrugged. "Didn't understand a word you said. I thought maybe you'd make sense in Irish."

Did he think he spoke more clearly with nonsense like that?

"For her to make sense, you'd have to actually hear with an open mind, Michael."

The human female seemed to have gathered her strength in the aftermath of the quaking. She extricated herself from her brother's protective embrace and pushed to her feet, dusting her hands together before offering one of them to Ash.

"I'd apologize for him, but he'd just do something else idiotic and start the cycle over again." The woman spoke with a wry curve to her lips. "I'm Maeve, by the way, if you didn't hear before."

Hesitant, Ash shook hands. The human custom sounded familiar in her mind, but felt awkward on her skin. "I heard."

With their fingers still touching, Maeve narrowed her eyes and peered closer. "This is why you're here, isn't it? Somehow, the two of you are linked. You and whatever it is that I saw coming."

That made Ash take notice. She tightened her grip and demanded, "What did you see?"

Those human blue eyes slackened and went unfocused as Maeve responded. "A black cloud. Fire. Blood. Shadows that can reach out and grab you and suck the life out while you scream and scream and no one hears you. Pain. Chains. And something . . . else."

The male scrambled to his feet and placed a hand on his sister's shoulder, as if he could protect her from her vision. "Maybe it wasn't even a vision. You've been working hard, Mae. It's late. Maybe you nodded off—"

"I know a vision when I have one, Michael Stephen. I've only had twenty years or so to grow accustomed to them."

Ash silently applauded both the confidence of the statement and the sharp tone in which it was delivered. The human girl had a backbone after all. Given her obvious fear during the tremors, Ash had wondered.

"But—"

"Once again, your sister judges the situation better than

you. What she has seen is the future the *nocturnis* would like to bring about." She ran her gaze over the female and frowned. She saw power in the girl, but not of the sort something told her she was looking for. "You have magic about you, but not the look of one trained by the Guild. Were you sent away because of your sex?"

The man stepped forward, putting himself between the two females. His expression had turned belligerent. "Again, no one here has any idea what you're talking about. Plain English will get you a lot further. If you can manage."

Irritation and amusement warred inside Ash. On the one hand, she disliked this Michael Drummond for the way he challenged her and the tone with which he often spoke to her. But on the other, she found the way he seemed determined to protect his sister from her almost . . . cute. As if she could not tear him limb from limb with very little thought and even less effort.

She found the chore of simultaneously suppressing a growl and biting back a smile more of a challenge than she had expected. The growl wound up backing up in her throat and making her feel as if she needed to sneeze.

"If you cannot understand the concepts of the Guild and the Order, human, then any explanation I might offer would take far more time than I feel is wisely spent here. This place is too open to attack, and I fear what other effects the Darkness might have in store."

"Come back to the Bones, then. Michael's pub," Maeve clarified when both sent her incredulous looks. Well, Ash just looked puzzled, she felt sure; Michael Drummond, though, looked a combination of shocked and appalled.

Maeve crossed her arms at her brother's expression and lifted her chin. "It's after hours, so the place will be empty. No one will see her if we bring her in through the back. And I have more questions."

"You want me to bring a monster into my pub in the

middle of the night so you can interview it like you're Ryan Tubridy and it's a guest on *The Late Late*?"

There went that tone again. Ash couldn't suppress the hiss. "I am not an 'it,' and I am *not* a monster."

His sister slapped his shoulder hard enough for the crack to register in the quiet. "Really, Drum. Have some manners in front of the lady, or I'm telling Ma."

He squeaked out, "The lady?" just before another smack caught him across the back of the head. Considering how far the small female human had to stretch to reach, Ash found herself almost impressed.

"Ow! Right, then." The man reached up to rub his skull. "This way, I suppose." He walked a few steps into the night before his posture stiffened and he turned. "Just one problem here, Mae."

"One problem aside from your poor stupidity, you mean?"

"Yes, aside from that. I brought a car, thinking I'd be driving you out to Ma's house tonight."

"And?"

"Aaaand . . . have you any brilliant ideas how I'm meant to fit th—"

Maeve narrowed her eyes, and Ash growled.

Drum quickly corrected himself. "How I'm meant to fit *her* into the back of my Toyota?"

Maeve turned to Ash and performed a quick visual survey. Ash had to fight the urge to shift her feet that struck her like an itch between her wings. She felt as if she were being scrutinized and found wanting, which made no sense.

She had been designed perfectly to perform her duty. She had long, strong legs to give her power on takeoffs, and huge, powerful wings that sliced through the air like a ship through ocean waves. Her tail acted as a rudder in flight and an extra weapon in the field. Her muscled arms allowed her to wield a heavy battle-axe for hours on end and added strength to her blows in combat. Certainly, she stood taller than the tiny human female and even the disrespectful male, but a warrior needed to be large and powerful in order to win her skirmishes and vanquish her enemies. There was nothing wrong with the way she was formed.

And still, the assessing gazes of these humans unnerved her.

"It's the wings," Maeve said, breaking the extended silence. "They stick up too high, and she'd have to sit on them to get them to fit. I don't suppose they fold any smaller?"

Ash bit back the urge to ask if the male's head folded any smaller and shook her head. "They do not. However, if I understand you correctly and we are meant to enter a confined area, I can perhaps offer an alternative."

She saw their expressions of confusion, but ignored them and focused on the process of concealing her true form under a disguise of humanity. It was a skill all Guardians possessed in order to allow them to pass unnoticed while investigating the threat posed by the Darkness on this mortal plane.

The human shape felt confining, like a set of clothing in a size too small, but Ash ignored the sensation. Perhaps with time, the disguise would stretch to fit more comfortably.

When the transformation was complete, she looked to the humans. "Will this do?"

They stared back at her with wide eyes and open mouths, which Ash found somewhat rude. She had no way of seeing herself as she appeared to them, but no matter how she looked there should be no cause for such scrutiny.

Maeve recovered first, her slack-jawed expression firming into a grin with a decided edge of mischief. She shot a sideways glance at her brother before she nodded briskly. "That will be perfect." She stopped and frowned. "I just realized I have no idea what to call you. Do you have a name?"

The urge to roll her eyes almost overwhelmed her, but Ash held strong. *Do I have a name? Hmph.* "You may call me Ash."

"Ash. I like it. I also like that jacket. I don't suppose you got it at Top Shop, huh?"

Reflex had Ash blinking down at her own body. The ability to alter her appearance came naturally, an innate ability for all Guardians. She simply thought of a shape that would fit in among her human companions, and the magic that lived inside her provided. The appropriate clothing was just part of the package. Still, Maeve appeared to be waiting for her answer.

"Uh, no, I did not," Ash managed. "I do not know where it came from. I made it, I suppose."

Maeve sighed. "Figures. Come on, though. I'm getting cold just standing out here, and I certainly wouldn't turn my nose up at a pint right now."

Through all of this, the male remained silent, but Ash noticed the way his gaze lingered on her human shape. Was he in awe of her ability to shift shapes as she willed? Or did he find something about this form of particular interest?

She didn't get a chance to ask. An elbow in his side provided by his sister had him turning and stalking off into the gloom. Maeve scurried after him, her short legs pumping to keep up. Ash found the pace no problem. In fact, judging by the view she had of the back of the bad-tempered human's head, she would guess her new form stood eye to eye with the man, or close to it.

That thought made something inside her grunt in satisfaction, as if she needed the height to keep her advantage against a human. She huffed. That was ridiculous. No matter what shape she wore, her strength could crush a mortal of either sex. After all, she was a warrior and a Guardian. She existed to battle the most powerful Demons the Darkness had ever spawned. Her prowess could not be matched on this plane, even if this was the first time she had ever visited it.

The thought made her frown, because it meant something very important had brought her here. She needed to discover that reason, and for that, she should have a Warden by her side.

Ash slowed to a halt. The man and woman had brought her away from the ancient buildings behind them and to the edge of a modern road. Black pavement glistened under a slick coating of rain and tall lampposts cast circles of light like golden puddles at regular intervals along the curb.

Glancing back over her shoulder, Maeve saw her hesitation. "What's the matter?"

"I have allowed myself to be distracted. I must leave you here." Ash shook her head and took a step back. She needed to refocus. Her duty included protecting humans, not socializing with them. Now that the immediate danger to them appeared to have passed, she should forge ahead with her tasks. A Guardian's first contact after summoning should be with her Warden.

Why did that thought make something in her chest pull tight? Her instincts warned her that all was not as it should be on this plane, and a lot of it had less to do directly with the Seven than one might first imagine. Curiosity nudged at her with unusual force.

"Are you certain that's such a good idea?"

Ash had already turned away, her attention turned inward and her focus on determining her next step, when the female's voice cut through her thoughts. "Excuse me?"

"Do you think leaving us here and heading off on your own is really such a good idea?" Maeve repeated while her brother stood behind her, brooding. "Based on what you said to us at first, it seems to me that you're not any more certain of what's going on at the moment than we are. In the circumstances, don't you think that it might be a better idea if we pooled our resources and tried to figure it out together?"

"Work together?"

"What? Us and her?"

Ash and the male human spoke at the same time, and with the same degree of incredulity coloring their tones. Their thoughts must be running along the same lines.

Somehow that gave Ash reason to pause.

This time, the man managed to dart out of the way before his sister's blow landed. "Hey, now, love, I never said a word of insult! I only meant that if the . . . er . . . lady wants to be on her way, we've no right to try to stop her. And based on what she's said since we met, it sounds like that's what she wants."

Ash started to nod in agreement, but again felt that jerk of uneasiness behind her sternum. Why would her instincts want her to remain with two humans who knew so little of her kind or the mission of the Guardians that they had never even heard of the Wardens Guild? It made no sense.

"It's hardly as if I'm attempting a kidnapping, Michael," Maeve said, crossing her arms over her chest. "I'm merely pointing out that perhaps we could help each other. After all, Ash appears to be, um, new to town, and Ma always says that many hands make light work. I'm all but certain that extends to many minds making light puzzles. Staying together until we know what's going on just makes sense."

The man scowled at his sister. "The saying I remember

about hands had more to do with the devil's work," he muttered.

Ash curled a lip and wished she hadn't changed forms. A flash of fang always added a certain something to that particular expression.

"Stop pouting, Michael. It's not at all attractive in a grown man." She turned to Ash. "Well? What do you think? Should we work together?"

Still, the Guardian hesitated. She knew that the only humans her kind traditionally worked beside were their personal Wardens and other members of the Guild, but her Warden seemed to be missing. He should have met her at the place of her summoning, but both of these mortals denied knowledge of the organization, and no other beings appeared anywhere near the area. That in and of itself told her that at least a few of the old rules might no longer apply.

What else might have changed between the collective knowledge she had inherited upon her awaking and her waking itself? Did these siblings have anything to do with it? Had they simply been in the wrong place at the wrong time, or had fate somehow put them in her path for a larger purpose?

Her lengthy pause must have registered with Maeve as a reluctance to answer the question, because the human woman pressed her lips together and narrowed her eyes.

"Before now, I would have sworn on the graves of all my grannies that not a creature on earth could outstubborn my darling brother, and yet here you stand, just to prove me wrong." She moved her hands to her hips and maneuvered herself to place both Ash and her brother in her field of vision. "I was trying to be polite about this whole mess, and to give the both of you the chance to come to a graceful agreement, but it seems you're each too pigheaded for anyone's good. So I'll just come out with it."

She shifted her glance between the two figures before her as if weighing the quality of their attention. "I've seen something very disturbing in the last few days," she told them. "Something big and dark and very, very unpleasant is coming our way, but that has me not half so scared as knowing that whatever is headed for us is only a small part of something far worse." Her expression softened, looking less angry and more haunted for an instant, before she lifted her chin and forged ahead. "There is a very bad future in store, not just for us, but for the entire world, Michael, something I can't even look at straight on, and I can't quite find words to tell you how much that frightens me."

Ash felt a rush of awareness jolt through her. Perhaps fate really had played a hand in this meeting. A wise Guardian never ignored the words of a woman of power. "You have true magic, then. You see the future?"

Maeve pulled a face. "I see *a* future. Sometimes more than one, but I can't tell you for certain which will come to pass, or even if any of them will. I see possibilities, but the future changes a thousand times before it's written in stone. A lot of decisions still need to be made before that happens."

The first of them seemed to rest on Ash's shoulders. Should she follow the path dictated by tradition and strike off on her own to find her Warden and fight her battle unassisted? Or should she explore the new trail that stretched before her, one that would place two humans at her side, at least for the moment?

She expected the decision to be more difficult. Guardians always kept to tradition. They all came from the same place, followed the same rules, and fought the same battles. All the knowledge she had inherited upon her summoning told her this. The collective history of the Guardians stretched itself out in her mind and she could see century upon century of her brethren, like an army carved from a single block of stone. Their faces might look different, their forms vary in size or shape, but inside, they were all the same.

And then she looked a little bit closer and she saw one other important detail—all the Guardians who came before her, from the first seven ever summoned to the one whose place she had taken this very night—every single one of those warriors had been male.

Which meant that something significant had already changed. Perhaps this was fate's way of telling her that this new battle would not be won by following the old paths. Perhaps it was time for Ash to try something new.

Blinking to clear her thoughts, Ash looked back at Maeve's expectant face and nodded once. "Let us go, then, and you can tell me what exactly it is that you have seen. Perhaps together we will find the answers I need."

And perhaps she would find the strength not to copy Maeve's blows to the back of her brother's head, though based on the way he muttered, "Bollocks," under his breath at Ash's last statement, she harbored some serious doubts.

Chapter Three

Drum felt the gargoyle's glare burning into the back of his skull, but he pretended to be oblivious. Partly to protect himself from another of Maeve's surprisingly vicious whacks, but mostly because it seemed to drive the creature crazy.

Did that make him petty?

Given how little he cared, the answer to that question seemed moot.

He unlocked the rear door to the pub with as much disdain as one could pack into the motion of turning a key and swinging open a slab of wood, which wasn't much. Since Maeve brushed past him to enter with no sign of violence, he doubted she had even noticed.

His sister chose the table right in front of the bar and made herself comfortable. She didn't bother to look at him as she said, "Guinness, please."

He scowled. "It's after hours, Maeve. The pub is closed."

"Well, since I don't intend to pay for it, you won't see any trouble for it, will you?" She gave him a supercilious look and waved one hand toward the bar. "I'm sure Ash could use something, as well. It has been rather a trying night."

Drum bit back a few choice words, ones that would have his mother brandishing a spoon, and opened the pass-through with a touch of extra force. He grabbed three glasses and started to build the pints. While the first pour settled, he splashed out two fingers of Jameson and threw them back. He'd damned well earned it.

He could feel the gargoyle watching him, a prickling against his skin that kept him on edge. His reaction to her was almost as unsettling. He felt so damned *aware* of her, of her presence, her attention. He knew exactly where she stood, when she sat, of her fingers tapping restlessly against the scarred tabletop.

It had to be fear, the natural wariness of any living thing that finds itself in the presence of an apex predator. Because she was that, no doubt about it. With muscles and fangs and talons, this creature had been designed to hunt and kill.

Of course, he found that a little difficult to remember when he looked at her now.

The change in her appearance had almost knocked him back on his arse, and seeing it happen before his very eyes almost set him to swooning like some Victorian female. One minute he had seen the monster, and the next a vision out of any man's fantasy. He wasn't entirely sure his head had stopped spinning, and after just one shot it wasn't like he could blame the whiskey.

Drum hadn't had time to reconcile himself to the monster walking and talking in front of them, and just as quickly he found himself confronted by a dream. He'd had a moment of panic that she'd plucked her appearance straight out of his head, but that had to be impossible. Right?

She was gorgeous. He was man enough to admit it, and terrified enough to curse the truth of it.

First off, she was tall, as long and straight as a runway

model. For a man well over six feet, who had lived his life surrounded by petite females, the importance of that couldn't be overstated. The idea of looking at, of kissing, a woman without getting a crick in his neck or kink in his back was more than appealing. And she wasn't tiny, either. If any woman deserved to be called an Amazon, it was her. She looked strong, her torso and limbs thick, not with fat but with muscle, the kind that came from work, not from working out.

Her body curved in a way that made a man's hands itch, with full breasts and round hips. It sent his mind wandering to how she might use that strength in bed, those thighs hugging and hips lifting, and that just made him mutter another curse under his breath.

Keeping his eyes on her face didn't help. Beauty he might have ignored, dismissing it as rank deception, but her face was *interesting*. Even her human visage looked carved from stone, not because it was hard and frozen, but because the lines were clean and sharp. She retained the high cheekbones and exotic eyes, but her skin had turned the color of rich cream and looked just as silky soft. A smattering of freckles could have been a dusting of nutmeg across the narrow bridge of her nose.

He tried very hard to ignore her lips, which were pink and full, and formed a perfect Cupid's bow. An appropriate analogy, he acknowledged, given how they drew tight every time she looked at him, as if ready to unleash an arrow in his direction. He ignored that, or tried to, as he finished the pints and carried them over to the table.

Maeve didn't even acknowledge him, occupied instead with shrugging out of her jacket and draping it over the back of her chair. "You said you made that coat of yours. I don't suppose you could whip one up for me?"

Ash looked surprised, then mildly confused. "No."

"So, it isn't like magic, then?"

The confusion remained. "Not the way you mean. I didn't create anything. It is part of this form."

"Oh. Can you do magic, though?"

Ash shook her head. Drum lifted his glass to his lips. It kept him from reaching out and tucking a stray wisp of hair behind her ear. She wore the dark length of it in a loose braid, but long pieces of fringe kept falling in her eyes and teasing her cheeks. Of course, if he had given in to his urge, he got the feeling she would have taken his hand off at the wrist. Knowing that helped a wee bit.

"My kind is nearly immune to magic," the woman said, "and we cannot wield it. We leave that to the Guild."

"And that raises a very important point," Drum said, staring at her. "What exactly are you?"

"Drum!"

He ignored his sister's gasp of outrage and kept his gaze level.

The woman—the creature, he reminded himself—had no trouble meeting his eyes. "I told you before. I am a Guardian."

"You say that as if it should mean something."

"It means more than you can fathom, human." Her eyes narrowed on him. "It means that your world still exists. That you still live. I believe I would call that 'something.' "

Maeve rolled her eyes. "Michael, drink your Guinness. Maybe if your mouth is full of stout, you won't be able to fill it with your foot." She turned to Ash. "Forgive our ignorance, but as Inigo Montoya said, 'You keep saying that word. I do not think it means what you think it means.' Guardian, in this case."

Drum saw the woman's eyes spark with impatience before she wrestled it back. For some reason, she seemed to respond to Maeve. He only seemed to irritate her.

She wrapped long fingers around her pint glass, but didn't drink. "I must remind myself that you are not with the Guild. My mind tells me that I should have met my Warden the instant I was summoned. Something here is very wrong."

"Maybe if you tell us what it is, we can help."

Drum muffled his snort in the head of his beer. To hear his sharp-tongued little sister sounding as soft and compassionate as Mother Teresa was one for the books. If it were just the two of them having this conversation, he'd already be bleeding from a thousand tiny wounds. But with the monster, she was all sweetness and light.

"I am a Guardian," Ash repeated. "We were created by the founders of the Guild to battle against the Seven Demons of the Darkness. We are all that stops those abominations from joining together and destroying this world. It has been so for longer than you humans can remember, thousands of years."

Maeve's eyes opened wide, and even Drum swallowed a little harder. "How many of you are there?"

"Seven."

"Wow. If those demons you mentioned can really destroy the entire world, don't you think you would rather outnumber them?"

"We began as seven, and we will end as seven. There has never been a need for more." She frowned. "Though I sense that this time, things are . . . different."

Different. That was one way to describe Drum's world at the moment. Not the one he would have chosen, mind you. But then he remembered his mother's spoon.

"Okay," Maeve said, dabbing at the foam that clung to the corner of her mouth. "I really want to ask you what 'different' means, but I think that first you had better explain this 'Guild' business. You've mentioned them more than a bit."

"The Guild summoned us into being. When they call upon us, we answer, and we fight until the Darkness withdraws. Then they return us to sleep. While we rest, they watch the Order, and alert us when a new threat arises."

Something about her words bothered Drum. No, he realized, not her words. Her tone. It was flat, even. Almost blank. She spoke with no emotion whatsoever, and that niggled at him. People didn't discuss their purpose in life without displaying some sort of feeling about it. But then again, she wasn't a person, was she? If he wanted proof, the fact that she still hadn't touched her Guinness offered plenty.

Maeve had drained half of hers, but now she pushed it away and leaned her elbows on the table, clearly fascinated by Ash's story. "And they can do magic, you said? Like, the casting-spells kind of magic?"

Ash's expression softened with a glint of humor. "You have said that you can see the future, and yet you doubt the existence of magic?"

"Of course not. I've just never seen it."

Drum didn't think he had done anything, but Ash turned to him and raised a brow. "And you, Michael Drummond? I believe you doubt me."

He scowled at her. Actually, it wasn't really at her; he just scowled. "Just 'Drum.' And it's nothing to do with you. I just see a difference between having the Sight and pulling rabbits out of hats."

"I do not recall that I am wearing a hat."

Maeve poked him. "Michael, behave."

Ash glanced between them. "Why did she call you Michael?"

"It *is* the name Mother gave him, but when he was twelve, he decided Drum sounded cooler. And then he went and named this place after himself. Thought he was very clever, I'm sure." Maeve shook her head, grinning. "Silly git."

"This place?"

Mischief glinted in his sister's eye. "The pub is called the Skin and Bone. As in a drumskin, and a bone is what people used to use to play the *bodhrán*. A traditional Irish drum." She shook her head. "Punny bastard."

Instead of rising to the bait, Drum drained his pint and slapped the empty glass back onto the table. It hadn't been his idea to bring Ash back to his pub, and now Maeve was going to turn it into an opportunity to harass him? She could have done that at their mother's house, in front of a warm fire and without the presence of what he wished had stayed a mythical creature.

"I understand." Said creature nodded. "It is humorous, a nickname joined to a play on words. I understand humans enjoy such things."

"What is it that you enjoy?" Maeve asked, pointing her chin toward Ash's untouched drink. "Clearly, it isn't Guinness. Do you fancy something else?"

Drum let out a growl. "For fuck's sake, Maeve, I let you drag her here for answers, not so you could host a bloody *céilidh*. She doesn't need a damned drink."

Before his sister could tear into him, Ash nodded. "I do not. What I require is to know how you can lend me the aid that you promised."

"I promised you nothing," Drum snapped.

Ash leveled him with a stare. "And I expect nothing of one such as you."

"Such as me?" he bellowed. "And what the bloody hell do you mean by that?"

Maeve placed a hand on his shoulder. "I guess she's referring to your manners, Michael. You've hardly made Ma proud with displays like this. Why don't you have another drink? If that's what it takes to calm you down."

"I'm perfectly calm," he said through clenched teeth.

"No, you're perfectly horrid. Now, *settle. Down.*"

His little sister wasn't physically strong enough to keep him in his seat, but the pressure on his shoulder at least reminded him to breathe. He did that, but it took several deep inhalations to get a firm grip on his temper. The gargoyle seemed to possess a talent for rousing it.

Maeve watched him for moment, as if expecting him to break his glass against the edge of the table and go after Ash with the jagged shards. The idea barely occurred to him.

Really.

Finally satisfied, she turned back to Ash. "I do think we can help you. In fact, I think we're meant to. I told you that I see more than one future until things are settled, but the only ones I see that don't go up in flames include all of us."

Drum slumped into his chair. And wasn't that just a kick in the pants?

Ash kept a tight grip on her impatience. Instinct battered at her, telling her to hunt, to search, to fight, the way her kind was meant to. It didn't understand strategy, and understood even less that something in this world was very wrong.

She had told the humans the truth of her kind. She was one of seven Guardians, each one summoned from the ether whenever the Darkness threatened the world of humans. Usually, a Guardian fought until his foe was vanquished, and then his personal Warden returned him to his stone state to wait until he was needed again. Each of the seven was essentially immortal, sleeping and rising in an endless cycle until the end of time.

That did not, however, mean that a Guardian could not be destroyed. Although immune to magic, possessing skin almost as difficult to cut as true stone, and able to heal physical wounds with amazing speed, in theory a Guardian could be killed by destroying its body. Over time, enemies had realized that the only practical way to achieve this was to attack the Guardian's sleeping form. Break the statue into pieces, and the Guardian within ceased to exist. A new one would have to be summoned to maintain their numbers.

That was how Ash had come to be. The Guardian she replaced had slept among the chapel's spires for hundreds of years. When it had crashed to the ground, the old warrior had been destroyed and Ash took his place, inheriting both his duties and his knowledge. The continuity insured that there would always be seven, but there were two things wrong with Ash's summoning: one, no one had summoned her; she had appeared without a Warden's call, which should be impossible. And two, Ash was female. The first female. Ever.

She should not exist.

It was for those reasons, the wrongness of them, that Ash had allowed Maeve to persuade her to return to the pub. She hadn't known what else to do, and that left her feeling both lost and infuriated. A Guardian never questioned what to do, but then again a Guardian never had to. As soon as he woke, his Warden stood before him and explained the threat he would face. Every Guardian knew this, and for every one before her, it had stayed true.

So what had changed?

Ash had a feeling that the answer to that question would solve more than one mystery. Too bad that she had no idea who to ask.

Pressing her palms flat against the table, she centered herself and attempted to take stock of anything she *did* know. It wasn't much, but it was the only place she had to start.

She looked at Maeve. "Tell me of your vision. Describe it to me."

"Which one?"

"I do not care. Any. One that does not 'go up in flames.' "

Maeve grimaced. "It still isn't pretty." She drew a deep breath. "I don't see things all smoothly put together like a film. Things are more disjointed than that, more like looking at photographs one after the other, faster than you can imagine. But I know I see something headed toward Dublin. Or, that is what I did see. Now, I think it's here."

"What is it?"

"I haven't any idea. It's nothing I recognize, nothing I can describe. It's just . . . blackness. It rolls in like a storm, but it's not a cloud. It's thicker and darker. And it's oily." She crossed her arms over her chest and pressed them tightly to her. "It's just wrong. That's the word for it. Just thinking of it turns my stomach."

Ash saw the way Drum's expression tightened with concern as his sister spoke. He might be hostile toward her, but clearly he wished to protect his sibling. She felt a grudging spark of respect.

"You see the Darkness," she said, returning her focus to the other woman. "Your sickness is an appropriate response, for what you see is the embodiment—the source—of all that is evil. If you have seen it come to this city, then things are already worse than I had imagined."

"And what the hell have you imagined?" Drum demanded.

She shrugged. "The usual. That the Order had grown too aggressive once more, that they had gathered a little power and sought to use it to weaken the defenses imprisoning the Seven."

"I think we need another definition," Maeve said. "What do you mean by 'the Order'?"

"The Order of Eternal Darkness. They exist to serve the Seven. It is their mission to free their demonic Masters and to set them loose upon the human world. It was one of their number I fought briefly when you first saw me."

Drum made a choking sound. "Who the fuck would want to go and do a stupid thing like unleashing a horde of demons into the world?"

Ash stared. Had he not heard her the first time? Or did the human possess a deficit of understanding? She made certain to repeat herself slowly. "The Order of Eternal Darkness."

He lifted two fingers in a V formation and accompanied the gesture with a rude expression. Ash might be new to this realm, but she had no trouble understanding his meaning.

"I meant *why* would they want to do such a thing."

"They are devoted. They have sworn to serve the Demons, and the greatest wish of the Seven is to be returned to the human world so they might seize it for themselves."

"Earlier, you made it sound as if these Demons wanted to *end* the world."

"They do."

"I think that's what's tripping us up," Maeve said. "After all, if the world ends, everyone dies. Including this Order."

Ash sighed. Human understanding was so limited. "The world cannot end as you understand the word, where life ceases to exist and a void takes its place. This is impossible, and rather arrogant of you. The earth and heavens do not go away if humans disappear. It is mainly the world *as you know it* that would stop. The members of the Order, whom we call the *nocturnis,* do not wish to die. They do not even wish especially that you die, for if you do, who will their Masters enslave and feed upon?"

"Ew." Maeve's face wrinkled with disgust. "Maybe it would be better if the world did end as we understand the word. It sounds better than *that.*"

Drum had grown visibly tenser the longer that Ash spoke. His hands lay on the table before him, fingers curled into white-knuckled fists. "So, you're telling us that my sister has seen the end of the world."

Ash looked at him, searching his expression. Either he no longer cared if she could read his emotions, or he had lost all ability to hide them. Rage, fear, and frustration had etched themselves into the lines that bracketed his eyes and his mouth, turning his blue eyes stormy. The urge to lie to him surprised her. It would offer no more than false comfort.

And Guardians did not lie.

She answered with the truth. The stark whole of it. "Yes."

Drum cursed in Irish, the syllables at once coarse and lyrical. His sister went pale as fog.

"But it isn't certain," Maeve said, a tremor in her voice. "I told you that. There are still other possibilities."

"And are any of them full of puppies and clover?" her brother asked.

Maeve pressed her lips together and shook her head.

"Did you imagine any of them could be? Given that your sister has seen that the blackness is already here." Ash felt a tingle in her hands, her fingers aching to wrap themselves around the shaft of her battle-axe. She existed for battle, and to sit offering explanations like a teacher to her pupils made her tense and restless. "There is no question that we have to fight. The only question is when."

"I think I would add how, where, what, and who," Drum said. "It might not bother you, but I would feel like a right idiot to be swinging my fists at a shapeless black cloud."

Ash had not expected that humans would be so literal. She could only assume that he did it to annoy her. Searching for patience, she opened her mouth to explain how the Seven used the *nocturni* to do their bidding, but something interrupted.

Something small and black that traveled in packs and stank of rot and sulfur.

Hhissih. Five of them. They burst through the door she had followed Drum through earlier, and scuttled toward them. Claws clicked and clacked over the wooden floor-boards, and the few lights Drum had flipped on when they entered seem to dissolve the instant the beams hit their slimy, fur-covered flesh.

At last. Something to fight.

Blinking back into her natural form, Ash reached for her axe and smiled. Time to go to work.

Chapter Four

Really? Someone really thought that Drum hadn't seen enough weird shite tonight? Oh, but he begged to differ.

Weird didn't even begin to describe the things that had hacked their way through the bottom of his door and into his precious pub. They were the size of small dogs, but no corgi he'd seen had ever looked—let alone smelled—like these beasts.

Like a furry oil slick, each creature appeared to be covered in hair long enough to obscure its feet, however many it might have. Yet each one seemed to glisten, as if encased in a slimy, chitinous shell. How something could look like a mammal and an insect at the same time, Drum had no idea, but the things managed it.

They sounded like insects, with their scurrying clicks across the floor. Even the way they moved was entomic, reminding him of cockroaches or beetles or scorpions. All the nasty things a sane person preferred remain outdoors.

He especially preferred that, given that these things appeared to view him and his sister as dinner.

Maeve screamed and scrambled up onto the table. She never had done well with bugs. His primitive instincts urged Drum to follow, but his pride and his protective streak told him to fight. Of course, neither of those latter emotions had the decency to offer him a weapon to fight with.

He picked up a chair and brandished it before him, like a charade player miming a clue for "lion tamer." He imagined he looked like an idiot, but beggars and choosers and all that.

Just before the first of the little monsters reached him, he found himself pushed aside by the smack of the gargoyle's giant wing. He ended with a mouthful of downy fur-feathers, and the attacking creature with a steel spike pinning its skull to the floor.

The gorgeous woman Maeve had led back to the pub had disappeared. In her place stood the monster from the abbey, all gray skin, sharp fangs, and talons like daggers. She looked fierce, like a warrior. Not princess, but queen. Her wings were half spread, crowded by the limited space, and in one hand she clutched a battle-axe. The weapon featured a shaft more than three feet in length, tipped with the lethal metal point. On the other end, the axe head was wide and heavy, and curved gracefully along each side of the double-sided blade. Behind her, her tail flicked and twitched like an angry cat's.

Ash pulled her weapon free and swung it around in front of her, sending a second black creature sailing against the far wall. From boogeyman to cannonball in one easy step.

The three remaining monsters hesitated before regrouping in what seemed like a coordinated attack. They rushed forward as one, darting aside at the last second to avoid Ash's axe and focus on Drum instead.

Wasn't he a lucky boy?

He swung the chair like a club, bringing the edge of a leg straight down onto a hissing mass of putrid ick. He didn't know how he had missed it at first, but these things stunk. They smelled like rotten eggs and red meat left out in the sun, like garbage and death. Bile rose in his throat, and he had to hold his breath in order to choke it back.

The gargoyle fought as if she didn't notice, as if the things were pretty as a poppet and smelled like summer roses. Well, hopefully she didn't go bashing in the heads of dolls and flowers, but still. The stench didn't appear to bother her. She breathed easily, her mouth open and smiling, as she dispatched two monsters with efficient grace.

The one pinned by Drum's chair continued to struggle, squirming and writhing and emitting a high-pitched squeal, like nails on a blackboard being run through an underlubricated food blender.

Cursing, Drum stomped his boot heel into the middle of the thing's back, pinning it in place. Then he lifted the chair, and used it to beat the creature until it went silent. It took longer than he expected, even when he put his back into his swings. Apparently, even evil had a survival instinct.

When he finally looked up and met Ash's gaze, he was breathing hard and pumping adrenaline. "Well, that was fun," he bit out. "Care to tell me who else might come visiting?"

Ash lowered her axe, bits of stinking, black something dripping from the blades. She shook her head. "I cannot tell you. The *hhissih* took me by surprise. I do not know why they would strike here. They are attracted to dark magic, but they are stupid, mindless creatures. Usually they must be sent to attack a human. They lack the intelligence to do so on their own."

"Intelligence didn't seem to matter when they were trying to gnaw through my leg." Drum probably sounded like he blamed her for this mess, but that was only because he did. Or mostly. "What about the little shite who ran off after throwing a fireball at our heads? Could he have sent them after us?"

Ash appeared to consider that. "I suppose he could

have, though I cannot see the point. He would know the
hhissih pose no threat to me, and why would he seek
to harm you? You would mean nothing to him."

"Please, enough flattery."

Maeve hadn't moved from atop the table where she had
waited out the attack, but now she sank down to sit cross-
legged on its clean, but battered surface. Her hands shook
as she tucked them close beneath her arms. *"Hhissih?"* she
repeated. "Is that what they were?"

Ash nodded, producing a cloth from somewhere inside
her tunic and using it to clean the gore from her weapon.

Drum dropped the cracked and battered chair and
slumped into another. "If they were an example of what
Maeve saw headed our way, I can't say I'm excited for
round two."

"The *hhissih* were nothing," Ash scoffed. "They are to
the Darkness as an ant is to the veteran of a thousand com-
bats. Nothing of consequence. Something to be crushed
under one's boot."

Drum wiggled his toes and looked down at his feet.
Dammit, that black shite covered his left boot. And this
was his favorite pair, too. He looked up and caught Ash's
gaze. "I didn't enjoy being taken by surprise. Next time,
I'd prefer to be a bit better prepared, and I think that means
we need a plan." He raised one eyebrow in the gesture his
mother found endearing and his sisters called infuriating.
"Suggestions?"

Ash shrugged and put her axe away. Literally. She set
it to one side, and it disappeared, as if she'd put it in her
pocket, but that pocket just happened to be in some other
dimension. Handy, that. "I know no more of the current
situation than either of you. A Warden should have greeted
me and apprised me of my immediate task."

Maeve looked up. "Well, if this Warden fellow didn't
come to you, why don't you go to him?"

"I cannot. I have never before visited this realm. I know his name, given to me by my fallen brother, but that is all. I do not know where to find him. Nor even where to look."

Something in that statement appeared to perk Maeve right up. It took Drum a second to follow her train of thought, and when he got there, he groaned. "Maeve, no."

"But Drum, you heard what she said. She's lost something. You could help her."

Of course. His baby sister only used his nickname when she was trying to butter him up. "You don't know that. A person isn't a bloody set of car keys."

Ash looked from him to Maeve and back again. "I do not understand."

"It's nothing."

"My brother can find things."

Drum closed his eyes, pressed his lips together, and counted to ten. Meanwhile, his sister continued to dig a pit and push him toward the edge.

"Talents pop up in our family in every generation," Maeve said, beginning to relax in her enthusiasm. "Our mother has a way with green things. She grows her own herbs and can make something to cure you of almost anything. Our older sister, Sorcha, is a bit like her, but she has a touch of independent healing, as well. She studied to become a nurse-midwife. You already know that I can see things."

Ash nodded.

"Well, so can Drum. Only the things he sees aren't in the future, they're happening right now. Not so much happening, actually, I don't think. He sees literal things. As in objects."

"Exactly," Drum said, "and a person is not a thing."

"No, but I don't see how it's so very different. You could at least try."

"It's entirely different."

He believed his own words, Drum assured himself. Performing what he thought of as his "parlor trick" to find the missing mate to his sister's favorite shoe was one thing; trying to locate a missing person was a trick he had never even contemplated, and he had no desire now to make the attempt.

The way Ash had begun to eye him, therefore, made him feel as if the seat of his chair had turned into the eye of the cooktop. And someone had just turned the knob all the way to boil.

"Drum," Maeve wheedled, "you can't say that if you don't at least give it a go. You've got nothing to lose. What could it hurt?"

Oh, so many things.

The only thing Drum could see was hurt—hurting Maeve when he failed. Hurting himself if he succeeded. Right now, he enjoyed the luxury of seeing his ability as nothing more than that "trick" he had called it. He felt comfortable with that. It made no demands on him. But what Maeve suggested had the potential to open up a Pandora's box of demands.

Say he tried and succeeded in locating this Warden fellow for Ash. If he did that, he would know—for certain—that he could. What then? Every time he watched a news program, or read a newspaper, or logged on to Facebook, he would see a story about another person whom no one could find. Except that maybe *he* could.

He could try to keep it a secret. If he asked, sincerely, he could persuade Maeve to stay quiet. No one would know that Michael Drummond could find the missing. But *he* would know. And knowing, could he live with himself if he didn't try? Every time. Every day. For the rest of his life.

The thought closed around his stomach like a fist and squeezed. Hard. Mind racing, he stood and stalked to the bar to pour himself another shot of whiskey. He tossed it back, wishing the fire would burn not down to his stomach but up into his mind to flash those thoughts into ashes.

No such luck. So much for being Irish.

"Michael?"

Drum kept his back to her. "Maeve . . ."

"Does your sibling speak the truth?"

The gargoyle's voice—with his back to her, he could force himself to think of her that way, as a creature and not a woman—made his shoulders tense. Her tone was neutral, the question asked evenly, almost idly.

"That's a matter of perspective. Can I find *things*? Yes. I'm fairly good at it."

"Brilliant," Maeve interjected.

He turned to glare at her and leaned elbows back against the bar. He held a new glass of whiskey clutched in tense fingers. "But I have never found a person."

"You've never tried."

"Maeve, leave it."

"I don't understand—"

Ash cut in. "Your brother fears this."

Drum felt the blood rush upward to stain his neck and face. Her gaze pierced him, cut through his defenses, and saw much too much. Anger stirred in his belly. "Look, you—"

"He is wise," the Guardian finished. "Such a talent carries with it a great deal of responsibility. It is not to be shouldered lightly. I think few humans would be up to the task."

Drum went from offended to relieved to grateful and back to offended in the space of two heartbeats, but it wasn't the whiskey making his head spin.

"In other circumstances, I would not ask one of your kind to take on something like this," Ash continued. "In this case, however, I fear I have little choice. At the moment, I am blind to the plans of my enemy, and that leaves me vulnerable. It leaves *you* vulnerable, and puts all of your race at risk. This is unacceptable."

"Interesting word, that." Drum swirled the liquor in his glass and fought to keep his voice level. "I have a feeling that to you and me, 'unacceptable' has two very different meanings."

"I disagree. I do not believe that you wish to risk the lives of yourself, your people, or your family. I do not believe you wish to encounter more of the types of creatures that serve the Darkness. I do not believe you wish for this world to end. I think that we would both call all of those things unacceptable."

Ash met his gaze and held it. Behind the blackness of her eyes, the flame burned steadily, barely flickering. Her gaze wasn't human, far from it, but he recognized it. The resolve, the strength, the need for justice, all of it seemed very human. Contained within something other, he could see all the best traits of humanity.

Better than his own.

The realization hit him like a fist to the gut. If he had that resolve, that strength, or that dedication to justice, he wouldn't be arguing with her now. He wouldn't hesitate. He would have the courage to do the thing that no one else could, and worry about the consequences later.

The last of the whiskey tasted sweet and bitter on his tongue and left him feeling not warmed, but chilled. He'd been trapped. No matter what he decided, he would pay for it in the end. If he did as his sister and the Guardian asked, he would face all of the problems he had already envisioned, and they would follow him for the rest of his life. But if he refused, his own cowardice would haunt him. One was his rock, the other his hard place.

In the end, his decision wasn't noble. He just decided

that he'd rather blame his future misery on someone other than himself.

"Fine. I'll give it a try, but I make no guarantees."

Maeve lit up like sunrise. "You don't have to, Michael. You'll be brilliant. I know it."

Only because he still had his eyes on Ash's face did he see the flicker of surprise. She had expected him to stick to his refusal. Whether she thought him that stubborn or that cowardly, he ought to be insulted, but he couldn't manage it. Not when he realized how epically, drastically tired he really felt.

Damn it all, he was even too tired to yawn.

"At least one of us does," he said, glancing at his sister. "But it will have to wait. Right now, I'm too bloody fagged to find my own arse with both hands and GPS."

Maeve pulled out her phone and glanced at the screen. Her eyes went wide. "Good Lord, and it's no wonder. It's nearly three in the morning. I had no idea it could be so late. I should have passed out ages ago. And Ma was expecting me tonight."

Drum gathered up the empty glasses—and Ash's full one—and dumped them in the sink behind the bar. "It's too late to drive out there now. We'd wake the whole house. And besides, I'd never be able to keep my eyes open. You can sleep upstairs and take the bus in the morning."

And then, as if she hadn't caused him enough trouble that night, his sister slid off the table and looked up at him with her big, blue eyes. "What about Ash?"

He froze. "What about her?"

Maeve wore the expression that said she thought he was an idiot. She'd been using it since her cradle. "Where will she stay?"

"How should I know? Where she usually does, I suppose."

"Weren't you listening? She doesn't *usually* do anything. She's new here."

Drum saw another trap looming and looked around for something to spring it with, other than his own cursed tongue. "Mae, weren't you *looking*? She's a gargoyle."

A gargoyle who growled, "*She* is standing right here."

Maeve braced her hands on her hips. "What? So, she should go stand in the garden for the pigeons to roost on?"

"Mae—"

His sister ignored him. As usual. "Come on." Maeve waved to Ash and headed for the door marked PRIVATE. "We can share the spare room. Michael's flat is right upstairs. One or another of us girls is always crashing here, so we make sure the linens are always fresh."

Drum watched, utterly helpless, as Maeve worked to arrange the world to her own liking. At least he was smart enough not to protest aloud when Ash looked his way before falling in behind his sister. He kept his screams in his head, and had the strained jaw muscle to prove it.

The women disappeared into the back, the faint sound of their footsteps on the stairs reaching him in the silence of the taproom. He felt sure they would make themselves very comfortable in the twin beds of the spare room under the eaves. They'd probably sleep like babies. After all, they weren't the ones looking forward to tomorrow as a date with the gallows. That was all on Drum.

He groaned and returned to his chair, letting his upper body slump onto the table.

Where had he left that bottle of Jameson?

Chapter Five

Ash had no desire to sleep. She had only just awoken, and she knew that the fate of her kind was to sleep through the passage of centuries. She felt no compulsion to start early.

Still, it would have been rude to protest against the fussing of the human female. Maeve kept up a steady stream of cheerful chatter that belied her avowals of exhaustion. As she spoke, she led Ash up a narrow set of stairs at the rear of the building to a heavy wooden door secured with a dull brass lock. A set of keys drawn from her pocket allowed them access into a small foyer, lined on the floor with shoes and on one wall with jackets and sweaters dangling from a row of pegs.

The space opened up into a large living area with pale walls and lots of dark oak trim. It outlined a square arch to left, through which appeared to be a kitchen, and to closed doorways on the right. The rear wall was lined with four tall, rectangular windows through which a bit of weak moonlight filtered in through the misty rain. A faded rag rug covered an area in the center of the scuffed pine floor, with a long battered sofa, a pair of well-stuffed chairs, and a low table positioned on top.

"Through here," Maeve said, opening the first of the

closed doors. "I need to find myself a bed so I don't accidentally break something when I keel over."

Ash had a moment of worry until she saw the smile the other woman aimed in her direction. She must have intended the statement to be humorous. Ash needed to remember she was dealing with humans. They could be tricky to understand.

She followed Maeve down a short hall to another door, which opened into a cozy room under the eaves of the old building. Another rag rug, this one smaller and more brightly colored, covered the floorboards between two narrow beds pressed against the walls on the right and left. Opposite the door, a window looked out to the alley beside the pub, but the only real source of light came from the frosted glass fixture overhead that blinked on when Maeve flicked a switch beside the door.

The room was small and slightly chilly, but the quilts on the beds looked thick with down, and their patchwork tops boasted colors just as bright as the ones in the rug. The small table in between held a lamp with a pretty yellow shade trimmed in eyelet lace. At a touch of Maeve's hand, it glowed with a soft golden light.

"The bathroom is the next door down," Mae said, bouncing down onto the bed on the left. "I would show you, but now that I've sat, I'm not certain that I can get up again. I really am knackered." She gave a quick laugh.

"I am certain I could find it if I should have need," Ash assured her.

She stood just inside the door and looked around the room, feeling awkward and unsure what to do next. She felt no fatigue, and though the beds looked comfortable and warm, the idea of lying on one and remaining motionless for several hours held little appeal.

It would not do, however, to be rude to her hostess. Following Maeve's lead, she crossed to the opposite bed and perched gingerly on the edge. Across the way, the human woman had pulled off her shoes, wriggled out of her denim trousers, and crawled beneath the heavy quilt.

"You have to forgive me for being so rude," Maeve mumbled through a yawn, "but I really can't keep my eyes open another minute. Sleep well, Ash. I'll see you in the morning, and we'll get Michael to do his thing. Promise." Two minutes later her breathing settled into the soft, steady rhythm of sleep.

Ash continued to sit there for several minutes and watch her sleep. She didn't know what else to do. She was a warrior who couldn't find the battlefield, and off it, her purpose became unclear. The only foe she could see at the moment was uncertainty, and against that, her axe was useless.

A Guardian should be better at waiting. Of course, a Guardian should be a lot of things that Ash wasn't. Like male.

Ash frowned into the distance. The thought bothered her more than she wished to admit. Not the fact of being female, but what the knowledge that she was might signify.

Her brow furrowed as she reviewed in her head the anomalies she had encountered since waking. The first was clearly the manner of her waking; a Guardian should only wake when being summoned at the hands of a Warden. So it had been from the first, and for something so fundamental to have changed indicated a disturbance at the very foundation of their existence. She could think of no reason for a Guardian to wake on her own unless no Warden existed to wake her.

The thought sent a chill down her spine. While each of the seven existing Guardians was served by a single Warden, the Guild itself boasted several hundred additional members, each of whom was a fully trained Warden in his own right. If a Warden in service were to die or be killed, another immediately took his place. Usually such positions passed along family lines, but they were never left vacant. Service to, and the summoning of, the Guardians was too important a task to allow for such carelessness. Could the fact that no Warden had greeted her awakening mean there was no Warden available? How could such a thing be possible as long as the Guild existed?

Then, there was the matter of the purpose for which she had been summoned. Her waking indicated a serious and immediate threat from the Darkness. Filling her in on the details of that threat would have been her Warden's first and most important task. He would have told her what the threat was, who posed it, and where to find the *nocturnis* or Demon behind it. Without that information, Ash was— half literally—flying blind.

The fact that she was female made for a subtler, but no less puzzling, question. Ash knew her own skills and strengths quite well. She knew her sex played no part in her ability to battle and defeat any enemy who stood against her. She wielded no less power than the next among her brothers and would perform her duty with equal determination and success.

But that didn't make her existence any less of an aberration. The first female Guardian. Ever.

Why? she brooded.

Not only had a female Guardian never before existed, one of the most significant and sacred of the tales about their origin involved the relationship between the *male* Guardians and human females. The human female of power, one with abilities beyond the ordinary—like Maeve's precognition—was, in fact, at the center of the story of how the Seven Demons of the Darkness had been imprisoned the last time they had all broken free. She was also the key to freeing a male Guardian from the endless cycle of waking and sleeping that defined his existence.

Such a female could become the Guardian's mate and their bond would allow him to retain his human shape forever, at the sacrifice of his immortal life span and inhuman abilities. In other words, love could transform the beast into the man.

But where did that leave Ash?

The questions tumbled around in her mind like pebbles at the ocean's edge. She had no answers, though, and continuing to ponder seemed unlikely to provide her with any. Taking care to keep silent, she rose from the bed and slipped out the door into the narrow hall.

The dim space was lit only by the glow coming from the living room at the front of the flat. With nothing else to do, Ash padded toward it and found herself back in the welcoming space. The empty room and the late hour gave her ample opportunity to explore.

She discovered after only a few seconds that Michael Drummond didn't have all that much to look at, at least not in this common space. Aside from the sofa, table, and chairs, the only furniture was a tall, dark bookcase that leaned against the wall near the entry. Nearly every shelf was crammed with titles, some paperback, some hardcover, and a few here and there bound in worn leather. She didn't recognize any, not that she would have, but the titles indicated an eclectic taste. A few pockets of space not occupied by books held an odd miscellany of objects—a rusted buckle attached to a frayed strap of leather, a framed photograph of four smiling women with their arms wrapped around each other's shoulders and another of a man and a woman who leaned against each other as they smiled, a handful of chipped and pitted coins that looked as if they had been dug from the earth. None of it said much about the place's occupant.

Ash found herself frustrated, and then found herself surprised by the frustration. She realized she had been looking for something that would allow her to understand this human called Michael Drummond. She wanted insight into what made the man tick, or at least that was what she told herself. Then it occurred to her that what she really wanted to understand was her own reaction to the man.

The realization knocked her off balance. The idea that a human male should cause her to react in any way at all mired her thinking like quicksand. She was not here for the sake of any one human, but for humanity as a whole.

Humanity as a whole, though, didn't leave her feeling angry, confused, and fascinated against her will.

Ash spun away from the bookcase, and the edge of her wing caught a precariously perched volume, knocking it to the floor. Human dwellings were clearly not designed for creatures with wings, especially not ones as large as hers. Muttering a curse, she bent to retrieve the book and shifted back to her human form. She might not find the shape as comfortable as her own, but it was safer for the moment. It wouldn't do to destroy the very place where she had been invited to stay.

She stood, book in hand, and found herself facing a doorway that had opened to reveal the very object of her thoughts. Drum stood frozen, one hand on the doorknob and the other braced against the wooden frame. His dark, wavy hair was rumpled as if he'd run his fingers repeatedly through the short-clipped curls, and stubble shadowed the firm line of his jaw. His blue eyes had locked on her, but she couldn't quite define the expression in them.

Her fingers clutched the book before her, and she felt a strange and unfamiliar urge to shift her weight from foot to foot. She stomped it under a mental boot heel and straightened her shoulders.

Ash waited for him to speak, but he remained quiet. The silence stretched between them, tightening in tiny increments like notches on a belt. She could feel the tension, could almost touch it, but Drum gave no indication that he sensed anything out of place, while it poked at her like a pebble in her shoe. Annoying human.

If he could think of nothing to say to her, then she certainly felt no obligation to initiate a conversation. They didn't need to utter a word to each other.

Pulling her gaze away, she half turned to set the book back on the edge of the shelf, then stepped toward the hall that would take her back to her borrowed bed. She had barely moved when Drum cracked the tension with a rough clearing of his throat.

"I thought you would be asleep," he said.

Ash faced him again and realized in a rush that she had no idea what to do with her hands. She looked down at them, wondering how a part of her own body could suddenly feel so awkward and alien. Was it because of their human shape? She told herself it was, because she had no wish to contemplate an alternate explanation.

Shoving the treacherous appendages into the pockets of her trousers, she lifted one shoulder toward her ear and let it fall. "I have not been awake long enough to require sleep."

Drum nodded and stepped the rest of the way into the apartment, closing the door behind him with a quiet click. "I—I, er, I was just downstairs. Clearing up. Our glasses and all."

Ash nodded. It seemed the thing to do, even if she wasn't certain why he had explained himself. This was his pub, his flat. Her understanding of human laws indicated he could do almost anything he liked here. It would be none of her business.

He took another step, and Ash noticed just the slightest waver as his foot landed on the edge of the rug. She narrowed her eyes and peered at him more closely. Had he been injured by the *hhissih* without her noticing? Or could he have taken ill? He had shown no signs of sickness earlier.

"I also had another little drink. Or two." He frowned, and the bridge of his nose drew up in a series of small wrinkles. "Or five. I may have been the slightest bit angry with you, Miss Call-Me-Ash. What sort of name is that, anyway?"

Ash recoiled in surprise. "Angry? You have no cause to feel anger at me, human. I am not the source of your troubles."

He continued as if she hadn't spoken. "That's something you find at the bottom of your fire grate. Not a proper name for a woman at all. Your parents should be ashamed of themselves."

He took another couple of steps toward her, not precisely swaying, but perhaps a little less than steadily upright. A small voice in her head whispered she should retreat. Such advice made no sense, went against everything she was, so Ash ignored it. Or rather, she raised her chin and took a step forward, meeting that slightly unfocused blue gaze head-on.

"I have no parents. I was summoned, not born. And my name is none of your concern."

" 'Course it is. I'm th' one usin' it. You're not callin' yourself by your name. That'd just be mental."

He leaned forward, and Ash reared back, raising a hand to brace against his chest. She could feel the heat of him through the soft cotton shirt. It warmed her cool fingertips and made her hesitate when she should have pushed him back.

Drum closed his eyes and drew a deep breath. She saw the way his nostrils flared and heard a low, satisfied hum pass between his lips.

"Your scent is . . . amazing." His voice had taken on a

purring quality that set off an unfamiliar fluttering sensation in Ash's stomach. Was she hungry? Anxious? Ill? "Fascinating. Like stone left in the sun, but sweet. Like honey. And sharp, like clove. It makes me . . ."

His words drifted off into silence, and Ash felt the most unexpected flash of frustration. She wanted to shake him and force him to complete his thought. Her fingers actually curled around the fabric of his shirt before she realized what she was doing, but she held on as she trained her features into a scowl.

"The hour is late for humans," she said, the brisk quality she was aiming for sounding gruff instead. "You should seek out your bed and sleep."

His eyelids parted to slits, revealing a glint of blue that looked a lot more like a superheated flame than a cool autumn sky. "Don't wanna sleep. But bed sounds brrrrrilliant."

He caught her by surprise, an event that for her kind could have proven fatal. But the blow he struck was something worse, something she had never thought to defend against. Something none of her strategies, none of her training, none of her abilities as a Guardian could have protected her from.

He kissed her.

Drum leaned down and pressed his lips to hers in the most devastating attack Ash could ever have imagined. Not only did the maneuver seem to come out of nowhere, but it disarmed her more swiftly than a sharp blow to the wrist of her weapon hand. Against it, she had no defenses, no instinctive counterstrike to use to bring the battlefield back to even ground. It shamed her to admit it, but she froze.

Then, she melted.

Not completely, she could at least say that much, but all around the edges. She softened, enough so that instead of spinning away, she remained in place. Perhaps even leaned just the tiniest bit closer. Later, she could be ashamed, but in that moment her mind had gone blank. She could not think. All she could do was feel. The warmth of his skin, the softness of his lips. The gentle pressure of his mouth on hers, urging her further along the path of her own undoing.

That pressure scrambled her wits. It left her with nothing but the sharp burn of curiosity and something else entirely unfamiliar. In her belly she felt a strange, tight gnawing sensation and something else even more disturbing. Something almost like . . . a-a-a . . .

A tingle.

Ash's head spun, a spark of horror weaving itself into the knot of other feelings flooding through her. At least the horror she understood. Guardians did not tingle. By rights, she should not even grasp the word, let alone experience its meaning. Yet this man, this human, had thrust it upon her.

Why did she not want to kill him?

Drum repeated that humming sound and parted his lips over hers. The tip of his tongue teased the tightly closed seam of her mouth, and against her own will, she felt it soften in instinctive surrender.

That was sufficient, finally, to drag Ash back to reality. A Guardian never surrendered. But more than that, Ash did not even know how. She would not learn here.

Shaking free of the strange spell holding her in place, she shoved against his chest and sent him spinning backward. She caught his expression of surprise and panic in the instant before the back of his shins caught on the edge of the coffee table and upset his balance. His already impaired body tipped backward and landed in an awkward heap of contorted limbs in the narrow space between table and sofa.

She stepped forward until she could see his face, but

she was careful to remain well out of arm's reach. Drum blinked up at her, his expression still startled and very confused.

"What the bloody hell was that for?" Despite his language, he sounded more baffled than upset.

Ash crossed her arms over her chest and glared at him. "Your thinking and your judgment are impaired by the alcohol you have consumed, human. Were it not so, I would beat you bloody for daring to assault me as you have done."

"Assault? It was just a kiss, you fecking she-demon!"

She ignored his indignant tone and hardened her expression. "Were I a demon, human, you would not wake in the morning with no more than a pounding head and a bruised ego. You would not wake at all."

Turning on her heel, Ash deafened her ears to the man's continued protests and stalked back to the small room under the eaves. He could say whatever he liked; it would make no difference. Now Ash understood that in spite of his harmless human appearance, Michael Drummond posed just as big a threat to her as any of the Seven ever had. From now on, she would remain on her guard.

If only she could turn *off* her memory. She had a feeling that would really help.

Chapter Six

Sororicide remained illegal in the Republic of Ireland, but Drum was willing to throw his support behind any political party who put it on their platform. He'd slap a bloody sign over the door of his pub and stage a rally, and the good Lord himself couldn't hold it against him.

His current reasoning—it changed daily, sometimes hourly—included the fact that she had nagged and harangued him until he had given in and arranged for his employees to cover today's shift at the Bone. So, instead of spending his day doing his books, building pints, and enjoying his life, Drum sat at his kitchen table with a pounding head, a sister he wanted to murder, and a woman he'd rather forget who was quite literally made of stone. Well, at least some of the time.

"I don't think today is the day for this, Mae," he grumbled. "I'm not up for it. Why don't we try tomorrow?"

"That's what you said yesterday. Last night, it made sense. Today, you're just being a dosser."

His fingers tightened around his mug of tea, and he supposed he should be grateful for the sturdy quality of old stoneware. "Sod off."

"Just as soon as you finish having a look." Maeve flashed him a smile full of teeth and empty of sincerity.

Drum cursed. He knew his sister well enough to read the determination behind her flippant words. Either he could give in and do what she demanded, or she would continue to pester him until he really did reach for a weapon.

Or even worse, she would drag their mother into it.

He swallowed a mouthful of tea and set his mug aside before he could use it as a bludgeon. "Fine. But I make no promises, and an aching head isn't likely to do anything for my concentration. I doubt I'll manage anything useful."

The woman—the *gargoyle*—called Ash had remained silent all morning. She hadn't even offered a greeting when she and his sister had emerged from the room where they'd slept. But she had certainly watched him closely enough. Her dark eyes kept him steadily in focus, and Drum wasn't sure whether their expression contained more wariness or spite. Nothing like waking up the morning after and wondering whether the woman from last night wanted to kill you. Especially not when you had absolute confidence that she could do it blindfolded. And with one hand tied behind her back.

It wasn't like he had done anything so terrible, Drum reminded himself. He had kissed her, just a kiss. He hadn't laid so much as a finger on her, let alone copped a cheap feel. And she had enjoyed it, anyway. He knew she had. Her lips had softened, her mouth heated, her breath caught in her throat. She had responded to him. Right before she sent him sprawling ass over teakettle on his sitting room floor. If anything, he was the one who deserved a temper tantrum.

And now he was working himself up all over again, which did nothing to help the whiskey-induced throbbing beneath his skull. Grimacing, he pushed aside thoughts of last night and focused on the now. Sufficient unto each day the miseries thereof.

He focused on his sister, because she, he knew, he could take. "What is it exactly that you want me looking for?"

Of course Maeve deferred to Ash. "What do you think?"

"You say he finds things?"

Maeve nodded.

"Then he should find my Warden," Ash said. "The Warden should know precisely why I was summoned, and why present circumstances do not adhere to tradition."

His sister turned toward him and waved a gracious hand. "You heard the lady."

Drum clenched his teeth. "Well, your *majesties,* it doesn't quite work that way. You know this, Maeve. I have to be able to picture what it is I'm looking for. If I haven't seen it for myself, I at least need a photograph." He looked at Ash. "Do you have a photograph?"

Her expression remained blank. Stony, even. "The Guardian I have replaced had slept for the last three hundred years. Photographs did not exist the last time he saw his Warden, who in any event is most certainly dead. I have never met mine, let alone seen his image. All I have is his name. O'Riordan."

Drum tried not to let his triumph show. "Then I don't see how I can help you, love. I can't look for it if I can't look at it."

"Michael." Maeve's tone held a warning. "There has to be a way you can help her. I know there is. You just have to try."

Frustration made him cranky, not to mention the pain. The pain didn't help his disposition.

But he was telling the truth. He didn't know where Maeve had gotten this idea of him as some great and powerful psychic phenomenon. Compared to hers, his "gift" could barely be called anything more than a tendency toward lucky guesses. Sure, he could find car keys, misplaced books, and even the occasional cat that wandered out of his mother's barn and up the neighbor's tree. Finding a person constituted a whole different kettle of chips.

Maeve continue to watch him, her lips pursed as she appeared to debate whether or not another smack on the head might rattle an agreement from his lips. "What if you had something to focus on?"

"What you mean?"

"Just what I said. What if you had an object associated with whoever you're looking for? Would that help?"

Reluctantly, Drum considered it. He'd never tried anything like that before. Then again, he'd never tried anything like this, either.

"I mean, what you're doing when you look for something is tuning in to its energy, right?" Maeve pressed. "That's how it works."

"Oh, is it? Why don't you explain it to me, Maeve? I'll sit here like a good boy and promise to raise my hand, all polite-like, if I have any questions."

His sister reacted to his sarcasm about as he'd expected, which was to say she gathered herself up for a physical attack. Ash spoke up before Maeve could strike. "The assumption is logical, but it matters not, for I have no object to offer with associations to my Warden."

"Of course you do." Just when he'd thought he might have found a way out of this ridiculous farce, his sister had to go and be helpful. "You said it yourself. He's *your* Warden. You're associated with him, just like he is with you. What better focus could you possibly have?"

Ash's gaze flew to his, and he saw mirrored there his own helpless dismay. Clearly, she was as horrified by Maeve's suggestion as he was. He just didn't know if she had the same reasons.

When no one said anything, Maeve pushed her advantage. "Come on. At least give it a try. What could it hurt?"

Drum looked around for a pencil before he caught himself. Did she need him to make her a list? Maybe he should show her the bruise on his hip from last night's tumble. Ash had made it plain that touching was right off the menu.

Because of that, her next words shocked him. "Perhaps your sister is correct."

He fought the urge to stick a finger in his ear and give it a wiggle. "Pardon? I don't think I heard you just there. Could you repeat that?"

Maeve smiled wide enough that the sunshine glinting off her teeth flashed at the edge of his vision.

"She has made valid points. Magic is energy, and whatever your family has chosen to call their talents, a Guardian would recognize all of them as magic. Therefore, what you are able to do is use your magical energy to recognize the natural energy of the object you seek. Theoretically, locating a Warden should be easier for you than locating an everyday item, because the Warden possesses magical energy of his own. In this realm, magical energy naturally stands out from mundane energy, thus making it easy to find."

Bollocks. He hated it when his opponent in an argument began to make sense. It was the kiss of death.

Through sheer force of will, Drum managed to channel his scream of frustrated annoyance into an ill-tempered grunt. He might have sprained something in the effort.

"All right, then. Let's have it over with."

And if Ash objected to his touch this time, the blame could fall on her head alone. Drum might even give it a little push.

Placing his hand on the table, he extended his arm

toward the Guardian and raised an eyebrow in challenge. Without saying a word, Ash both acknowledged and accepted. She placed the tips of her fingers against his palm and let him not just hold them but hold her in place.

Electricity jolted through him. He tried not to jump, but knew the others had to at least see him stiffen. His whole body sat up, spine straightening and shoulders pulling back as his vision went gray.

Drum didn't black out, and his eyes didn't close so there was no darkness, but the world went out of focus. It was as if the thickest fog man had ever seen rolled in behind his eyes. He saw nothing, if nothingness could have a texture. Then, something new exploded in front of his mind's eye, and he knew that what he saw now wasn't happening at the kitchen table in his flat above the pub.

What he saw didn't look like a Warden. Not that he knew what a Warden looked like, but he assumed it would be a person and not a single person appeared in his vision. Instead, the first thing he saw was fire, red and yellow flames licking up from the blackened ground. His mind blinked, and he saw the ground moving, like lava flowing across an open field. Nothing else survived. There was no grass, no trees, no vegetation of any kind. Not even a stone was left standing. He saw nothing but fire and molten earth, and the skies above were a dark, poisonous gray lit occasionally by flashes of unnatural crimson lightning. It looked like the deepest pit of hell.

He blinked again, and the nightmarish vision dissolved. In its place something infinitely cooler filled his sight. It looked familiar and comforting, the opposite of the last image. Rich Irish fields, outlined by ancient rock walls and dotted with sheep and cows lazily grazing, stretched out before his mind's eye. In the center, the earth sloped gently higher into a flat-topped hill, and from the top of the hill rose an ancient round tower. The roof and at least two stories had long since collapsed, leaving rubble scattered about the earth nearby. Vegetation had come to occupy the space abandoned by man, with trees and shrubs growing beside and through the aging walls. It was a scene you could find a hundred times a day in a country with Ireland's long and rich history.

Drum was ready to dismiss it as a dead end, was already tasting the sweet savor of "I told you so" on his lips when he realized something about the scene was more familiar than just another postcard picture. He realized that he recognized this particular tower ruin as one he and his sisters had explored throughout their childhood. Across the fields beyond it, just out of the range of his sight, his parents' house sat near one of those limestone walls, less than a mile from the village of Clondrohitty. He knew exactly what he was looking at.

Drum shoved the vision away and snatched his hand from Ash's. He shook his head to clear away the last of the fog. Maeve's face hadn't even come into focus before her voice started chittering at him.

"—see, then? Michael? Michael, answer me. Drum!"

As if his head hadn't already been throbbing. Using his talent had turned the throb into sharp, rhythmic blows from an ice pick. Pressing the heel of his hand to his forehead, he squeezed his eyes shut and groaned. "Shut it, Mae."

"But we need to know if it worked. What did you—"

Ash interrupted, an unexpected voice of reason. "Your brother appears unwell, Maeve. Perhaps a glass of water would help him collect himself. If you would?"

Without opening his eyes, Drum heard Maeve rise and walk around to the kitchen behind him. The faucet squeaked and water tumbled into a glass before her soft footsteps returned to the table. The glass knocked softly against the wood. Drum reached out blindly and brought it to his lips, guzzling it down like a drunkard's gin.

"Another?"

He set the glass down and shook his head. "I'm fine."

"You do not look fine. Your skin looks very pale and moist. Your hands also appear to be shaking."

"Gee, thanks, Tinkerbell," he growled, wondering why his eyelids felt as if they'd been epoxied shut. "I appreciate your concern and am flattered by the assessment."

"I'm sorry, Michael." Maeve managed to sound contrite. "I let my excitement at the idea of finding something get ahead of me. But you've never looked like this before. You always made finding things look so easy, like you just pictured them in your mind and there they were."

He managed to open one eye and saw genuine concern in her expression. As usual, he became an instant sucker. "Don't worry yourself, love. I'll be fine. It just took me off guard, is all."

Maeve squeezed his hand. "I guess you were right about finding a person being different, eh?"

While his sister apologized, Ash took his empty glass into the kitchen and refilled it. She returned it to exactly where he'd left it and resumed her seat. "Now can you tell us what it is that you saw?"

He winced. "Well, I didn't see a person at all. Just as I told you, it didn't work that way."

"But you did see something."

A couple of things, Drum acknowledged to himself, but he had no intention of discussing the first half of his vision. Last night, Ash had stirred things up with her talk of demons and their servants, of evil and destruction, but it was a new day and the sun was shining. In the bright morning light, her words sounded like nothing more than ghost stories told around the fire after nightfall. None of it was real, and certainly his vision of fire and brimstone had been a figment of his overworked imagination.

"I saw a place, not a person," he said. He felt uncomfortable revealing even that much. "Just a scene of somewhere out in the country. Nothing very special."

"Describe it."

Drum glared into steady, dark eyes that never wavered. Being made of stone gave her an unfair advantage in outstubborning him. And here he'd always thought Maeve was the only one who could manage it.

"A ruin," he said. "This is Ireland. We've got them coming out our ears." She just stared; he got cranky. "It was a tower," he bit out, "or what's left of one. Stone, three or four stories at some point, now more like one and a half. It's on a hill surrounded by farmland. Like I said, nothing very special."

Ash continued to watch his face, her expression inscrutable. No one spoke for a moment, then Maeve stuck her freckled nose into things. Again.

"Michael . . ." Her tone held a caution and a threat, one he was familiar with.

He ignored her, but Ash turned her head and her attention to the little meddler. She didn't even have to ask; his own personal traitor turned on him cheerfully.

"He might not think it's special, but it sounds awfully familiar." His sister ignored his glare almost as easily as Ash had done. "There's a ruined tower near where we grew up, not far from my mother's house. I'd say it more than fits his description."

Drum said, "Whether it does or not, she was looking for a person, not a place."

Maeve shrugged. "So you didn't see a face. Maybe the Sight just showed you where he's staying instead of him directly."

"Where he's staying?" Drum scoffed. "So this Warden

fellow she's looking for is camped out in a pile of rubble with no roof, where sheep do their business as they wander through? In Ireland. In the autumn."

Maeve had a long-standing appreciation for sarcasm, but apparently only when *she* was using it. Her eyes narrowed. "How are we to know if he has the sense God gave a billy goat?"

Ash spoke before their conversation devolved along the usual lines—into physical violence. "Wardens are highly intelligent and magically gifted. One would not subject himself to such primitive conditions without taking measures that would leave some visible evidence of occupation. However, I do not believe what you have seen to be without truth. Perhaps a clue was left in this place. I must go and look for myself."

"Be my guest," Drum muttered beneath his breath.

Of course, his sister heard him. "She is your guest, Michael," Maeve said, "and she's not from around here. She doesn't know how to find the tower; we do. It's only right that we take her."

Not from around here? Drum swallowed a bitter laugh. He supposed you might say that.

Ash shook her head. "This is my mission, not yours. You have been generous with your assistance, and in pointing me in the proper direction. I cannot ask for more, and I cannot risk placing humans in danger."

"Don't be silly. We're happy to help. Besides, we're not talking about jumping off a cliff or fighting those things we saw last night. We've both played in those ruins since we were babies. It's perfectly safe."

Drum just leaned back in his chair and set his teeth until he felt the muscle in his jaw jump like a March hare. He knew arguing with Maeve would only make her dig her heels in further, but Ash appeared to have a penchant for hopeless causes.

"No. While I am grateful for your offer—"

Maeve continued forward like a piece of earth-moving machinery. "Besides, Ma is expecting to see me this morning, so we'll be driving out there anyway. It would be silly for us not to give you a ride."

We? "*You* are taking a bus, missy. *I* have a pub to run and books to do. I'll see Ma on Sunday, like always."

"Oh?" Maeve arched her brows at him. "You mean that when I see Ma and introduce her to Ash, you'd like me to explain that you forced me and my guest to ride the bus rather than driving us out yourself? Why, I would be happy to do just that, brother dear." She fluttered her lashes at him and smiled widely.

"Blackmail is a nasty habit, Mae."

"But effective, no?"

Her trap snapped shut around Drum with a nasty click of wicked sharp teeth. Damn her for pushing, and double damn her for knowing his kryptonite. Now he could either acknowledge defeat, or he could face the wrath of the person he felt certain even Saint Patrick himself feared to cross—his mother.

What was a man to do?

Chapter Seven

Green stretches of land rolled past the windows of the car almost as swiftly as if Ash soared above them with powerful beats of her wings. The novelty of riding in such a piece of human machinery had not worn off during this, her second experience. Last night, the streets had been dark and misty, but today the sun shone through the fluffy cover of clouds to illuminate the lush scenery.

If she hadn't known better, Ash might think she was feeling a sense of well-being, but that was impossible. Everyone knew that Guardians did not feel.

While her kind experienced physical sensations, like the heat of fire or the pain of a wound earned in battle, they did not possess anything like the human range of emotions. A Guardian existed to vanquish his enemy—*her* enemy—and so had no need for any feelings beyond those of a warrior: fury, determination, rage, and hatred for the enemy.

She knew, of course, of the legend of Guardians who found their mates among human females of power. Those brothers began to experience other emotions in the company of the women who would eventually free them from the prisons of their stony forms. No story existed that spoke of a female Guardian, let alone one with a mate or the ability to feel love or any other human emotion. Therefore, Ash remained as she had been summoned—cold as chiseled granite.

Were it not for Maeve's friendly chatter, the drive from Dublin to the siblings' native village would have passed in silence broken only by the grinding sound of Drum's clenched teeth. Ash was likely the only one who could hear it, her senses being so much keener than humans', but the steady soliloquy on the scenery, the Drummond family, and local history drowned most of it out. It could not, however, disguise the white of his knuckles clenched around the steering wheel, nor the continued stiffness of his posture. The man didn't have to utter a word to make clear his dislike of the situation.

He wasn't alone. Ash would have much preferred to follow the trail to her Warden without a couple of humans along for her to worry about. Drum's vision may not have indicated a threat at the ruin he had seen, but Ash would not have been summoned had dark forces not been stirring in the area. Allowing him and his sister to accompany her chafed against her instincts. She would do her duty to protect them at any cost, but that could interfere with her principal mission—find her Warden, then identify the threat from the Darkness and eliminate it.

An abrupt break in Maeve's speech interrupted Ash's brooding. The woman made a sound of interest and tapped a nail against the car's rear window. "Ooh, Michael. Isn't that Peadar O'Keefe?"

Drum cursed. "Where?"

"There. Crossing McSweeney's field. He must be on his way to check the post. Look, he's waving at us."

"Perfect," her brother grumbled. His fingers tightened further until Ash heard the vehicle's control wheel creak in protest.

"And he's off again, over the stile and down the lane to the post, right past Ma's house."

It was impossible to miss either the glee in Maeve's tone or the hostility radiating from her brother's tense form. It appeared as if the woman deliberately tried to annoy her elder sibling, a habit Ash had first remarked upon the previous night. It confused her. She could sense genuine affection between the two, yet each leaped on any available opportunity to taunt the other. If this was a human custom, Ash found it a bizarre one.

But maybe she had missed the human girl's true intent. "Do I miss the significance of a familiar person walking in this area?"

Drum answered over his sister's smirk. "Maeve is pointing out—needlessly—that now he's seen us, our neighbor is certain to tell our mother we're here to visit."

"This is undesirable?"

"I intended to drop Maeve off without stopping and take you right to the ruin. Now I can't."

Truly, the course of human logic eluded her. "I do not understand."

"My brother is just being grumpy. Ma would be crushed if you just ran off like that. She's always saying how she doesn't see enough of her only son. It won't kill you to spend a minute or two humoring her."

"But it might kill you."

Maeve made a rude noise, but otherwise ignored her brother's threat.

Ash shook her head and held her tongue as Drum steered the car through the narrow lane between the hedgerows. They turned a corner, and the road opened to reveal a white farmhouse less than a quarter of a mile farther on. They slowed and turned into a gravel yard beside the building. In front of them, an old barn appeared to have been converted into an automotive garage, while fields stretched beyond a stone wall to the left. On the right, a woman stood just on the other side of a low picket fence with her arms crossed over her chest and an expression on her face that Ash could not read.

Maeve opened her door almost before the vehicle had stopped. She flung it wide and jumped out to catch the strange woman in an enthusiastic embrace. "Ma, I'm famished. To look in his kitchen, you'd think Michael lives on bread and water."

"Well, we all know your brother is no monk, so I think it's more likely he couldn't be bothered to do the marketing." The woman's voice was rich, and her accent held even more of Ireland than either of her children's. "I thought you said you'd be here last night."

"My research took longer than I expected. By the time I finished and called Drum to come and fetch me, it was after midnight. We didn't want to wake the whole house, so I stayed with him and decided to come out this morning."

The elder Drummond female pursed her lips. "So I can see, and I see you've brought himself with you. And a guest."

Ash saw Drum tense when he heard that. He blew out a long breath, then pried his fingers from the steering wheel one at a time and climbed from the car. Ash followed suit and watched as the man stepped over to greet his mother.

"Hello, Ma." The man had to lean down a considerable distance to kiss her cheek, even though she stretched to meet him. "How are you?"

"Well enough, you don't need to ask," she said, "but you and your sister both are rude beggars for standing here and not introducing your friend."

Her words might have included both of her children, but her eyes remained steadily on her son as she spoke. Ash

saw Drum flinch and wondered at his reaction. "Right,
Ma, this—"

"—is Ash. She's a—"

"—friend of Maeve's."

The siblings spoke over each other, each glaring when
the other's voice rose louder. Mrs. Drummond looked between them but quickly turned her attention to Ash. She
extended her hand. "It's lovely to meet you, dear. As my
children have forgotten every manner I've attempted to
drill into them, I can tell you I'm Maddie Drummond.
Welcome to my home. Now, is Ash short for Aisling?"

Ash shook her hand, feeling both warmth and strength
in the elder human's lightly callused fingers. Maddie
Drummond stood even shorter than her daughter, barely
skimming two inches above five feet. Her face was round
but for the determined point of her chin, and her blue eyes
were exact replicas of Maeve's. Her mouth echoed the
shape of her son's, only softer, and bracketed by lines that
indicated frequent smiles and hearty laughter. Similar
lines framed her eyes, but otherwise her fair, freckled skin
looked smooth and fresh. Her dark brown hair was pep-
pered with gray, and her figure was trim, though softened
by age. She appeared to be in her late fifties, but guessing
the ages of humans was not a skill Ash could brag of.

"No, ma'am," she answered. "It is simply Ash."

Maddie held her gaze for several seconds, seeming to
look behind the dark but human-shaded irises of Ash's
mortal disguise. For a moment, the Guardian felt a stirring
of unease.

But then the woman smiled and pushed open the low
gate. "Well then, I'm very pleased to meet you, simply
Ash. Now come in the house, and have a cup of tea while
I feed this brat here. I know it's near to lunch, but breakfast will be quicker. Are you hungry?"

From the corner of her eye, Ash could see Drum's tension ease, while on her other side Maeve's seemed to tick upward a notch. Still, neither spoke while they followed Maddie around the side of the house, bypassing the front door to enter through another at the rear of the structure.

They stepped directly into a small kitchen filled with warmth and the smell of baking bread. Through an archway to the right, Ash could see a large table spread with a cheery red cloth and surrounded by six chairs with worn wooden seats. Several more stood back against the walls, and she would guess that beneath its cover, the table could extend to accommodate at least a dozen in total.

Maddie shooed them toward it with one hand, the other reaching to pull a kettle from the top of the range. "I'll start a new pot while one of you tells me what brought you out here this morning."

Drum slid into the chair at the foot of the table, his expression wary. "Maeve told you it was too late to bring her out last night."

After taking her own seat, Maeve nudged Ash to the one beside her, putting Drum to her left and the archway directly opposite. It gave her the perfect view of Maddie's face and the skepticism written over it.

"And as you know lying is a sin, that's as may be. But it doesn't explain why Peadar O'Keefe told me he saw your car on the road from Dublin instead of just Maeve walking here from the bus stop in the village."

"He was telling Ash just this morning about the ruined tower in McGinty's far field," Maeve said as her mother brought a plate of sliced brown bread and a crock of fresh butter to the table. "It seemed silly not to bring her out and let her see it for herself. Any marmalade?"

She ignored her brother's scowl and reached for the bread. Ash could read the threat of strangulation in the man's eyes and marveled at Maeve's lack of concern.

Maddie set plates and silverware before each of them,

along with a glass jar filled with orange marmalade near her daughter. "Oh? Did the two of you have other plans for this morning?" she asked with a pointed glance at Drum.

He shook his head. Ash guessed that his nonverbal response owed to his inability to unclench his jaw. She wondered if perhaps, for Maeve's sake, she should move his knife out of reach.

She attempted a distraction. "I told your son and daughter both that I did not require an escort to visit these ruins. I had planned to come alone and not disturb anyone."

Maddie had placed several rashers of bacon into a hot pan and began cracking eggs. Over her shoulder, she shot Ash a look of dismay. "Come alone? And without stopping for a visit? I'd never have forgiven you."

Ash refrained from mentioning that if she had not stopped, Maddie Drummond would not have known her to forgive. It seemed like a detail the older human would not appreciate.

"Michael, how many eggs, dear?"

"None, Ma." He pushed his chair back from the table. "While Maeve has breakfast here, I'll walk Ash to the ruins so she can look around. We'll be back in an hour and get out of your hair. Maeve can catch the bus back to Dublin before her next class."

Maddie spun away from her stove and brandished a spatula. "Michael Stephen Drummond, you sit back down in that chair and possess yourself in a little patience. Did I forget to teach you manners while you lived under this roof? You will not hustle this young lady in and out of my door like some sort of shameful secret. You will eat your breakfast, drink your tea, and engage in a civilized conversation. Do I make myself clear?"

Drum dropped back into his chair and snapped his jaw shut. "Yes, ma'am."

"Good. Maeve, come fetch the tea."

The young woman jumped up to obey while Ash watched their mother with appreciation. The human woman had impressed her with the ability to plow straight through her son's objections. Her fearlessness in the face of what Ash knew to be powerful determination would make a warrior proud.

Maeve returned carrying a tray loaded with a steaming ceramic teapot, four cups, a bowl of roughly shaped sugar cubes and a small pitcher of milk. While she distributed and poured, she and Maddie struck up an animated conversation surrounding local events, Maeve's graduate work at the university in Dublin, and other assorted items of mutual interest. Through it all, Drum remained silent and brooded over his teacup, speaking only when asked a direct question. Neither woman commented on his surliness as they finished preparing and serving breakfast.

When everyone had taken seats behind plates piled with bacon, eggs, potato scones, and fried mushrooms, Maddie lifted her teacup to her lips and turned her gaze on Ash. "So, dear, tell me a little bit about yourself. You have an unusual accent. I'm not sure I've ever heard a thing like it. You're not English, and you're not American, are you?"

Ash froze, a forkful of bacon poised in midair. Her gaze flew from Maeve to Drum before darting back to their mother. "Uh, no. No, I am not. I was . . . er, born . . . in Dublin, but most of my time has been spent, uh, elsewhere."

"Really? Is your family in the military, then?"

She nodded slowly, feeling her eyes widen. "You could say that."

"I hear that's a very difficult life for a child, to be always on the move." Maddie made a clucking sound. "But you plan to make your home in Dublin now?"

"Ma, give her a chance to eat," Drum interrupted. "It'll get cold if you keep her talking like this."

"Sorry, sorry. You're absolutely right. Ignore me for a nosy gossip, Ash, dear. Go on and finish your breakfast."

She felt a surge of relief and immediately dropped her gaze to her plate. She owed Drum a debt for his distraction maneuver, but it had pointed out to her that she should perhaps think of a story to explain her human presence, at least until she found her Warden. The search might require further interaction with humans, and it would be best to continue concealing her true identity when possible. She did not wish to alert the *nocturnis* ahead of time that a Guardian walked among them. It would give them more time to conceal their actions and intentions.

Ash, Drum, and Maeve tucked into their breakfasts. Though she could go a considerable time without water or sustenance, Ash found the meal delicious. The salty bacon was tender at the center and crisp at the edges, the eggs clearly fresh, and the scones flavored with snips of bright green chive. She ate eagerly while Maddie sipped tea and confined herself to sharing the latest village gossip with her children. The woman also brought them up to date with stories of their other siblings and assorted nieces and nephews. The evidence suggested that the Drummond clan was a close-knit one.

"That's the other reason why you and Ash can't just go tearing back to Dublin, Michael," Maddie said. "Síle and Meara are both coming to dinner tonight, and if Bridget Sorley delivers by seven, Sorcha may come by for a nightcap. You can't deny me a chance to have all five of my children in one place at one time, now can you? You wouldn't be so cruel."

Ash saw Drum surrender before the deep sigh passed his lips. "Madelaine Connelly Drummond, world's foremost wielder of guilt," he proclaimed, but his lips curved up at the corners. "You win, Ma. When Ash and I are done at the ruins, we'll come back and stay for dinner. But we're leaving tonight. I'm opening the pub in the morning, and Ash deserves to be home at a decent hour."

Maddie smiled in such a way that Ash now understood how a person could be said to beam. Previously, she had thought only bright lights and stars capable of that action. "Of course, of course. We'll eat early, at six. That way you have plenty of time for the drive back."

"Then it's settled." Maeve stood and reached for the jacket she had tossed on the next chair. "We should get going. It's only a mile or two, but Ash will want plenty of time to ramble about."

Drum's eyes threw daggers at his sister. "I thought you were going to stay here and help Ma with the washing up, Mae."

Maeve sent the blades right back. "Whatever gave you that idea, Michael?"

Maddie simply ignored them and began gathering the soiled dishes. Both of her children watched as if waiting for her to speak. Ash had the feeling that Drum expected his mother to back him up, while Maeve believed she would win the woman's support. Maddie herself gave nothing away as she carried her tray back to the kitchen.

"You'll not cut me out of this, Michael Stephen," Maeve hissed, checking to see if their mother was listening.

"This is none of your concern, Maeve Rowena," he shot right back, keeping his voice low. "The only one who needs to see the ruins is Ash, and only one of us needs to show her the way. I'm going. You're staying here."

"I'm not. Have you forgotten who had the vision that started this whole thing?"

"No, but I think you've forgotten that I am your older brother, and that it's my job to keep you out of harm's way."

"To hell with that! Let me tell you, big brother . . ."

Rolling her eyes, Ash shrugged into her own jacket and walked around the table to the kitchen door. The arguing siblings didn't even seem to notice. She recalled spying some sort of stone ruin in the distance when she had climbed out of the car earlier. She felt confident that she could find the place Drum had described all on her own. Maddie Drummond winked as she walked past and stepped out into the dappled sunlight.

It was obvious who had the brains in that family. Too bad the trait had not proven hereditary.

Chapter Eight

Drum thought smoke might still be pouring out his ears when he caught up to Ash as she crossed the border of his parents' property. Technically, since his father's death more than a dozen years ago, the place belonged to his mother alone, though she leased out most of the fields to local farmers, but old habits were not just hard to break; sometimes they felt indestructible.

The Guardian did not acknowledge his presence. She simply continued into the neighbor's field, taking the most direct route toward the ruin on the hill.

"You won't want to continue this way," he said after a moment of matching his stride to hers. The novelty of doing that with a woman was not lost on him. Most of the time he had to slow his pace to accommodate the disparity in length of leg, but Ash stood only a couple of inches shorter than he and had legs that lasted forever. He remembered that from last night. Among other things.

"Why not?"

She sounded snappish, and he felt another wave of gratitude that he'd succeeded in browbeating Maeve into staying behind. He wouldn't come out and say that blackmail had been involved, but he had set aside some very interesting photos a few years back in case of emergency.

"Because after the next field, you'll hit the pasture where Billy Evers grazes his prize bull. Fionn mac Cumhaill has a wee bit of a temper."

"Your neighbor named his bull after a legendary leader of warriors?" She glanced at him skeptically, but slowed her pace a little.

Drum shrugged. "As a calf, he felt more inclined to bang himself in the head than have a nap."

Ash snorted. "Which way then?"

"We'll head right. There's a path through the corner there that will take us around where we need to go. It's not much out of the way."

They walked for a while in silence, for which Drum was grateful. It might not be entirely comfortable, but an hour in the car with his magpie of a sister followed by his mother's gentle inquisition had brought his headache roaring back. The pain only served to remind him of all the whiskey he'd consumed last night, and that in turn made him think of last night's other big mistake.

He should never have kissed her. Ash had made that clear when she'd sent him flying with no more than a casual shove. He would hate to think of the force she might have brought to bear if he'd tried to take things any further. He probably would have woken up with his teeth on the pillow beside him.

Drum wanted to blame the whole thing on the liquor, but not even his own conscience was buying that story. He had done a lot worse with a lot less alcohol in his belly, which perhaps indicated that his problem had more to do with a sorry lack of basic intelligence.

He didn't enjoy calling himself stupid, but the shoe was beginning to slip on with disturbing ease. It would be much more to his liking if he could blame his lapse in judgment on Ash instead. The trouble with that was that the female hadn't flirted with him, hadn't even so much as batted her long, dark eyelashes in his direction. She hadn't invited the kiss. He had simply fallen on her like a ravening beast. Unless he could prove that she exuded some sort of irresistible pheromone that short-circuited the wiring of the male human brain, the only one to blame for the debacle was himself.

But that wasn't the worst part. The worst part was that every time he looked at her, he wanted to do it all over again.

There must be something wrong with him. They could barely speak to each other without arguing. They agreed on nothing. They approached everything from opposite perspectives. For fuck's sake, they weren't even the same bloody species, and yet he hardened every time she turned those fathomless dark eyes his way.

He should thank his maker she wasn't watching him right now. Hiking through muddy fields with an erection was no man's idea of a good time.

Clearing his throat, he attempted to focus on something other than the way his companion affected him. "You've read a lot of Irish mythology, then?"

"I have read nothing," she said. "I did not exist before you saw me last night. But all Guardians have knowledge of warfare, both how to wage it and how others are said to have waged it in the past."

"Fionn mac Cumhaill is a legend, though. And the Fenians. No one knows if those battles were ever actually fought."

"No one knows they weren't."

Right. So much for conversation.

They tromped across fields, avoiding Billy Evers's, until the tower ruin loomed before them atop an isolated hillock. A cloud had rolled across the sun, leaving the landscape dulled and the stone a stained and dingy gray, where before it had glinted white and silver in the bright light. Trees and bushes had grown up all around the tumbled stone, and vines of woody nightshade crept up an outer wall, fighting a carpet of ivy for its foothold. The place looked empty and forgotten, one of the thousand remnants of a bygone age.

Drum looked over to Ash. She stood at the base of the hill, one foot forward and braced on the slope upward. Her hands rested on her hips, and her narrowed eyes were locked on the ancient pile of rubble. For a moment he wondered if she might see something he couldn't, because her gaze seemed fixed on a specific point. But she said nothing.

Instead, she let her hands drop to her sides and pointed her chin toward the top of the hill. "Let us go."

She climbed the short distance quickly, her strides long and steps sure. Drum followed without comment, and in moments they stood in front of the yawning archway that had once been the tower's entrance. He expected her to hesitate, but she pushed forward into the dim confines of the enclosed space without a second thought.

"Be careful," he called as he scrambled after her. "The roof may already have fallen and the upper floors rotted away, but the ends of some of the beams are still up there, and the tops of the walls are none too stable. Keep your eyes open for something falling on your head."

Ash didn't bother to answer, but he thought he heard a grunt. He supposed he would have to satisfy himself with that.

While she inspected her surroundings, Drum took the opportunity to look around him with fresh eyes. He'd spent many an hour with his sisters chasing and being chased through and around this old heap. It didn't require much imagination to recall the sound of childish giggles and taunts shouted in Irish, as if it were their own secret language.

He and his sisters had grown up learning their native language in schools alongside English, but his grandparents had been educated in a time when teaching the old tongue was still forbidden and his parents in a time when using it was seen as backward. So for the five Drummond siblings, Irish really had seemed like a private code no one else could crack.

Drum had been back a few times over the years, usually on quick passes by when he took rambling walks during his visits home. He had seen the evidence of time marching on. The walls stood less tall than he remembered, partly because he had grown, and partly as they continued to disintegrate under the fingers of the wet and windy Irish weather. The space seemed less vast, as well. What had felt cavernous to a child now seemed no larger than half of the front room at the Bones.

Ash paced around him, the soles of her boots crunching against the floor, whose cobbles had long since disappeared beneath a layer of crushed rock and spreading moss. She frowned as she examined the walls, from the crumbling remains of a demolished hearth to the large hole where a narrow arrow slit had grown through age or violence into a gap through which the two of them could have passed abreast.

She looked at Drum. "There is nothing here."

"I told you that before we left Dublin. It's an empty ruin. What did you expect?"

"Something more than this." She threw her hands into the air and growled. Not simply a growllike sound of frustration, but an actual growl. If the last Irish wolf had not been killed before the turn of the nineteenth century, he would have checked over his shoulder to see if one lurked in the shadows. "Why would your magic have shown you this place when you attempted to locate my Warden if it offered no evidence of his existence?"

"If you'll recall, I pointed out the lack of a relationship between an unknown person and a familiar place. Also before we left Dublin."

Okay, Drum acknowledged to himself. That may have been a little snippy. But between the frustration of finding himself in a situation so far out of the realm of normal that it featured magic and gargoyles, and the torment of the inexplicable arousal he experienced just from looking at the gargoyle standing next to him, his temper was what you might call slightly frayed.

It didn't help when a sudden tremor that made those of the night before seem like a case of hiccups rattled the earth beneath his feet and tossed him right on his arse. It felt the same as before, as if someone had just shaken out the ground as if it were a giant rug, only Drum was standing on it when those cosmic wrists gave their powerful flick.

At least this time he wasn't the only one to go flying. Ash landed beside him with a thump and a curse in what he thought might be Latin. "No force of nature has caused these earthquakes," she hissed.

"I told you," he said, gasping a little to regain his breath. "Ireland doesn't have earthquakes, not ones we can feel."

"You felt that one."

"I did."

He also felt his stomach drop when he heard a sudden crack of stone, louder than the blast from a cannon, ring out in the ruined tower around them. Adrenaline rushed through him as instinct had him throwing himself— literally—at the woman he'd been lusting after since midnight. He wasn't making a pass, though; he was reflexively and idiotically attempting to shield a being made of stone from being crushed beneath the rocks falling from the tower walls. The structure was coming down on top of them. That was where the noise had come from, and to his surprise Drum discovered in himself a willingness to die in order to protect a woman he barely knew.

Who would have thought?

Only he didn't die, and the stones never fell. Instead of doom falling from overhead, it approached from below. The ground at the center of the tower's interior split open, a giant seam appearing in the mossy rubble. The edges spread apart like a great, yawning maw and exposed the darkness beneath.

At least the sight gave them some warning of the next tremor. Fat lot of good it did them. The motion sent them rolling toward the chasm too fast for them to scramble away. Drum felt them hit the edge, and then the sickening sensation of the earth falling away beneath him. He screamed, a small part of his mind shaking free of the terror to wonder whether or not he sounded like a little girl. Not that it would matter when he died the instant they landed.

He felt the sting of air whip across his cheeks for a moment before the momentum of the fall jerked to a sudden stop. Beneath his frantic, clinging fingers, he felt a tingle of electricity and the shifting of cloth and flesh into something very different. As they spun through the air, Ash cast aside her human form and spread her wings in the darkness. They caught the air and arrested their drop to the center of the earth.

At least, it looked like the center of the earth. He couldn't say how far they had fallen, but then, the air around them was utterly black. The tear in the earth above them looked a very long way off, and the light from it didn't filter down more than a few feet. They hadn't reached the bottom yet, but at least they hadn't gone splat.

Drum bit off his cry, snapping his jaw shut with the

click of teeth hitting teeth. Maybe he would survive until dinner after all. Good. That would save Ma the trouble of killing him.

He heard the heavy beat of Ash's wings stir the air. Moments later, he felt solid ground beneath his feet an instant before his knees gave out. He collapsed into a gasping, panting pile of spent terror and blinked up into near-total blackness. Ash touched down beside him with a quiet rustling sound. Unable to see her, he reached out a hand and fumbled around until his fingers brushed the smooth skin of her bare calf. To hell with personal boundaries. She would need that axe of hers if she wanted to make him let go.

"Are you all right?" Her voice had taken on that growling tone again. Apparently, she appreciated being thrown into the bowels of the earth as little as he did.

"I'm alive, and I don't think I broke any bones, but that doesn't make me any closer to all right than Dublin is to Timbuktu." Drum levered himself into a seated position but kept his fingers wrapped around her leg. "How the bloody everlasting hell did that just happen?"

"As I told you and your sister last night, this must be the work of the *nocturnis*. I can feel the earth objecting to their defiling touch."

"Brilliant. But now that I think on it, I suppose the more relevant question would be, 'How the bloody everlasting hell are we going to get out of here?' Any ideas?"

As he spoke, Drum used his free hand to fumble in the pocket of his jeans for his key fob. Since buying the pub almost five years ago (with a great deal of help from his family), he had taken to working some very late nights. It hadn't been long before he realized that bumbling around in the dark only led to frustration, curses, and large amounts of wasted time. He had quickly begun to carry a small but powerful LED flashlight on a ring along with his keys. He located it and pressed the button just in time to intercept Ash's expression of disbelief at his ignorance.

In the circle of bright light, he saw her point a finger behind her own shoulder. At her wings. "The same way we avoided a most unfortunate landing. But first, I must look around."

"What? Down here? Is this Warden fellow of yours some sort of cave troll?"

She turned away from the beam of his flashlight and peered into the darkness. "Do not be foolish. The last troll on this plane went extinct centuries ago."

"Well, that's a relief," Drum mumbled, releasing his grip on her calf as she stepped away. He pushed himself to his feet and swept the light in a circle around them.

If he hadn't remembered—in vivid detail—how he and Ash had landed in their present circumstances, he might have thought they had simply walked into a natural cavern. He could see the walls of stone to the right and slightly ahead of them, as well as those curving around behind on the same side. To the left, however, the flashlight's beam petered out into the thick, inky shadows.

"Aim your contraption at the floor," Ash snapped at him. "It interferes with my vision."

Drum gaped at her. "You can see in this?"

"Many of the evils against which a Guardian fights are more comfortable in the darkness."

His heartbeat sped up, and he obediently pointed his light down before stepping closer to her. "And, ah, are any of those evils here right now?"

"Relax, human. Were a creature of the Darkness lurking in the shadows, we would already be engaged in combat." She sounded almost as if she were laughing at him.

"No need for rudeness," he said, ignoring the fact that he hadn't exactly put on his best manners around her since their initial meeting. "My name is Drum, not human. Especially not the way you say it. Like an insult."

She didn't respond. She prowled forward in the darkness as if she expected to stumble on some sort of lost treasure, or a neatly written summary of the cause of current events.

"I do not understand," she muttered, running her hand across the rough face of the cavern wall. "There must be something here, something I am meant to find. It is the only explanation, both for your vision and for this place being revealed to us."

He could see her frustration as well as her confusion in the dim glow of his averted light. Her brows drew together, wrinkling her pale gray skin, and the way she chewed on her lip made him wonder how she managed not to pierce herself with her own fangs. She stared into the shadows as if waiting for the secrets of the universe to be revealed.

Instead, what revealed itself was more bloody darkness. Drum felt fecking well sick of it. He could see no more than a few steps in front of him even though the echo of their voices told him the cavern around them must be huge. He had fallen an estimated sixty feet through a hole in the earth that shouldn't have existed, and even though his companion had softened his landing, he still felt as if he'd had the wind knocked out of him. Figuratively, if not literally. Said companion also appeared to have about as much respect for him as he had for the soccer hooligans who occasionally stumbled into his pub before realizing it wasn't their sort of establishment.

And to top the whole thing off, it almost looked as if the blackness beyond the circle of his flashlight was moving, sort of throbbing and shimmering like a heat mirage over the Sahara. Drum blinked and shook his head and peered a little closer.

As it turned out, that may have been a mistake.

If the odd motion of the air had provided him with advanced warning, as far as Drum was concerned, it did a piss-poor job. His eyes might have seen the shadows coalesce into a hulking, slavering form with eyes like burning coals and grotesquely long arms tipped with claws like shards of obsidian, but his brain almost fried itself trying to make sense of the picture.

The shadow creature leaped forward, somehow managing to travel at roughly twice the speed of sound while still investing its movements with the unnerving, sinuous quality of a serpent. It reached for him with those glittering talons, and Drum reacted on pure instinct. His hands flew up, one arm covering his face while the hand holding the flashlight pointed straight at the monster. He opened his mouth to release another girly, wordless scream and heard instead his own voice bellow in an unfamiliar tone of command.

"Get back!"

The words accompanied a blinding flare of light, a warm, golden tone that provided sharp contrast to the pale beam of his flashlight. It emerged not from the tiny clear bulb of the device, but from the palm of Drum's hand. It crashed into the shadow figure as if both possessed actual mass. Drum swore he could hear the impact. The creature howled, a wordless combination of pain and outrage. It flew backward away from the golden light, then spiraled toward the ceiling of the cavern before splintering into a million tiny shards of darkness and dissolving into the atmosphere.

Drum watched with his eyes wide and his mouth agape. What the fuck had just happened? One moment he had seen his own death staring him in the face, and the next he had done a fair impression of a character straight out of a Marvel Studios film. Maybe he really had lost his mind outside the abbey last night, and this was all a hallucination he was experiencing in a hospital mental ward. It sounded a more reasonable explanation than anything else he could think of.

He heard Ash stirring beside him and turned to stare at her. If anything, her eyes appeared even wider than his felt. She looked at him as if he had just revealed himself to be a Hollywood version of a leprechaun, complete with green suit, red hair, and obligatory pot of gold. He nearly caught himself looking around for a bowl of sugary American cereal.

"You," she whispered, and he couldn't decide if her breathless tone held an accusation, or utter disbelief. "It was you all along."

Drum dropped his hands to his sides and rubbed the palm of the one that had blasted the shadow creature against the leg of his jeans. "What are you talking about?" he asked uncomfortably.

"You are my Warden."

Chapter Nine

Drum shook his head in startled denial, but Ash felt the truth of her statement all the way down to the talon on her rearmost claw. The moment she had seen the magic pour from the human man's hand and dispatch the shadeling, she had felt as if a veil had been ripped from before her eyes. Michael Drummond was her Warden, and now her summoning made even less sense than it had when she had first burst free from the nothing.

The knowledge that Ash had inherited from the memory archive of her kind made her certain that she alone had been woken to a female form. It told her with equal certainty that a Warden should never be ignorant of his calling. Men—and rarely women—of talent came to the attention of the Wardens Guild early in their lives, soon after puberty, when evidence of their abilities first began to emerge. The Guild immediately took them under its wing and instructed them in the use of magic and their role in using it to defend against the Darkness. No potential Warden should be left to his own devices, let alone one destined to provide personal service to a Guardian. Not ever.

So how could she explain Drum?

"You're having me on." His tone of near panic did not make the task any easier. "You said this Warden buck was somewhat different. You bleedin' asked me to find him for you. I can't be him."

Ash drew a breath to steady herself. "I know what I said, but I was mistaken. I should have seen it sooner, but I ignored what stood in front of me, and instead attempted to blindly follow the traditions of my kind."

"Traditions are fine old things." He jerked his chin in a desperate nod. "My mother adores them, thinks they're vitally important. You shouldn't abandon yours. We'll keep looking."

"It is futile to search for what has already been found."

"You haven't found a fucking thing," he snarled. His shaking hand sent the beam of his flashlight bouncing wildly about the cavern. "I'm not your fucking Warden."

"Denial of the truth does not change it."

Ash could almost have felt sympathy for Drum's obvious distress. Never before had she stopped to consider how the discovery of a Warden's calling might prove itself more of a burden than an honor. The war against the Seven and the Order of Eternal Darkness had raged beneath the noses of humanity for millennia and would likely last for many more. To be drafted against one's will into either side's army would change that life forever. Not everyone embraced change.

Unfortunately, Drum had as little choice in the matter as Ash herself. From what she understood, although he had been born with his talent for remote viewing, the event she had just witnessed marked the first time he had come into his Warden's ability to wield magical energy. He could deny the truth, and resolve never again to perform such an action, but he could not change the past. He was a Warden, and now any agent of Darkness could gaze upon him and know it. Sooner or later, they would come for him, and without Guild training or the protection of a Guardian, they would kill him.

Ash felt something inside her recoil at the thought. Michael Drummond's life would not be cut short by the enemy. She would not allow it, no matter what powers they threw in his path. Ash would destroy them all.

The violence of her thoughts took her by surprise, and she stuffed them away in the back of her mind. At the moment, she had more important things to worry about. Like convincing Drum that she was not the thing that had just ruined his life.

Ignoring his attempts to evade her, Ash wrapped her arms around the man and flew both of them up and out of the underground cavern. The moment their feet touched the solid surface of the earth, she shifted back to her human form and released him, holding her hands up beside her. Drum cursed a blue streak in two languages, spun on his heel, and stalked out of the ruined tower.

Ash hurried in his wake and tried to give him some time to think as he led her back down the hill and onto the path through the surrounding fields. She thought she understood his anger, but she only had so many moments to spare before they would be back at his mother's house, surrounded by other humans.

After fifteen minutes of tense silence, she ventured a careful prod. They were halfway to their destination, and both of them had run out of time. "Drum, while I do not understand the emotion you must be feeling—"

"Really?" His mouth curled up in a sneer. "You think that a thing made of stone that didn't exist before last night might not understand my emotional reaction to having the bloody rug of my entire fucking life yanked out from under my feet? I'm gobsmacked."

His sarcasm had teeth, and they bit deep, even through Ash's tough hide. She felt herself stiffen and had to beat back the impulse to respond with cutting words of her own. Arguing would only make things worse.

She kept her tone even as she made another attempt to penetrate the bubble of anger surrounding him. "Becoming a Warden is something no one chooses, Drum, any more than they choose to become a Guardian. But someone must stand and protect the world from evil."

"I don't doubt you're right, Guardian." He spat her title like an epithet. "I just don't see that it has to be me." He didn't look at her and didn't slow down, just continued trudging across the muddy field toward the home of his boyhood.

"Who else should it be?" She tried to keep her voice gentle, because the question was not. "The Darkness cannot be fought by ordinary human soldiers with tanks and guns and bombs. Such weapons are useless against it. Only humans gifted with powers beyond the ordinary can hope to cause it harm. You have those powers. Even you cannot deny that."

"So what? I'm not the only bugger in the world with a touch of the Sight. Shite, I doubt I'm the only one in County Kildare."

"You would suggest someone take your place? It would need to be someone else with power. Your sister, perhaps?"

He rounded on her so quickly and with such fury that she had her hand up to deflect the blow. It never struck. Drum merely stood before her, trembling with rage, his hands clenched into white-knuckled fists at his sides.

"Don't even think it, gargoyle," he hissed. "I don't care if you can put that axe of yours through twenty feet of solid steel. If you even try to drag Maeve any deeper into this epic fucking nightmare than she's already gotten herself, I will find a way to end you."

"And I am attempting to explain that if you do not accept your place in the nightmare, as you call it, you will be putting yourself, Maeve, and your entire family at risk. You cannot ignore the Darkness, Drum, any more than you can hide from it. You can either prepare to face it on your own terms, or you can allow it to catch you unprepared. Only one of those choices gives you any chance of survival."

He watched her, his entire frame still vibrating with a combination of rage and frustration. Something inside her wanted to reach out, to offer him comfort and reassurance, but neither of those things would help him.

After a moment he spoke, his voice still tight and clipped. "As soon as you woke, you said you needed to find your Warden. You said if you did, he could tell you why you were here and what you needed to do. I can't do any of that. Neither can my sister, or anyone else in my family. We're no use to you. You should find a Warden somewhere else."

She shook her head. "It is not so simple. You are the Warden who is meant to work at my side. I know this. I realize you have no training, no way of knowing the things another Warden might tell me, but it changes nothing. You feel you have no choice, that I am trying to rob you of it, but I have no more than you."

Drum opened his mouth, and Ash didn't know how long they might have stood in that empty field arguing back and forth had they not been interrupted by a boy of eleven or twelve years who ran up to them at a dead sprint. He came from the direction of Drum's family home. When he reached them, he relayed his message in breathless pants, his brown eyes wide in his pale face.

"Mr. Drummond," he gasped. "Your ma sent me. I was bringing by some lamb for my da when it happened. You gotta get home quick. Something's wrong with Maeve. We was all in the kitchen havin' the *craic* when she turned white as chalk and toppled over like Mr. McGinty did at

Christmas. Only she wasn't fluthered like him, I'm sure of it."

Drum didn't wait to hear about Mr. McGinty's drinking habits. He had taken off running before his sister's name had finished falling from the young boy's lips. Ash followed close on his heels.

They reached the house in minutes. Drum burst into the kitchen like an avenging angel and found his sister stretched across the vinyl floor with her head cradled in their mother's lap. He sank to his knees beside them while Ash hovered behind, unsure what to do.

"Did she hurt herself?" Drum asked in a rough voice. He didn't sound panicked, though. Just concerned.

Maddie Drummond shook her head. "No. We were standing side by side when I saw her knees start to go, so I helped her down. Johnny Evers jumped so high, though, I thought he might knock his empty skull on the ceiling. I sent him out to fetch you just to keep him from doing himself a caution."

Drum blew out a breath. "He gave me a fright. He said something was wrong with her, and I just bolted home."

"He's a daft chiseler," his mother said with a sound of exasperation. "She'll be fine in a moment, but it was a fast one, and it took her hard."

Understanding finally dawned on Ash. Maeve had been struck with a vision and lost consciousness, which had frightened the young boy, and Maddie had sent him after Drum not because the young woman was in any danger, but simply to get Johnny out of the way. Drum's panic had likely resulted from his own state of heightened tension. There had been no reason to fear for Maeve's safety. Other than the ones Ash herself had pointed out.

Drum looked up, and Ash followed his gaze over her shoulder to find Johnny returned and watching from the open door, his expression at once sheepish and interested.

Drum shot the boy a level gaze and used his chin to gesture outside.

"Thank your da for the lamb, Johnny," he said, "and
thanks to you for chasing after me, but you can be off now.
Maeve has had a little spell, but she'll be fine now. She just
needs a bit of a lie-down."

The boy's eyes remained wide and curious, but he nodded and departed reluctantly, pushing the door closed
behind him. Ash rested her back against it and watched as
Drum got his feet beneath him into a crouch. He reached
for his sister.

"Give her to me, Ma," he said. "Let's get her off the
floor before she takes a chill." He scooped Maeve's limp
form into his arms and rose, turning toward the kitchen's
other door.

Maddie darted in front of him to turn the lever, and then
repeated the process at the living room entry. Ash trailed
behind, stepping in last and pulling the panel shut. Drum
deposited his burden on the fluffy cushions of a flowered
sofa, while his mother opened the lid of a stamped tin box
and began to stack bricks of peat in the fire grate. She soon
had a neat blaze going, and she bustled back toward them,
wiping her hands on her embroidered apron.

Maeve remained pale and unmoving as her family
fussed around her. Drum pulled a chair close up beside the
sofa, then unfolded a knitted blanket and draped it over his
sister's legs. Maddie settled into the chair and took her
daughter's hand between her own.

Ash estimated that the girl had lain unconscious for at
least ten minutes. She frowned as she considered the ramifications. The gift of prophecy was a rare and powerful
one, but if the visions always affected Maeve this way, it
was also a dangerous one. To lose consciousness for even
a second or two left one open to enemy attack. A *nocturni*
could strike while Maeve was helpless, injuring or killing

her while she lay oblivious to the peril. It made her unsuitable for training as a Warden and vulnerable to anyone who knew the truth. No wonder Drum acted so protectively.

Edging closer, Ash asked, "Is it always like this for her?"

Drum nodded. He half sat on the arm of the sofa and braced his hands on his thigh. "Sometimes it only lasts a minute or two. Once, she stayed out for almost four hours. We've tried waking her, but nothing works. We just have to wait until she can tell us what she's seen."

"That's right." Maddie hummed her agreement. "Whatever questions you have will hold a few more minutes. Maeve will answer just as soon as she wakes up, Guardian."

Chapter Ten

She really had to stop underestimating the Drummond family, Ash noted as her mind reeled. Every time she did, one of them managed to surprise her. First Maeve, then Drum, and now even sweet, maternal Maddie, who called her Guardian as if she had done so from the very beginning.

"How did you know?" she croaked out after a minute.

The older woman smiled. "I come from a long line of very special women, young lady. It only stands to reason that one or two of the men along the line have had a little something extra of their own."

"What's that got to do with anything?" Drum demanded, a note of shock coloring his words.

Maddie met her son's gaze calmly. "Your great-great-great-uncle Daibhí was a Warden, Michael. Of course, it was well before my time, but I heard the stories right enough."

"No one ever told them to me," he protested.

"There didn't seem a need. Other men in the family had a touch after him without another one being chosen. No one thought it would ever happen again. Especially once you were grown. Those that are chosen are chosen early."

"I still should have known."

"Perhaps, and if I had your sister's gift, I certainly would not have kept it to myself. I'm sorry, dear. I had no desire to hurt you with this, and no thought that I possibly could."

Ash could see the rapid play of emotions making their way across Drum's face, but even had she had the experience to identify them, she didn't believe she could have. They passed so quickly she wondered if he could identify them himself.

"Does that mean that you understand all of this about Darkness and Demons and Guilds and wars?" he asked after a moment.

"Good heavens, no." Maddie laughed. "All I know is that there are Wardens and there are Guardians, and it's their job to protect us from anything that the good Lord might ask them to." She looked up and caught Ash's gaze. "And I know that a fire of protection burns behind a Guardian's eyes."

Ash had not thought that the flames visible in the black eyes of her natural form carried over to her human disguise. Or maybe Maddie Drummond saw more than the average human.

She offered the woman a nod of respect.

A soft sound came from the girl on the sofa a moment before her blue eyes fluttered open. Her gaze locked on her brother's face and tears began to stream onto her cheeks. "Michael. Michael, it was so horrible. So dark and so cold. And so much blood. Everywhere."

The broken whispers brought Ash to immediate attention. She stepped close and leaned down to hear Maeve better. "What did you see, Maeve? Where was the cold, dark place?"

"Back off, Guardian," Drum growled, gathering his sister into his arms and sliding down to sit beside her.

"Give her a minute, for fuck's sake. Can't you see she's crying?"

"Michael! Language!"

Maddie's outrage at least made Drum stop glaring at Ash. He turned all his attention back to his sister and used a corner of the blanket to dry her tears. "Hush, Mae, love. You're home safe. Nothing is going to hurt you."

Ash bit back her anger and reminded herself that Drum still did not understand the true extent of the threat posed by the Darkness. If he did, he would not think her urgency so intrusive.

She tried to explain. "I can see that Maeve's vision has frightened her, but that is why it is so important that she share it. We cannot hope to stop what we are not prepared to face. I only wish—"

"I don't care about your wishes! I care about my sister, my family, and right now you're making their fear worse. Get out. I don't have time for you. I'll deal with you later."

"I am trying to ensure that there is a later, Michael Drummond." Ash bit the words out, frustration closing a fist around her throat. "I would not be here if you, your sister, your family, and the rest of your bloody country were not in imminent danger. Do you understand that? A Guardian is not called from sleep unless the threat is so dire that the battle would be lost without us. That is the truth, but right now I do not even know where the battle will be fought. Your sister might be the only one who can tell me. Now, would you rather protect her from me? Or from those who would harm both her and every other human around you?"

"Michael, it's all right." Maeve still spoke softly, and her words held both tears and exhaustion behind the low tones. She curled a hand around her brother's wrist and patted in reassurance. "Ash is right. So many people could die. What I saw . . ." She shuddered, and squeezed her eyes shut for a moment. "It was awful. If those things are what's in store for us, Ash will need every advantage she can get. I can't even describe to you what they were like. I tried to look, but it was like staring at the sun. My eyes would close whether I wanted them to or not. I just know that their presence made me sick to my stomach and so afraid I couldn't move. Couldn't even scream. I just stood there and watched while they tore the world into little bloody pieces."

Ash cursed under her breath in Ancient Sumerian. She had the very bad feeling that Maeve was describing more than the ordinary servants of Darkness, that she had seen one of the Seven itself. Humans did not look upon those Demons and walk away. More powerful than any entity to ever cross into the mortal plane, the Seven could join together to give life to the Darkness itself. They were the reason the first Guardians had ever been summoned. Since their defeat, they had been kept imprisoned in separate, extradimensional planes that existed only to contain their evil. If one or more had escaped, human deaths were inevitable until they could be defeated and taken captive once more.

"Maeve, I need you to tell me what you saw," Ash said with quiet insistence. "Please. Start at the beginning."

Maeve shook her head. "There was no beginning. I told you, my visions don't play like a film inside my head. They're just images that flash into my mind one after the other, but they're not joined together, and they're not always in order. Besides, I thought you'd want to hear about the other Guardians first."

Ash drew up in shock. "Other Guardians?"

"My vision contained four others," Maeve said. "Two of them were helping you attack that thing, but there were another two someplace else who were also somehow supporting what you were doing. I'm not sure I understand it, but the visions don't always make sense to me."

Ash almost choked on her own surprise. "You mean that you saw three Guardians together in one place?"

"Yes, and I think there were Wardens there. I mean, these were women, but they seemed linked to the Guardians somehow, and they were using magic to fight against some other people in these strange, black robes."

Shock after shock exploded in Ash's mind like little land mines of revelation. Her archive of information inherited upon her summoning told her that what Maeve described was impossible. A Guardian worked alone unless the threat was so large he had to call on one of his brothers for aid. For three to join forces against one foe could only mean that one of the Seven had not only escaped its prison, it had regained its full strength on the mortal plane. The thought was enough to make even a Guardian go pale.

The vision also indicated that more unexpected changes to tradition had occurred in recent days than just the summoning of a female Guardian and the existence of an untrained Warden. Maeve had seen female Wardens, which were uncommon to begin with, linked in service to active Guardians. As far as Ash knew, such a thing only happened when those Wardens were destined to be their Guardians' mates, and multiple Guardians had not mated at the same time since the very first among their kind.

Everything Ash thought she knew was being called into question by a single human female's precognitive vision. Confusion seemed to well up inside her until she feared she would drown. Instinct urged her to trust in what Maeve was telling her, but its voice almost disappeared beneath the shouting of her logical mind. How much stock could she really place in the accuracy of a girl who had never been identified by the Guild, let alone gotten proper training in how to handle and interpret the images she received?

Ash hadn't realized she was shaking her head until Maddie placed a gentle hand on her shoulder. "I know how you feel, Guardian. The first time Maeve fainted, I thought it was because she had a touch of the flu. But then she opened her eyes and told me, as plain and certain as Sunday roast, that her big sister Síle would be coming home from school in a white car with a red fella and would be getting married before Brigid's Day. And sure enough, on the very next Saturday what should happen but that Síle pulls up to the house in Colin Faraday's white car and introduces that sweet, ginger boy as her future husband. Maeve scattered rose petals down the aisle before them on the last Saturday of January."

It occurred to Ash to point out that predicting an engagement and wedding was a far cry from predicting a possible apocalypse, but she understood Maddie's meaning. Maeve's family had faith in the accuracy of her visions, and they wanted to assure Ash that she could trust in them, as well; but Ash could not help but remember everything at stake. Trusting in the gifts of a human woman she had met less than twenty-four hours ago would mean gambling for stakes that were murderously high.

"I'm never wrong," Maeve said softly, bringing Ash's attention back to her. "Often enough I've wished I was. I understand, though. Maybe there's a way to get proof about what I saw. If Michael could use his gift to find another Guardian, would that make you feel better?"

Drum protested. "Wait a minute. I never said I had any intention of trying such a thing. Didn't anyone notice that the last time I tried to locate a person, the only thing my bloody *gift* showed me was a broken-down pile of stone?"

"Not true." Ash saw Drum's frustration, along with his anger at those around him who continued to push him into using his sight. She also saw that underneath the others, the emotion that most continued to plague him was fear. She could not pretend to understand his relationship with the power inside him, but Maeve was correct that it might be the only thing at this point that could save them. Ash caught his eyes as she reminded him, "It showed me the identity of my Warden."

This time when Drum released a long and heartfelt string of curses, he spoke them in Irish. His mother pressed her lips together and gave him a sour look. "Just because I can't understand exactly what you're saying doesn't mean you should be saying it under my roof, Michael Stephen. I'll thank you to watch your language—both your languages—in my presence, boyo."

Drum lapsed into brooding silence.

Ash shared his frustration. She enjoyed their current predicament no more than he. A Guardian had not been designed to sit idly by while danger loomed, nor to rely on the aid of others before taking action against the enemy. The Wardens who served them might control their sleeping and waking, but once a Guardian was summoned, members of the Guild became support staff rather than the key to a mission's success. It chafed her to ask him to use his gift as much as it chafed Drum to use it, but he could likely read her emotions and know her thoughts better than she did his.

In the end, it mattered not what either of them wanted. It mattered that the Darkness be stopped.

"I need to know," Ash said. "I need to know if the Guardians your sister has seen have already awoken. If they have, then I need to know where they are, and if they have not, then I need to know that as well so I may search for them myself. Maeve has seen what is at stake, and I know the extent of the danger that awaits. You must help me, Michael Drummond, or all will be lost."

He stared at her for several long seconds that seemed to stretch into lifetimes. His anger was obvious in the narrowing of his eyes and the clenching of his jaw. In that moment, she knew he hated her, and deep inside something strange and unfamiliar cringed and wailed at the thought.

"Fine," he bit out, the capitulation bitter and familiar. "I'll do it, on one condition. If I tell you where to find these other Guardians, you go after them alone. You leave me and my family and you forget that we even exist."

Maeve made a soft sound of distress. "Michael, she can't do that. I told you that my vision last night said we have to work together—"

He cut her off with a sharp shake of his head and a raised palm. "No. That was last night. You know as well as I do that every choice we make creates changes in the possible future. What we did today may have made that last vision obsolete. In the new one you said you saw the Guardians and female Wardens using magic. The only Guardian here is her, and even if she's right that I'm a Warden, I'm sure as f-feck not female."

It took a force of will for Ash to keep her temper. Fury might be one of the Guardians' very few emotions, but they felt it deeply. Drum might see himself as only refusing to be dragged into something he had never asked for, but to Ash his choice amounted to a betrayal. For him to turn his back on his duty as a Warden served to strengthen the enemy and weaken the forces of the Light.

It also meant that the only things he felt when he looked at her were anger and dislike.

He had placed her between the sword and the executioner's axe. In order to have any hope of victory, she would have to concede to his terms, leaving her without a Warden to aid her cause. She had to grit her teeth and take a very deep breath before she could force herself to agree.

She barely managed the nod.

Drum's was equally abrupt. Once he gave in, he pushed to his feet and turned to leave. "We'll do this outside. My sisters are bringing their families for dinner in a few hours. I don't want any trace of this to touch them."

Ash straightened her shoulders and trailed after him. She did not wish a single particle of Darkness to affect his family, either. That was why she had demanded his assistance.

"Ash, do you need my help?" Maeve called softly from her nest on the sofa. "He needed to touch you to look for the Warden . . . ?"

"No." Ash shook her head. "He knows what a Guardian is. If he has the ability to find them, he'll be able to do it without you showing him what you saw."

Maeve nodded, her face still troubled with worry. Ash ignored the urge to offer comfort. She didn't think she had any to give. Quietly, she traced Drum's steps out to the kitchen and drew the Drummonds' door closed behind her.

Chapter Eleven

Drum stepped out of his mother's house for the third time that day. Unlike on the last occasion, he was followed not by a relentless Guardian intent on using him to further her own ends but by the sound of laughter, happy chatter, and familiar voices raised in song. His family remained inside to overflow the bounds of the sitting room and occupy every seat they could scrounge together. Bellies were full, drinks still flowed, and the Drummond clan had settled in for an impromptu bit of *craic*.

He had to get away for a moment.

Gravel and crushed stone crunched beneath his boots as he crossed the drive and open parking area. A dry stone wall, built generations before his great-grandfather had first farmed the fields beyond, lay a few yards past the barn his father had converted to a garage when he opened his own business as a mechanic. The fields had been leased to the neighbors for more than twenty years now, and while Drummonds still crawled all over the place, none of them made their living tilling soil and planting seed. A lot had changed.

They still maintained the section of wall though, and Drum leaned his arms upon it as he gazed out onto the starlit night. He drew in a lungful of crisp, fresh country air, held it for a moment, then blew it out in a slow, steady stream. The tension in his gut didn't follow. It stayed put, a tight fist kneading in his belly. He'd had a rough evening.

He snorted at his own mental understatement. Rough was one word for it, but probably not the most accurate one. It had started with his failed search for the Guardians, and even the company of his tight-knit family hadn't been able to salvage it. He'd been trapped by his own words and his own failure. Because he hadn't been able to point Ash toward the others of her kind, he would be forced to continue working at her side.

When he had opened his eyes after his search attempt, the temptation to lie had nearly pulled him under. His first thought had been that she couldn't read his mind. She had no idea what he had seen or not seen. He could have made up anything, sent her on a wild-goose chase to the deepest part of the Amazon or the most remote point on the Mongolian steppes. She wouldn't know the difference until it was too late. His lips had parted, his tongue poised to utter the words that would free him from this surrealistic nightmare of obligation, but she met his eyes steadily, her expression calm but expectant, and he hadn't been able to do it.

He told her exactly what he had seen.

"I can see four," he said in a flat tone. "Maeve got that right. Four are up and moving. Two more statues, but they're still frozen." He saw triumph and excitement start to fill her and hurried to finish. "But there's no way on earth I can tell you where to find them. Just not here. Not in Ireland. But I imagine that's as helpful as telling you they're not on Mars. Maybe at least one is in America, because that certainly narrows it down."

Ash grunted and closed her eyes, her chin dropping to her chest as she absorbed the blow. After a moment, she looked up and her expression had cleared to show nothing but firm resolve. "Thank you."

"Don't thank me," he spat. "I didn't find a fucking thing. It looks like this is the start of a beautiful bloody disaster."

Then he had stomped back into the house, leaving her behind in the deserted garage and letting the kitchen door slam behind him.

She hadn't deserved that. Regret filled him. She bore no responsibility for his failure. Even if he'd told her not to expect any answers, his logical mind understood why she had taken the chance, that she hadn't had any choice. Ash wasn't the reason he'd found himself in such a situation; that was on fate. Someone up above was having one hell of a laugh at his expense.

> MICHAEL STEPHEN DRUMMOND, WARDEN
> INCOMPETENT PSYCHIC. THINGS *NOT* FOUND.
> ONE SPELL, ACCIDENTALLY CAST.

He should get himself a Web site, drum up some business, in case the whole publican gig fell through.

God's mercy, what a mess.

And as if the whole gargoyles, demons, magic, end-of-the-world situation wasn't complicated enough, he had discovered that not even rage, hatred, or bitter resentment could hammer so much as a dent in his attraction to the inhumanly beautiful Ash.

He felt ridiculous. The woman didn't even belong to his bloody species, and he couldn't keep his eyes or his mind off her. Hell, he wasn't even sure if calling her a woman was the appropriate terminology. After all, didn't the word imply a humanity that the female Guardian had never claimed to possess? There was no doubt she was female, though, so he supposed the question didn't much matter.

Ash was female, Drum was male, and his hormones wasted no opportunity in reminding him of the relationship between those two facts.

Just thinking of her generated enough heat to keep him warm in the chilly night air. He hadn't bothered grabbing a jacket, as the air inside had gone overheated from the collection of bodies pressed together in the confined space. He had wanted cooling off, but if he intended to get any he would have to find a new direction for his thoughts.

He almost swore he heard the angels laughing at him when the object of his obsession appeared beside him and mirrored his pose braced against the wall of stone. He tensed, but when she said nothing and simply looked out over the darkened countryside, he returned to contemplating the same view and felt himself gradually relax.

For a good while, neither of them spoke. The only sounds were the rustle of leaves and grasses, the buzzing of insects, and the occasional call of a night bird. He wouldn't label the interlude peaceful, since nothing seemed to dissolve the tension that had accumulated between them, but it was quiet and empty of sharp words or resentful glances, so he would give thanks for small mercies.

"Your family shares a great deal of affection for one another," Ash finally said, her voice a bare ripple in the air. "You are fortunate to have one another. Though I think that they become a little overwhelming at times."

He gave a short chuckle. "You aren't the only one to have mentioned it."

Hadn't that been part of the reason why he had left the party to stand out here alone? He was surprised Ash had lasted as long as she did surrounded by the chaos. But he hadn't missed the note of wistful envy that twined through the background of her words.

"Two of your sisters are older? Those who have children."

"Síle and Sorcha. Síle is the oldest. She and Colin are parents to Stephen and Isabel. Sorcha and John have to take responsibility for the other three."

"And Meara is younger."

He nodded. "Three years behind me, four ahead of Maeve. She and Sorcha both inherited Ma's talent for healing. Sorcha is a midwife and Meara is doing her residency at a hospital in Cork."

"Your mother was very pleased to have you all together in her home tonight."

"Usually it only happens that we're all in one place like this at Christmas." He shrugged. "That's what happens, I suppose. Everyone gets busy with their own lives."

Ash lapsed back into silence, and Drum considered the impact of his words. Had the last time his family gathered together really been almost a year ago? Sorcha and John's youngest had been only a couple of weeks old last Christmas, so the family had jumped right from their reunion at the christening into the holiday madness. Since then, he'd seen each of them from time to time, but no more than two or three in any place at once.

It seemed so strange, he reflected as the reality of it sank in. When his father had been alive, the family had seemed to constantly be stepping on each other's heels, tripping over each other even—or especially—when Drum had longed for a little privacy. But Stephen Drummond had died shortly after Sorcha's engagement, more than a decade ago, and since then his children had grown and moved on to establish lives and families of their own. What would his father think if he could see them now?

The question only increased Drum's feeling of confusion. He felt as if everything that used to make sense had turned into a giant puzzle, and he couldn't even figure out what image the pieces were supposed to make when he managed to fit them all together again.

Once more, Ash's quiet voice drifted into the silence. "I will not force you to continue aiding me, human," she said. "I release you from any obligation to me. I just wanted to tell you that."

For the first time, being called human didn't make Drum feel as if he had just been insulted. She hadn't used the word as if she couldn't be bothered to remember his name, but simply because that's what he was. And what she wasn't.

She pushed against the stone wall and turned to leave. Reflexively, Drum reached out and grasped her arm, stopping her.

"What did you say?"

Ash stilled, but she didn't try to pull out of his grip. "You heard me. I will no longer force you to help me, nor expect you to go any further in fighting this battle. I accept this fight is mine, and mine alone."

If he had expected to feel relief at her words, at being released from a bargain that fate had made without so much as consulting him, he got a rude surprise. Instead of feeling relieved or unburdened, Drum felt only angry at the thought of Ash walking away from him and taking on this mysterious threat all on her own.

No, it didn't make a single, bloody lick of sense, but he didn't care. Now that the moment was upon him, he couldn't bring himself to let her go.

"What if I want to help?" he demanded in a low, harsh voice. "What if I don't want you to do this alone?"

She stared at him for a moment, then threw up her hands and laughed without humor. "Then by the Light, I have no idea what to do with you, Michael Drummond. You have done everything in your power to run from me, since the moment your eyes first lit on me. Everything you have done for me, I have had to drag from you with threats and bribes and coercion. And now that I have finally given in, have finally tried to give you what you ask for, now you decide that you want the exact opposite? In the name of all that is sacred, I do not think I will ever understand you."

"Don't worry," he rasped. "I don't understand it, either."

Then, with a sharp tug he pulled her into his arms and took her mouth in a blazing kiss.

Ash felt herself begin to fall before she realized that her feet remained planted on solid ground. It was reality that disintegrated around her.

She hadn't expected the kiss. To say the least. After his failed attempt to locate the Guardians Maeve had seen in her vision, Drum had said no more than five words to her over the course of the evening. Maddie had taken over introductions between Ash and the steady arrival of family members young and old. Drum's sisters, their husbands, and their children had been warm and welcoming, and had immediately gone out of their way to include her in the lively dinner conversation and the raucous gathering that followed.

Drum glared and brooded when he was not obvious in his attempts to ignore her very presence. Ash had grown increasingly uncomfortable as the hours passed, until she found herself entertaining fantasies about changing forms and launching herself into the night air through Maddie Drummond's sitting room window. Luckily, Drum had excused himself before she had entirely betrayed her hostess's generosity. But it had been a very close thing.

She had remained perched as unobtrusively as she could manage at the fringe of the gathering for another quarter of an hour before Maddie caught her gaze and sent her a wink followed by a meaningful glance toward the kitchen door. Grateful for the opportunity, Ash had escaped without any real intention of chasing after the woman's son.

Outside, the fresh air and open space had allowed her

to breathe for the first time in what felt like forever, and she had wandered away from the house with no firm destination in mind. With her thoughts scattered and her gaze on her own boots, she hadn't caught sight of Drum until she stood less than ten feet behind him.

Her feet had frozen in place, and her internal debate on whether to approach or to turn and flee had quickly evolved into a much more complex argument with herself. She had known from the beginning that Drum had no desire to become a part of her world, with its never-ending war and its constant threat of danger. He had made that abundantly clear, but she had needed his help, and she had told herself that dragooning him into assisting her was all in service of the greater good. She had still believed that, all the way through the end of his failed afternoon vision quest. She had believed it right up until this very moment.

But now?

She squeezed her eyes shut and closed her hands into fists, but she could not shut out the images this evening had shown her. Tonight she had met Drum's family. Not just Maeve, but his mother, his three other sisters, his brothers-in-law, his nieces and nephews. She had heard stories about his aunts and uncles, about his father and his grandparents, the latter group long since passed away. She had seen him not as an isolated and useful human, but as a son, a brother, an uncle.

Under her very eyes, he had been transformed from a tool into an integral thread of his family's tapestry. If she bound him to her service and dragged him into battle behind her, the risk to his life would be equivalent to holding a match to the end of that thread. Not only would Drum burn, but the fire would spread until the entire fabric was compromised. The only way to prevent it was to cut herself off from him and remove herself from the picture.

Even then, Ash didn't realize she had made the decision until she heard herself speak the words. She told him that she was setting him free and felt the statement ring with truth. Then she felt a hollow space empty out inside her, and she turned to walk away.

That's when he grabbed her. That's when he kissed her, and that's when Ash lost her mind.

He tugged and took her by surprise. If he hadn't, she told herself, she never would have fallen into him and found herself leaning against his chest, dependent on him for balance.

He didn't provide it. Instead he stole what little remained by parting his lips above hers and tracing the seam of her mouth with the tip of his tongue. It was the same trick he had attempted the night before, but instead of bringing her to her senses, this time it set fire to the pit of her stomach, and made her head spin in a dizzying whirl.

She parted her lips and let herself dive under. Her arms rose without her conscious control. One hand gripped his shoulder, while the other ventured higher, her fingers tangling in the silky, black thickness of his hair.

Drum groaned and thrust his tongue forward to tangle with hers. She felt a start of surprise before sensation overwhelmed her, heating her until she melted against him. His grip shifted, his arms closing around her and pressing her tight against him.

It shocked her how well they matched. She had known he was tall, that he had the lean, muscular build of an athlete and enough strength to carry his sister around as if she weighed no more than a down feather. She had eyes, after all. But she hadn't known that a simple tilt of her head could put their lips into perfect alignment, or that when they stood this close, her breasts flattened against the firm plane of his chest and her hips cradled his erection in a way that seemed to excite him as much as it did her.

He devoured her mouth, but it didn't take long for Ash to follow his lead and begin to challenge him for dominance. She didn't think of it that way—she couldn't think at all—but she knew that she didn't want to be left behind, that she wanted them racing forward stride for stride and breath for breath.

Her fingers tugged at his hair, and he made a deep, hungry sound as he lifted his mouth from hers. She hissed her displeasure and tried to drag him back, but he bared his teeth in a feral display and resisted, only to lean down and use them to nip at the skin along the line of her jaw. Her hiss turned into a breathless moan, and she arched her neck to grant him greater access.

Teeth scraped and tongue laved a trail from her jaw, across her neck, to the sensitive hollow behind her ear. The first touch there made her whole body shake as if she'd been struck by a bolt of lightning. She felt so hot and disoriented she couldn't guarantee that she hadn't. Drum nuzzled the spot, his warm breath teasing her skin before he closed his teeth around the tender lobe of her ear and tugged gently. Her knees turned to water, and she would've fallen if he hadn't caught her.

In that moment, Ash did not feel like a powerful warrior, but like a woman pliant under the hands of her man. She would have sunk to the ground and let him take her in the cool, damp grass. And she would have gloried in it.

But somewhere above them, the Light was laughing.

"Ash? Michael? Where are you?" Maddie Drummond's voice rang out from the kitchen doorway, dragging them to earth in an entirely different way. "Come back inside before one of you takes a chill. John and Sorcha are getting ready to leave and they want to say good night."

Drum lifted his head and gazed down at her, his eyes glinting in the starlight. His breath came fast and ragged, and the way his fingers gripped her hips told Ash he had been as far gone as she was. They stared at each other for a long, tense moment before Drum gave her hips a squeeze and put a deliberate step between them.

"I hope that makes my position very clear, Guardian," he said in a near growl. "You'll not be getting rid of me quite so easily."

Ash could only blink. She had seen in the cavern that this man possessed more magic than either of them had first thought. It would seem his talents included the ability to rob her of the power of speech.

Dropping his embrace, Drum took her hand and kept it in his as he turned and tugged her toward the house. She tried to follow, stumbling over her first two steps before the worst of the fog of desire blew away on the night breeze. At that point she at least managed to keep her balance and school her expression into something resembling neutrality before she had to face his family again.

Then the devious human went and ruined it.

"You'd also better not be forgetting where we just left off, *mo chaomhnóir,*" he purred. "For I mean to take it up again just as soon as we can be alone."

She tripped over the kitchen threshold and met his family again with her mouth hanging open and her cheeks stained the color of ripe strawberries. Behind her, Drum laughed and rejoined the party with a grin of male satisfaction.

Bastard.

Chapter Twelve

Drum set the new land speed record on the return trip to Dublin. He did it with muscles so tense he expected that at any moment, one would snap like an overstretched rubber band and knock him unconscious with the recoil. Beside him, Ash clutched the edges of her seat and vibrated like a tuning fork. And it was all his own damned fault.

He had been the one to initiate the kiss that had nearly killed him (for several minutes, his heart had beat so hard and fast he wouldn't have been surprised by a cardiac arrest), and he had been the one to throw petrol on the fire with that final taunt. He didn't know what he'd been thinking, probably hadn't been thinking at all, but based on the current fit of his jeans, Ash could not possibly have been suffering worse than he.

By the time he parked the car in the spot behind the pub and hustled Ash inside and upstairs, the restriction the denim had placed on blood flow to certain parts of his anatomy made him doubt his future ability to father children. When he flipped the lock to seal them inside his flat, though, all futures beyond the next few hours lost any claim on his attention. So did anything else that didn't involve him getting his hands on the dark-haired, dark-eyed, not-quite-human woman in front of him.

They reached for each other simultaneously, flying across the space that separated them like boxers at the start of the round. Combat, though, was the last thing on Drum's mind. The first thing was the taste of her lips, and the second was the feel of her lush curves under his hands. Everything else faded away like a summer sunset.

This time, she opened to him at once, her lips parted in an invitation echoed by teasing little flicks of her tongue. She wrapped her arms around him and pressed every inch of that toned, female flesh against him, until she tore a ragged groan from the back of his throat.

The feel of their bodies straining together made Drum acutely conscious of the layers of fabric keeping them apart. The denim and cotton and wool suddenly became as offensive to him as the idea of watching this woman walk out of his life. Quickly, he shrugged out of his jacket and sent hers to the floor along with it. Ash offered no sign of protest but began to tug the hem of his shirt free of his jeans.

It spurred him on as if she had actually dug sharp little wheels of metal into his flank. He pulled her top overhead, cursing every second that it forced their lips to part. But then his eyes locked on the curve of her bare shoulder and the enticing slope of creamy skin leading down to her breast. The kiss drifted from his mind, and his mouth watered.

He lowered his head and dragged his mouth from the hollow of her throat to the sweet, scented valley where her bra dipped to a small plastic catch. He tasted her skin and detected a hint of sun-warmed stone and sweet anise beneath the tang of salt. His teeth worried the fastening of her bra for a moment, teasing them both, but before he could flick the device open, he felt her shift and heard a ripping sound, followed by a series of rapid pings. She had torn his shirt open and sent the buttons flying.

Maybe they had both had enough teasing.

Drum shrugged out of the tattered remains of his shirt and quickly dispensed with her bra. Ash's hands fumbled with his belt, undoing the buckle and quickly abandoning the ends to move on to the button of his jeans. She had the zipper down and his fly open before he managed to release the breath that had been trapped in his throat the moment he saw her breasts completely bared.

They were larger than he had expected, pale, full mounds perfectly proportioned between her broad shoulders and narrow waist. Her nipples had pale, blush-colored peaks that darkened to a deep rose beneath his gaze. He trailed one fingertip along the outer curve, marveling at the warm, living silk of her skin. He could hear her breath speed up, coming quick and shallow as she arched into his touch.

Had she lifted her battle-axe high above him, poised to make a fatal strike, he still could not have resisted. His mouth closed around a beaded nipple, and he curled his tongue about the little nub with a rough sound of pleasure.

Ash cried out, a breathless noise choked off by a sharp inhalation. She buried her fingers in his hair, fisting tightly enough that he would have winced were he not so delightfully occupied. She growled a definite warning as he released her nipple, but the sound faded when he shifted to capture the other peak.

She held him in place. As if there were anywhere else on earth he would rather be. Though actually, a bed would come in handy at the moment.

Drum started to step forward, intending to steer her to his bedroom without releasing his new favorite treat. The problem with his strategy became apparent when he realized that in abandoning her intention to remove his clothes,

Ash had left his jeans hanging just above his knees, effectively hobbling him.

He lifted his head only long enough to strip out of his remaining garments, his fierce expression making clear to the world just how he felt about the interruption. The world excepting for Ash, he realized, when she let out a fierce snarl and attacked him with all the ferocity of an angry tiger.

They tumbled to the floor in a tangle of limbs, one quarter of which still sported an unfortunate amount of fabric covering. Never one to shirk a task, Drum had her boots and jeans stripped away in under thirty seconds.

In less than three more, Ash had him pinned beneath her with his wrists beside his head and her strong, shapely thighs bracketing his hips. If she thought he intended to struggle, she had another think coming.

He responded by stretching upward far enough to capture her lips in a scorching kiss. She had clearly taken to the odd human activity over the last twenty-four hours, because she tangled her tongue with his and gave just as good as she got.

His blood heated to the boiling point, and his erection hardened well past the point of discomfort. He had to get inside her, and it had to be now.

If there had been a little more blood flow directed to his brain instead of to points south, Drum might have spared a concern for the hard wooden floor and potential bruising to Ash's knees. As it was, he could barely spare the breath for a combination of begging and demanding.

"Let me inside you, *mo chaomhnóir,*" he panted. "Now. Please."

She gazed down at him, her skin flushed and glistening in the light from the windows. Her eyes had gone completely black, the eyes of her natural form, and the fire behind them blazed higher than ever before. Her lips parted, and he thought he saw a hint of fang. Instead of frightening him, it only made him hotter.

"Hurry," he urged.

Her mouth twisted, and she let out a low rumble of frustration. "How?" she demanded. "Show me."

"Like this."

He didn't bother trying to flip their positions. It didn't matter to him who was on top. He just needed inside her.

She released her grip on his wrists and leaned back. Immediately, his hands shot to her hips, fingers guiding their bodies into alignment. Her hot, wet center dragged along the length of his shaft, making him experience the tortures of the damned, as well as reassuring him that her arousal matched his own. The head of his cock notched into her tight opening, and he felt his eyes roll back into his head.

With firm pressure he tugged her down even as he thrust his way up into perfection. Their bodies joined in one smooth motion, and Ash let out a long, shuddering exclamation of wonder and delight. Drum was too busy trying not to come to make any noises of his own.

Her body closed around him with the most perfect pleasure his body had ever known. He felt it in his soul, the way she stretched to admit him, then closed tighter than a fist around his length. She had taken every last inch of him and thrown her head back as if she couldn't contain the ecstasy. He knew the feeling, because neither could he, and this was before either of them had started to move.

He was almost afraid to. If this was how it felt just to be inside her, he concluded that when he began to thrust, his heart would explode, his lungs would deflate, and the top of his head would blow clean off. Then Ash's channel tightened around him, and he knew it would be worth every messy second on his way to the hereafter.

She waited for no further instructions. Guardian instinct, it seemed, was not that different from the human variety. She leaned forward and braced her hands against his belly, her long braid falling forward until the end teased the skin of his chest. Her gaze locked with his, and she began to move.

The torment began with a slow swivel of her hips that had both of them moaning. She experimented with clockwise and counterclockwise rotations, both of which had him clenching his teeth and praying for strength to a merciful God. Then she eased her weight forward, and he felt her thighs tighten against him a split second before she lifted her hips.

She rose until she was in danger of losing him, and the slick slide of her inner walls along his shaft drove him another step closer to the edge. She paused for a heartbeat and then lowered herself again, sheathing him to the hilt. He endured two more of the slow-motion thrusts before his control snapped and he began to wonder which of them was really the beast.

His fingers dug into her hips until he knew he would leave bruises on her fair skin. He couldn't stop himself. Using the tight grip, he began to push and pull her against him in a fast, pounding rhythm. All the while, he thrust himself up against her with all the force he could muster.

Ash uttered not a sound of protest. Rather she purred like a big cat and answered his movements with equal fervor. Her nails scratched across his chest, adding another layer of sensation to nerves already overloaded with pleasure. He retaliated by jackknifing forward until he could draw a tightly beaded nipple into his hungry mouth. Her keening wail sliced through the night, a desperate female calling to her mate.

Drum thrust in and out, burying himself over and over in her wet heat. It became harder to draw breath, and he let her slip from between his lips to suck in a desperate lungful of air. They moved together like two halves of a great machine, each part wholly dependent on the other, and the entire time their gazes remained locked together in the most intimate part of their embrace.

Ash made the mewling sound of frantic hunger and ground her hips against him, using her weight to drive into his pelvis and provide pressure to her needy clit. Her movements grew jerky, her rhythm floundering as she reached out to grab at her climax.

He helped her, changing the angle of his thrusts so that each deep penetration hit the perfect spot inside her. He felt his own orgasm nearing, felt the tingling in his spine, and the tightening in his balls. He didn't know how long he could hold out, but he refused to go over without her.

Releasing her hip, he wrapped her braid around one hand and used the other to pinch the tip of one flushed breast. Both hands applied pressure to drag her toward him, inch by steady inch. Her panting turned to high-pitched whimpers as she slowly bowed to his silent demand.

Their bodies continued writhing together as she sank toward him. The grip of his hands hardened, and with a final tug he yanked her down until their lips met.

That's when the world exploded.

Ash screamed into his mouth as her body contracted tightly around him. Her inner walls squeezed and rippled, massaging his cock until the unbearable sensations set off his own climax. He lacked the breath to scream, but a low groan rumbled in his throat as he poured himself into her depths.

She collapsed onto his chest in a movement that was less graceful than it was endearing. Drum wrapped his arms around her and felt her nuzzle against the hollow of his throat as their breathing began to slow and their skin began to cool.

Exhaustion reached for him and began to drag him

under, but his last thought was not for the hard floorboards under his back or the cold night air against his skin. His last thought was that the woman above him had just changed his life forever. After this, he would never have to watch her walk away, because wherever she wanted to go, he would go right behind her.

Chapter Thirteen

Ash opened her eyes and found herself staring into the dark space underneath a battered sofa. She blinked, startled to realize she had drifted into sleep. She hadn't expected to need rest for a very long time, but apparently Drum had managed to drive her to exhaustion—he a human and she an immortal warrior. Who would have guessed?

She recalled collapsing atop him, wrung out and boneless from pleasure. At some point while she slept, she had slid to his side and curled against him. She had one leg bent, her knee draped over his thigh, while her head rested against his shoulder and one hand lay on his chest above the steady beating of his heart. A second rush of surprise accompanied her realization that she had no desire to move from the spot. She felt as warm and comfortable as a drowsy cat and could have drifted back into sleep out of sheer contentment.

Except that something had woken her, something that continued to tickle at the edge of her awareness and prick at the skin at the base of her neck. She kept still, suddenly wary of calling attention to the fact that she was alert now to a potential danger.

She remained in place but swept her gaze around the

bits of the apartment that she could see without turning her head. They lay on the floor not far inside the entry. They hadn't been able to wait any longer than that, but it actually gave Ash an advantage. Because while the furniture blocked her from seeing the lower half of the far side of the sitting room, she wasn't confined behind the bedroom door.

From here she could see the entry to the kitchen, as well as the doors that lead to Drum's room and the spare room hallway. She could also see most of the windows on the apartment's back wall and the thin black mist that had begun to seep in around the edges of the casements.

She hissed and shook Drum roughly awake. His eyes snapped open and his gaze immediately focused on her face. He drew the correct conclusion from her expression, because he wasted no time in asking, "What's wrong?"

"Shadelings." She drew herself into a crouch just as the mist coalesced into the same sort of misshapen humanoid form that had confronted them in the cavern yesterday. Or this morning. She didn't exactly have the time to check a clock.

Ash sprang to her feet and shifted to her natural form. The confined space prevented her from spreading her wings, but this shape still possessed the advantages of greater size, strength, speed, and endurance. Plus, it could absorb significantly more damage, the advantage of which could not be understated when she realized that two more shadelings had already formed, and still mist continued to pour into the room.

Knowing her axe to be useless against enemies lacking solid flesh, Ash did not bother to call it forward, and instead simply stepped into a position that kept her body between the windows and her Warden. She could hear Drum cursing behind her as he scrambled to his feet, but she kept her attention on the oncoming threat.

Ash had always counted shadelings among the most minor of the creatures serving the Darkness. Their teeth and claws could slice through mortal flesh like paper, for all that they were made of mist and shadow, but her tough hide deflected all but the most vicious blows. They appeared like something out of a human nightmare, but their lack of intelligence and tendency to appear in packs kept them on par with the *hhissih* in the minds of most Guardians.

The one thing that elevated the shadeling above a *hhissih* as a threat was the fact that the shadeling rarely appeared on the mortal plane without the intervention of a *nocturni* magic user. Sometimes the mage would leave a magical trap that would summon the creature when tripped, but in other cases they manifested in response to a direct summons. Given the present number, Ash suspected this to fall into the latter category.

All of that came from the perspective of an immortal, stone-skinned warrior. While she and her brethren might be immune to the average shadeling attack, the human would not be so lucky. That meant these creatures had not come into the flat seeking to destroy Ash. They sought a more tender piece of prey.

The idea made Ash curl her lip and flash her mouthful of razor-sharp fangs. She braced herself against attack and dug the ends of her talons into the floorboards for better purchase. Any entity seeking to harm her Warden would have to go straight through her to do it. And Ash didn't give a shit that the shadelings' incorporeal forms made such a thing possible in theory. In reality, she would do whatever it took to stop them.

She heard a series of thumps behind her and glanced over her shoulder to see Drum hopping in place as he tried to pull on his jeans. She scowled at him. "Stop wasting time! Get out of here! Run!"

He returned the expression with interest. "Not happening! And if the Garda is going to find me torn to bits on the floor of my flat, I don't want them telling my ma that the first thing they saw when they broke down the door was my bare, white arse."

Ash scowled and spun back to face their attackers with a growl. "Irrational human," she muttered.

"I heard that," Drum called out, "but I'll let it go if you tell me how we get rid of these things."

"We do not. They are only vulnerable to magical strikes, so I cannot kill them, but neither can they harm me. You, on the other hand, must flee. Get out, and once you are safe, I will hunt down the sorcerer who set them upon you. Then he will find himself the one torn to bits."

"Set them on me? You think these things are here for me?"

Ash couldn't see Drum's face, but she could hear the incredulity in his voice. Then one of the shadelings made a feint to get past her right side, and she slashed at it with her long, curved talons. The thing hissed and allowed its misty form to evaporate where she would have struck. It fell back, but re-formed quickly and continued to watch her with those burning eyes.

"Not the time for a discussion!" she shouted. "Just leave! Quickly!"

Again, he ignored her advice, stepping forward until he stood just behind her left shoulder. "I already said that wasn't happening. Besides, if they are here for me, what makes you think they won't just leave you here and follow me wherever I go?"

She snarled her displeasure and lunged forward to cut off another creature who thought to slip past her. She hated the fact that Drum's theory made sense. In fact, he was probably right. The shadelings had to be here for him, and that meant that sending him off by himself would only increase the danger. She needed another plan, and fast.

It turned out that fast was already too slow. Before she could think, four of the entities converged on her in a shroud of black shadows. She saw the others fly past toward Drum, and then her sight was cut off by the shadelings' attack.

They began to circle around her at an ever-increasing pace until they blurred into something like the walls of a miniature cyclone. It was a tactic they employed often to confuse and disorient their unwary victims. Luckily, Ash was neither unwary nor the victim.

She dropped low where the concentration of mist thinned out to almost nothing. Creatures without bodies, after all, didn't have legs or feet to obscure the view. She was able to see Drum stumble backward away from the shadows streaking toward him and gathered herself to rush to his aid just as he caught himself. She couldn't make out the look on his face, but she heard the fierce anger in his voice when he raised both hands in front of him and yelled, "Leave us the fuck alone!"

He surprised her a second time by following the command with a stream of bright golden light just as he had in the cavern yesterday. This morning. Whatever. Without training, he should not have been able to gather his magic to him like that, let alone focus it into an effective energy weapon. One time could easily be written off as a fluke, but a second indicated the potential for her Warden to become a gifted combat magic user.

Provided he didn't get himself killed before they could find someone to train him.

Pressing her lips into a grim line, Ash unfurled just the tips of her wings with a sudden upward thrust. The movement created a quick gust of air that shot through the circling shadelings and interrupted their own rising currents. She heard the screech of protest but she was already rolling out from under their cage shadows.

A second high-pitched wail told her that Drum's magical blast had found its mark. She surged to her feet just in time to see the black veil in front of him dissolve like a lamp turning on to dispel the darkness. Or the Darkness.

With her wings tucked back into place, Ash raked her glance over him to be sure he remained uninjured and then placed herself once more between him and the approaching threat. Less than a second later, she felt a rapid ding to the back of her head like a pebble bouncing off her skull. It took her a moment to realize that Drum had smacked her the same way she had seen his sister do to him.

"Don't be an idiot," he said, when she jerked her head around to shoot him an incredulous look. "You said yourself you can't fight these. I can, but not with you standing in the bloody way."

"I did not," she protested. "I said I could not kill them. There is a difference."

"Not a big enough one. Move so I can blast the others. Go do whatever it was you were going to do to find who sent them. I've got this."

Ash hesitated, uncertain whether or not the human's confidence was misplaced. He still could claim no training in the use of magic. Had his first two shots merely been well-timed examples of good luck?

As if in answer to her unspoken question, Drum cursed and shifted behind her. His hands came up and his elbows came to rest on her shoulders a split second before he released a third stream of golden light at a rush of animated black fog.

"Go!" he shouted, and this time Ash listened.

She charged through the remaining shadelings like a

rugby player through a scrum and emerged on the other side to race to the darkened glass of the windows. Her claws scratched at the oak frame as she scrabbled for her grip and threw open the sash. Later she could apologize to Drum, but for now she had a sorcerer to catch.

The narrow opening of the old windows made for a tight squeeze between her size and the bulk of her wings, slowing her down on her way outside. It allowed the figure in the cramped parking area below time to see her coming. She saw the *nocturni*'s shoulders stiffen beneath the drape of his black robe as he debated whether to turn and run or to stay and face the Guardian. Apparently, this one thought quite a bit of himself, because he lifted his hands and shouted a word of power in the corrupt tongue of his demonic Masters.

Ash gave a mighty shove and freed herself from the window a bare instant before a bolt of kinetic force exploded against the brick where her head had been just a moment ago. She spread her wings and soared upward, reaching for her axe as she flew. She could almost feel the satisfying impact resonating down the haft as the blade slammed into its target. It was a bloodthirsty thought, but hers was a bloodthirsty race. Wars, every Guardian knew, were not won without bloodshed. All one could do was ensure that the enemy spilled more in the end.

She executed a graceful tumble in midair that changed her direction to face the evil below. Hovering just above the rooftops, she let her wings extend to their fullest spread and glared down at her foe. "Name your Master," she ordered, investing her tone with the full weight of her authority as a Guardian and her fury as the lover of the target of this villain's attack. "Tell me which of the Seven you serve, minion, and reveal your plans to me, or I shall bring the wrath of the Light down upon your head."

The *nocturni* tilted his head back to meet her gaze, and

even at a distance she could see the light of madness in his eyes. "You will fall, Guardian, you and your pet War- den, and all the others of your kind. My Masters are risen, and your precious Guild is no longer here to help you. Four have returned to us and the fifth waits below our feet for his chance at freedom. It's not long now, female abomina- tion. Your existence shows that your kind have grown weak, while we have only gained in strength." He laughed, the mad cackle of an excited zealot. "Not long at all till you *die!*"

With his last exclamation, he hurled his power into the sky. The sickly, blackened stream of red light surged forth until it gathered in a solid mass not ten feet from where Ash remained treading air. The corrupt energy twisted and writhed until it took the shape of a skeletal firedrake, a miniature dragon with wings made of ragged flame and claws like rusty sabers. It opened its bony muzzle to pour out a deafening roar, followed by a ball of polluted fire.

Ash cursed and dodged to the left. She recovered quickly and twisted to meet the creature's charge with one of her own. She felt the heat and rush of air that accompa- nied its approach and realized that this thing had mass, making it something she could fight. She swung her axe at its head. It ducked, causing her to miss, but the move- ment sent its next missile to sputter out uselessly in the night air.

A shout from the window distracted her for a second, and she turned to see Drum stick his head out to assess the situation. She yelled for him to get back inside, which served both to thwart the drake's next attack, and to draw the *nocturni*'s attention to the man in the window. A fiery claw raked across her rib cage, slicing through her tunic and the tough hide beneath.

In the same moment, Drum gave a hoarse shout and at- tempted to hit the drake with the same burst of magic that had driven off the shadelings. This time, however, the energy bounced harmlessly off its target, and the monster didn't so much as twitch. The *nocturni* got luckier. His blast missed hitting Drum straight on, but it did glance off his shoulder and send the man stumbling back into the flat with a cry of pain.

Ash screamed her fury and threw herself at the firedrake. The dumb creature had not anticipated a frontal assault and failed to dodge in time. Using the slightly smaller blade on the back of her axe, Ash hooked the edge of her weapon in the vulnerable spot beneath the thing's front leg and spun it around like a discus before sending it flying straight at its creator.

The monster belched out another stream of fire, but this time it found a target. The flame ignited the *nocturni*'s black robe, lighting up the demon worshipper like a Roman candle. The man screamed and ran, which only fed the fire, but it also broke his concentration so that the firedrake blinked out of existence.

Ash turned immediately and flew back to the open window. The minute her hands closed about the frame, she shifted back to her smaller human form and threw herself inside. She found Drum sitting on the floor propped up against the back of the sofa. He swore a blue streak through a grimace of pain as he pressed his head into the upholstery. She could see the skin on his left shoulder had already blistered, and the red of the burn continued down over the upper portion of his biceps. She fell to her knees beside him and leaned in to get a closer look at the injury.

"Are you all right?"

"Hurts like bloody everlasting hell," he hissed through clenched teeth. "But I suppose I should be glad it wasn't my head. Burned hair smells like shite."

"Was that meant to be funny?"

"Guess it doesn't matter." He straightened his head and

looked down at her side. "What about you? I thought I saw that dragon thing get a good whack at you."

Ash had forgotten all about that. She had been too worried about Drum to remember the slice she had taken in her side. She paused to assess. She could feel a slight sting but no serious pain, so she shrugged. "It is nothing serious. Come, we should apply ice to your shoulder."

She reached forward to drape his right arm across her shoulders, intending to get him to a more comfortable seat while she tended to his wound. He pulled away with a frown, his eyes focused on a spot just below her left breast. Had his burn somehow affected his eyesight?

"Bullshit," he growled. "That's blood on your shirt."

"I told you, it's nothing."

Drum ignored her. His right hand darted out and caught the fabric of her shirt. He raised the hem to reveal a long, shallow cut that ran all the way along the curve of her lowest rib. He cursed again, this time in Irish. She had noticed he tended to do that when he was most upset. "We have to get this cleaned up."

Ash slapped his hand away. "It barely broke my skin. Guardians have tough hides. Your burn is much more serious. Ice. Come on."

He scowled at her. "Won't help. Once the blisters form, it's too late for ice. Ma makes a cream, though. I keep a jar in the drawer in the kitchen." She rose to her feet without a word and turned toward the archway to the other room. She hadn't taken more than two steps when he called out behind her. "Bring a soapy flannel, too, so we can clean that slice of yours."

She ignored him. She rummaged through two drawers before she found a small jar filled with a white cream. A flowered label on the glass read simply BURNS in neat block letters. She grabbed it along with a clean, white towel with blue stripes. She ran it under a cold tap, but ignored the soap. Her wound didn't require cleaning, and the stuff might irritate Drum's burned skin.

Returning to the sitting room, she found that he had managed to lever himself off the floor and around the side of the sofa. He had slumped against the far side with part of his back and his right shoulder against the rear cushions, leaving his left shoulder and upper arm out in the open.

He looked at the items in her hands and held out his own. "You first."

Ash held the cloth out of his reach until she could drape it over his burns. He hissed and then relaxed as the cool compress provided a small amount of relief. He narrowed his gaze on her. "Ash—"

She rolled her eyes at the warning in his tone. Did he think he could overpower her, wrestle her to the ground, and clean her scratch by force? Ha! Not even had she been the one sporting second-degree burns. But she didn't want him to exert himself in the attempt, so she lifted her shirt herself this time to show him her torso. The cut had already sealed itself and scabbed over. Within a few more minutes the scabs would come off and shortly after that, no one would be able to tell that the drake had even touched her.

As she had said, Guardians healed quickly.

Drum looked surprised for moment before relaxing back into the sofa cushions. His eyes closed on a grunt. "Fine. Do your worst."

Ash took her first stab at sarcasm. "Why, thank you."

The corner of his mouth quirked upward, but his eyes stayed closed.

Refocusing on her task, Ash lifted the cloth from his shoulder and noted that the fabric felt warm now. The heat of his skin had raised the temperature by several degrees, and she could easily see why. The burn stretched straight across the top of his shoulder and down onto his chest and upper arm. Turning her head, she could even see reddened areas on his ear and the side of his neck. The blast of fire had gone directly over his shoulder, probably less than an inch from the surface of his skin. The blistered areas had gotten closest, but if the flame had actually touched him, the burns would likely have been even worse. His chest and upper arm had escaped the blistering and instead appeared more like an angry sunburn. It probably caused no less pain, but it would heal faster and more cleanly.

It took an effort of will for Ash to rein in her anger. Her first instinct was to scold Drum for putting himself in danger after she had repeatedly told him to leave their attackers to her. Her lips actually parted to let out the sharp words before she caught herself. She might not have known Michael Drummond for very long, but she already knew him well enough to understand that haranguing him would get her nowhere. He would only dig in his heels and insist that his actions had been justified.

While Ash would not go so far as to agree, she could at least understand his reasoning. He had already held his own against two attacks by the shadelings, and he'd had no way of knowing how much greater the threat outside would be. She could also admit that she possessed no greater skill than he at standing on the sidelines when she saw another in danger.

All this ran through her mind as she smoothed a thin layer of the cool cream over his injury. Drum remained silent, but she could see him wince now and then when her fingers hit a particularly sensitive spot. She could only hope that his confidence in his mother's abilities as an herbal healer were not misplaced. She could admit that the balm felt pleasant and silky on her undamaged skin and bore a light, refreshing scent of citrus and herb, but the proof would be in the pudding. She wanted to see his wound healed before she passed judgment.

Drum opened his eyes as she replaced the cap on the jar. "Do you think that was the same idiot who attacked us at the abbey?"

She shrugged. "It is impossible to be certain. I did not see the *nocturni*'s face during that first confrontation, and tonight I caught no more than a glimpse. But I cannot tell you whether it would matter either way. If it was one cultist or two, they both had the same intent. Both belong to the Order, and both serve the same Masters."

"Then that means that Maeve's visions were right."

Ash thought about his sister's revelations that afternoon and then recalled the words the sorcerer had spoken. Maeve had said that she had Seen that five Guardians were awake and confronting something so terrible that her mind's eye could not bear to look directly at it. That described one of the Seven quite well. But their attacker tonight had said that four of the Demons of Darkness had already been released into the human world.

She shuddered. Was it possible? Or had it been an idle boast designed to strike fear into the hearts of those who opposed the Order's plans? The idea of four of the Accursed Ones loose together on the mortal plane would be a greater disaster than Ash had allowed herself to imagine. Even with five of the brethren working together, it could take months, or even years, to recapture that many Demons. They could hope the creatures remained weak, not at their full power, but they could not count on such good fortune. They would need to be prepared for a battle the likes of which had not been seen on earth in thousands of years.

"It would mean that we must move forward as if she has seen the true future," Ash said. "The chance exists that the future remains in flux, but it is a Guardian's duty to prepare for the worst."

He reached out with his good hand and hugged her into his lap. "And a Warden's duty?"

"That does not change. A Warden serves his Guardian, and when the battle is won, he revokes the summons to return us to stone."

Drum made a noncommittal sound. His gaze swept over her face as if searching for something. Had she known what he looked for, she would have provided it gladly. He gave nothing away, but pulled her closer to his uninjured side and forward until his lips hovered a bare inch from hers. "I told you I wasn't Warden material," he murmured before closing the distance and capturing her mouth in a kiss.

Ash didn't bother arguing. She was too busy trying to devour him whole. They could discuss destiny and duty another time. Or argue about it. She didn't care. At that moment all she cared about was the rising tide of desire she felt for this man. Everything else could be sorted out later.

Including the other feeling that swept in beneath the tangle of heat and attraction. The soft, inexorable force that threatened to upset her balance forever. There would be time enough for contemplation when she was trapped once more in layers of unyielding rock. For now, Ash had better things to do.

Chapter Fourteen

The phone rang well before Drum had any intention of clawing his way to consciousness. Try following wild monkey sex with a frantic battle against the forces of evil and see how perky you felt after less than five hours of sleep. He let voice mail take the call. Seven seconds after the ringing stopped it started up again.

He cursed. In his head, because he lacked the energy for full-on vocalization. Ash stirred beside him.

"You should answer."

No, she was the one with the power of audible speech, he thought. She could get it. He lay still. The ringing stopped only to start again after five seconds.

Did Warden training cover the ability to lay curses on people? If so, maybe he should look into enrolling after all.

"What if it is important?"

He managed a grunt, which he supposed signified progress, and a twitch of his fingers. She still had him beat.

And the phone kept ringing.

A finger poked hard between his ribs, and Drum muttered a word that would have made his mother's wooden spoon quiver. A superhuman feat of strength brought his fumbling hand to the bedside table and closed his fingers around his mobile phone. He tried bringing it to his ear, but Ash's head lay nestled in the way, forcing him to switch hands. He brought the device to his other ear and winced when his burned shoulder protested the movement.

"H'lo?"

"About time, lazybones," Maeve chirped into his ear. "It's after nine and you're still lounging in bed like a pasha, hm?"

"Hanging up now," he muttered, sliding his thumb around in search of the appropriate button.

"Wait! I have news. You'll want to hear this, Michael."

"Doubt it."

"Well, I know that Ash will. I think I found a way to find those other Guardians."

Ash stiffened against his side, her supernatural hearing allowing her to eavesdrop without difficulty, and lifted her head to meet his gaze. Drum knew this because his own eyelids had finally opened in reaction to his sister's news.

"How?"

"After you left last night, in such a hurry"—Maeve emphasized the last phrase with a note of mischief—"I had an idea, so I decided to do a bit of research online."

Drum scoffed. "Online? You? How long did Ma's computer hold out? Three minutes?"

His sister sniffed with disdain. "Don't be a child, Michael. I asked Meara to help me."

"I'd have thought she'd have left right after we did."

"Don't be daft. You think she came all the way from Cork just to stay for dinner? She's visiting with Ma through the weekend."

"Oh, right." He hadn't been thinking all that clearly over the last couple of days. He should have known that.

"What did she find?" asked the distraction snuggled

against him. She had raised her upper body and braced her forearm against his chest, while her gaze monitored his expressions.

"Right, then. So, what did you come up with?" Drum asked.

"Well, I got to thinking that no matter how ancient the Guild and the whole Guardian organization might be, in this day and age there would have to be something about them floating around on the Internet. So, I asked Meara to Google a few keywords."

Drum let a note of skepticism seep into his voice. "And you found the home page of the Wardens Guild? Tell me, did they have an application and a list of classes scheduled for next semester?"

"Honestly, Michael, you can be such a child." He could almost see Maeve rolling her eyes at him. "What I found was a series of very interesting news articles from America. It turns out that they had their own little dustup at the same time that the Easter riots were turning Dublin on its ear."

Drum frowned. "Okay . . ."

"Apparently, this all happened in Boston. There was some sort of high-profile conference being put on by that American philanthropist fellow. Richard Foye-Carver. It turns out that the event was interrupted by a very violent incident, one of those terrible mass shootings that keeps happening over there."

"What does this have to do with the Guardians?"

"Patience, big brother. I'm getting there," Maeve said. "I told you we were searching for keywords and some interesting ones popped up around this conference. Apparently, a few of the attendees who had witnessed the attack claimed that it wasn't a couple of men with assault rifles like the police said, but real-life monsters who killed the victims."

Ash met his gaze as he felt the hairs at the back of his neck stand to attention. "Monsters, huh?"

His sister hummed. "Monsters," she confirmed. "And to make these witnesses sound even crazier, a couple of them said that a few of the creatures seemed to be trying to protect the conference attendees. They described those as being huge, muscled figures with gray skin and wings."

Ash murmured something under her breath, but Drum's heart beat in his ears too loudly to hear. He had to force himself to calm down enough to listen to the rest of Maeve's story.

"The authorities, of course, dismissed all the talk of monsters," she continued. "The official version of the story is that three men with ties to a white supremacist organization and individual histories of mental illness registered for the conference for the sole purpose of staging the attack. Apparently, the medical examiner felt that what looked like bite wounds could be explained away as the damage inflicted by rounds of fragmentary ammunition and homemade grenades tossed into the crowd. The other stories resulted from mass hysteria, simple hallucinations induced by the trauma of the events."

"Fools," Ash muttered under her breath. Drum agreed, but he also understood the impulse to attempt to explain away something a human mind didn't really want to understand. It took a lot less effort to cope with the reality where such things only happen in movies and scary stories.

"We start looking for the Guardians in Boston, then," he said. He tried to think of a strategy to begin with but came up blank. "That's an awfully big city for a clue that's already half a year old. But I suppose it's more than we knew an hour ago."

"And less than you'll know in a minute or two, if you

let me finish," Maeve said. "I haven't even gotten to the most interesting part yet."

When she paused and left that statement dangling like a baited hook in a fish pond, Drum had to pray for patience. "Stop teasing, Mae. Just spit it out already."

His sister chuckled. "You're no fun, but all right. One of the reasons that the stories about monsters got any traction outside of the tabloids is because at least one of the 'hallucinations' reported claimed that the helpful monsters were getting help from Kylie Kramer."

"Kylie Kramer," Drum repeated. "Where have I heard that name before?"

"Uh, how about everywhere? Honestly, Michael, I sometimes wonder if it ever rains in that cloud your head gets stuck in. I think ninety percent of the human population has heard of her. She's the American girl genius who sold the app she developed to one of the major tech companies in the world for about twelve gajillion dollars. It made the top story in everything just a few years ago. It turns out that she lives in Boston."

Ash leaned across his uninjured right side to speak into the phone. "And she worked with the Guardians during this battle?"

"That's what the lunatics said right before the authorities dragged them away from the scene and to the nearest hospital," Maeve said. "I'm not sure whether the stories held up once they got a few doses of antipsychotic medications in them. Meara says probably not. Kylie Kramer, of course, declined to comment."

Drum nodded at Ash. "It sounds worth checking out. But how well-known is this woman? It might be difficult to get close enough to her to ask the necessary questions."

"I would say so, since the fellow standing next to her in some of these news photos is variously identified as either

her boyfriend or her bodyguard. He's built like an American football player, and he looks about as friendly as Fionn mac Cumhaill on a rainy day. He also looks protective, whatever his relationship to Kramer."

"He is a Guardian." Ash's voice held not a trace of doubt. She looked at Drum. "She may be his Warden. How soon can we travel to Boston?"

Maeve spoke again. "Not so fast. If you'll remember, our current troubles are happening here, not in America. It seems to me that it would be more helpful to bring this particular mountain to Mohammed, so to speak. I've already sent an e-mail. Well, Meara did. Mama didn't want me crashing her hard drive again."

"What good is an e-mail going to do?" Drum grumbled. "Who's to say she'll even see it? If she's a famous millionaire, she probably has an assistant who goes through that stuff and screens out the unsolicited junk. But even if it got through, are you really so gone in the head that you came right out and told her about what's been going on here?"

"Give me a little credit, Michael. I told you this is all about keywords. The e-mail was perfectly bland and sane sounding. I just made sure to bury a few words here and there that only someone who already knew about the Guardians would pick up on."

"But who's to say she'll even answer? Maybe she doesn't care about a bunch of people in Ireland she's never heard of?"

Ash shook her head. "If she understands, she will answer. Only one affiliated with the Guild or the Guardians directly will know of what your sister has written, and such a person cannot refuse an earnest call for aid. She would have to respond. There would be no choice."

Drum could feel his brows draw together. "Unless the reason she understands the bloody e-mail and knows about Guardians is because she's working for the other side."

"Impossible. Were she *nocturni,* no Guardian would have let her walk out of that battle alive." Ash sounded very certain.

"Okay," he acknowledged reluctantly, "but we still have to wait for her to respond, and based on last night, I doubt we can wait forever."

"Last night?" Maeve pounced on his slip. "What happened last night?"

"Nothing."

"We were attacked."

Ash spoke over his denial, making Drum frown and Maeve gasp. Dammit, if his sister heard about last night, it would be another ten seconds before his mother knew the whole story, as well. At that point, he would have to go into hiding to avoid her fussing followed by her scolding. In Maddie Drummond's eyes, he might as well have still been eight years old and prone to bloody accidents. Last night did not count as any kind of accident.

"Attacked! Merciful heavens. Drum, are you all right?" Maeve demanded.

"I'm fine, Mae. I promise."

"He received a burn on the shoulder, but he will recover soon." Ash avoided his attempt to cover her mouth with his hand and ignored the dirty look he gave her. It was an entirely different kind of dirty than the looks he had given her last night. "There is no cause to worry. I made certain to treat and bandage the wound."

"Thank you, Ash. Did you use Ma's burn cream?"

"Liberally."

"Good."

"Yeah, it's fan-fucking-tastic," Drum snapped. "But do you think we can get back to important matters?"

Maeve made a clucking sound of chastisement. "He's never been one to stay in good spirits when he is under the weather. Bit of a whinger."

"Maeve!"

"My goodness! Fine, have it your way," she said. "I promise that I'll let you know the very minute I get an answer."

"And in the meantime?"

"First thing, I suggest you practice your dodge, big brother." Maeve disconnected before he could respond to that pithy suggestion.

He stared at the phone for a second and nearly gave in to the urge to hurl it against a wall. Only a sharp twinge in his shoulder restrained him.

Ash patted his chest. "In the meantime, we wait. And, we keep our guard up. I will not allow the Order to sneak up on us a second time."

Drum forced down his anger and frustration until he could release the worst of it in a sigh. He replaced his mobile on the bedside table and wrapped his arms around his lover. "Good," he said as he began to relax. "The first time wasn't all that grand."

She smiled at him and slid her hand to the south. "Perhaps you need assistance in focusing on something more pleasant."

His eyebrow quirked upward. "Perhaps I do," he murmured an instant before her hand closed around him, drawing his breath out in a hiss.

"Let me help with that," she said, and settled her mouth over his.

Drum's last coherent thought was that he was happy to accept this woman's help. In fact, he wasn't sure if he'd be able to manage without it.

Chapter Fifteen

The next three days crawled by like a narcoleptic turtle. If he hadn't had the pub to keep him busy and Ash to keep him distracted, Drum figured he'd have lost his mind by the end of the third hour. Kylie Kramer turned out not to be the sort of neurotic technology addict who checked her e-mail every thirty seconds and responded to each message as it arrived. Damn her.

Maeve stopped answering his calls after the seventh time he dialed her number. She got tired of explaining that the world didn't revolve around his demands, that people took vacations, and that very well-known people often got behind in responding to large quantities of incoming mail. He knew all that, recognized it as a perfect example of calm and rational thought, but he still wanted to tie her shoelaces together every time she said it. Which was probably why she stopped answering.

By Monday evening even Ash had begun snarling at him with preemptive threats every time he opened his mouth while looking in her direction. Maybe she was right about that whole Xanax suggestion, though he still found himself unwilling to let her administer it via the route she wanted. That wasn't his brand of kink.

She had accompanied him down to the tap, and occupied the far corner stool while he stood behind the bar filling orders and building pints. It was a quiet evening, as Mondays usually were, especially since his kitchen operated only for lunch. He spent a good deal of time turning to speak to the Guardian, only to be warned off with a discreet flash of fang. He had worn his way down to her last nerve, and given how easy it would be for her to knock him into a coma with that slap Maeve had taught her, he found himself retreating several times an hour.

And bribing her with cider. It turned out that her distaste for alcohol only extended to Guinness. She liked a pint of Bulmers well enough, though she nursed it through most of the night.

It was after seven, and the pub sat almost empty but for a handful of regulars scattered about the place. He looked up from drying glassware when the door opened and a couple of strangers stepped inside. Out of the corner of his eye, he saw Ash stiffen, and he drew himself up warily.

"Evening." He nodded to the newcomers, a man a couple of inches shorter than him but bulky with muscle and a tiny, dark-haired sprite of a woman less than half her companion's size.

They stepped up to the bar, and it was the woman who offered him a smile and a greeting. "Hi. Things are certainly looking better after a few hours of sleep." She had pretty dark eyes and an obvious American accent. "Transatlantic flights are the worst. I'm dying for some caffeine. Can I get a Coke? With what you would consider ridiculous amounts of ice, please?"

Drum glanced at the man hovering behind her, but he had his eyes fixed on Ash. He had the battered face of a boxer and little more than a stubble of hair covering his head. The expression on his face didn't offer many clues to his thoughts, but Drum would be willing to bet on confusion mixed with hostility. The hostility made his eyes narrow and his hand reach for the sap that rested under the bar. His fingers had just closed over the grip when Ash's voice cut through the rising tension.

"Brother." She nodded at the burly man, leaving Drum confused. Someone without family shouldn't be calling anyone brother, and her tone remained cool and wary. She pointed her chin at the petite American. "Is she your Warden?"

It took a moment for her meaning to sink in. When it finally hit him, Drum felt as if he'd taken a blow from his own weapon. He had been expecting a suspicious e-mail, not an impromptu and in-person visitation.

The small woman turned toward Ash and lifted her eyebrows. "Well, I was going to take a minute and work up to asking if there was a Michael Drummond here," she said, "but it sounds like you are the one I should be talking to. I'm Kylie Kramer, but you don't much look like any of the Guardians I've ever met."

"Because she is not." When the muscled mute finally broke his silence he did it in a voice that sounded like gravel doused in whiskey and dragged backward through a smoke-filled midnight. It also sounded like he had just rejected Ash's claim of being a Guardian.

Drum's fingers tightened again around the sap. He narrowed his eyes at the stranger. So did Ash.

"You deny what I am?" she asked.

"I know only that you are female, and since the dawn of our kind only males have been summoned."

He opened his mouth to defend Ash's honor, but Kylie spoke before he could get a word out.

"Boy, are you lucky Wynn isn't here when you make a comment like that," she said, snickering. "She might hex something you consider important. You guys calm down.

It's not like we can ask her to show us the real her out in public like this."

Her words made Drum realize that they had been speaking about a rather sensitive topic in front of several local regulars. He'd rather not find himself trying to explain the concept of Guardians and Demons to some half-langered neighborhood gossips. Luckily, when he swept his gaze around the room, no one appeared to be paying them much attention. A couple of glances shifted their way at the sound of an American accent, but no one seemed interested in the actual words.

He thought back for moment, reviewing the conversation, and was struck to notice that no one had said anything worth paying attention to. Words like "Warden" and "Guardian" now had very specific meanings for him, but for the rest of the world they simply meant people employed to watch over someone or something. Pretty dull stuff when you dispensed with the capital letters and the forces of evil.

Ash's verbal challenge pulled him back to the matter at hand.

"Would you truly require such a sight in order to recognize that which stands before you?" she asked.

"I don't, and I'm the one who's human." Kylie tilted her head at her companion. "He doesn't either, not really. He's just confused. I would blame it on not getting all the rock out of his head, but I admit I have a couple questions myself. I kind of thought that you guys were always, well, *guys*."

Ash relaxed just a little, but it was enough for Drum to notice. He brought his hand reluctantly back to the bar.

"Were I not a witness to my own existence, I might doubt as well, but I have no answers to give you. I know I am the first among my kind, but I do not know why or how I appeared as I am. I only know that I am here and that I share the memory and the purpose of all of my brothers."

Both of the newcomers stared at her for the space of two heartbeats before the woman gave a brusque nod followed by another smile. "Good. In that case, how about you tell us your names and why I got a really unusual e-mail telling me to contact someone at this pub named Michael Drummond about a guy in a robe and earthquakes without any fault lines."

Her companion grunted and lifted her onto the stool next to Ash before sliding into the one beside it. "Guinness," he said. "Might be here a while."

Drum grabbed a fresh pint glass and shook his head. The surly bastard had no idea.

They sat at the bar till closing and then adjourned to the flat upstairs. As they settled into their choices of seats, it wasn't Ash and Drum who were still talking. As it turned out, their story so far couldn't hold a candle to the adventures Kylie and Dag had already been through. It didn't bode well for Dublin city.

Ash listened to every word with careful attention. She heard about the first stirring of a Guardian in this time when her brother Kees awoke on the West Coast of Canada and became the first of those to claim a female Warden, an art historian named Ella. Then Kylie told her about Spar and Felicity in Montréal, and Knox and Wynn in Chicago. Dag had been the last of the four, rising from sleep in Boston just that spring in time to fight a bloody battle against the Order. The same one covered in the news reports Maeve had unearthed online a few days earlier.

It enraged Ash to hear about the *nocturni* attacks on Ella, the deaths of the young men and women on a deserted island in the St. Lawrence River, and the measures required to release Wynn's brother from the power of the

Demon Uhlthor. It disturbed her to hear of the machinations of the Hierophant and the lives lost during the horrible events in Boston, which sounded a thousand times more chilling when related in the words of one who had fought through it. It made her want to do violence when she listened to the story of the destruction of Guild headquarters in Paris and the near annihilation of the ranks of Wardens, with hundreds dead and any survivors assumed to be in hiding.

But what really disturbed her, what made her spine tingle and her stomach tighten, was the news she had most desperately wished she would never hear. She wanted to utter a denial, but it took a single glance at Dag's tight jaw and stony expression to convince her that her fears had been realized.

"Of course, we're a hundred percent certain about Uhlthor, and almost that much about Shaab-Na," Kylie said, her voice quiet and grave. "They are both here and both have already gathered a significant amount of strength. Nazgahchuhl was being hosted inside the Hierophant, but between the energy they got in Boston and what they would have raised at the riots here in Dublin, we can't be entirely certain it hasn't regained its own form. In fact, we can't swear the sacrifice wasn't big enough to at least open the door for another."

Ash felt bile rise in her throat. "Four."

Dag shot his Warden a warning look. "That is uncertain. We tried to find evidence of a fourth Demon, but right now all we have are theories and speculation."

"And if we're going to *speculate,* my *theory* is that the fourth would be Hrathgunal, since it's apparently pretty tight with Shaab-Na. You know, 'The Unclean' and 'He Who Walks in Filth.' They've got, like, a theme going." Kylie rolled her eyes when Dag tried to shush her. "Come on. If we're going to fill them in, we might as well tell them everything. So some of it is guesswork. So what? Unless the Order wants to give us a neatly bound copy of their manifesto, we'll be doing a whole lot of guessing before this is over."

"There is a difference between guessing and needlessly inciting panic."

"I'm not so sure about panic being needless," Drum muttered, slumping back against the sofa cushions. "Let's not discount it out of hand."

Kylie chuckled. "No. Dag and I disagree about the value of educated guesses, but he's right that it's not time to panic. Especially not now that we have you guys on our side. Ash makes five Guardians who aren't stoned anymore, and you're our fifth Warden. That equals ten of us against three, maybe four, of them. That's not bad odds."

"Those numbers only apply if you ignore that the three or four are Demons of the Darkness, and that they likely have thousands, if not tens of thousands, of *nocturni* servants to do their bidding." Ash scowled. "Ten of us against an army of ten thousand led by the greatest evil this world has ever known sounds a little less pleasant, does it not?"

The American rolled her eyes and leaned far forward in her chair to pat Drum on the knee. "Don't listen to her, Drum. These Guardians could teach night classes on worst-case scenarios. They need us around to keep them from depressing themselves into blubbering masses of immortal angst."

Dag rumbled a growl that sounded more like a habitual response than a legitimate complaint. Ash, however, gave serious thought to ripping the woman's arm from its socket and beating her over the head with it. Oh, she was grateful that the Warden had responded so quickly and personally to Maeve and Meara's e-mail, but if the American touched Drum one more time, Ash could not be held responsible for her actions.

Her hands curled into fists until Drum took one in his and tugged her closer against his side. She settled for cuddling against him and sending the other woman a hostile glance.

Kylie just grinned. "So, I guess the big question here is whether or not anyone has any clue what this new stuff happening in Ireland means."

Her Guardian, who had been prowling restlessly around the perimeter of the flat, returned to the sitting area and lifted Kylie out of her chair. He took the seat and arranged her in his lap. The Warden didn't react, telling Ash this was something of a habit for these two.

"We should hear the story again," Dag rumbled. "From the beginning, in case we missed something."

Ash appreciated her brother's urge to be thorough even as she felt Drum heave a sigh. She placed a hand on her lover's thigh. "I'll do it."

And so she took everyone through it again, step-by-step, relating each event from the moment she woke on the abbey grounds to the instant when Kylie and Dag stepped inside the Skin and Bones. She even included the first vision Maeve had seen, though it had struck the girl before Ash's summoning. The only things she left out were a couple of kisses and some wild monkey sex. Some things should simply remain private.

When she finished, both of their visitors appeared thoughtful. "It sounds as if the *nocturni* who attacked you here several nights ago confirmed that four of the Seven have indeed been freed," Dag said, his harsh features pulled into a frown. "That is grave news."

"Provided he's telling the truth," Kylie said, pursing her lips. "Yeah, I know I play devil's advocate a lot, but guys who sign up with an organization that calls itself the Order of Eternal Darkness, and that has a mission statement about ending the world through unleashing unspeakable evil . . . Well, they're not the most trustworthy nuts in the rugelach."

Ash shrugged. "You speak the truth, but I am unsure if we can afford not to imagine the worst."

Kylie winked at Drum, but included Ash in her smile. "See what I mean, Drum? Pessimists, every single one of them. I'm thinking of nominating them all for honorary Jewishness."

Dag tightened his arms around her until his Warden squeaked. "No war has ever been lost by an army who faced its opponent while overly prepared."

"It would help if we knew exactly what to prepare for." Drum sighed. "My sister's visions have been disturbing, but not what I'd call clear. Still, I can't shake the feeling that these earthquakes we've had are important. They're just too unusual. One, I could have written off, but not a handful. And not after having the ground near home open up and swallow me. I've never heard of any natural cave in that area. That place we fell into shouldn't even exist."

"Well," Kylie said as she jumped to her feet. "That sounds like a good place to start. Tomorrow we can all head out that way, and you two can show us these ruins and this cave that shouldn't be there. In the meantime, Dag and I will go back to our hotel. I need to get on video chat with the others and let them know that you guys are the real deal. They'll kill me if I keep them in suspense."

Ash felt a little bit as if she'd fallen under the wheel of an oncoming steamroller. She had seen one of the machines in a film Drum had persuaded her to watch, and she imagined this was how it would feel. She just hadn't expected that the vehicle would have such an air of energetic intelligence about it. Kylie Kramer had proven to be a fascinating human.

Drum climbed to his feet as well and tugged Ash along with them. "I can call you a taxi, if you'd like."

"Ooh, that would be awesome. I guess it's a little late to be standing outside, hoping one happens to drive by."

"Especially with *nocturni* on the loose," Dag growled down at his mate.

Kylie reached up—way up—to lay a hand on the Guardian's cheek. "You worry too much, *zeisele*."

"Impossible."

Ash did not recognize the pet name the American had used for her Guardian, nor the language to which it belonged (it resembled German, yet was not), but Ash recognized the tenderness in the tone and the gesture. Drum had already turned away with his mobile phone to order the cab, so he missed the sweet interaction, for which Ash was grateful. She could see that Dag had found his woman of power, the true mate who would eventually free him from returning to his stony prison. When the war had been won, provided they survived, Dag and the other mated couples would be allowed to live out their mortal lives together. The legend of the first Guardians proclaimed it so.

But Ash was different. She was not male, and so the legend could not apply to her. She could not help but think that she would once again be trapped in granite until the next threat from the Darkness emerged. The thought caused an odd sensation behind her breastbone. It felt as if a thick chain had fastened itself too tightly around her heart, both squeezing the muscle and weighing heavily upon it. Had she been human, she might have labeled it grief.

Drum stepped forward, slipping his mobile into the pocket of his jeans. As soon as his hand was free he wrapped his right arm around Ash. It still aggravated his wound to do much with his left side, so she had been careful to avoid it.

"Cab will meet you downstairs in front," he said, interrupting the quiet moment between the other couple. "Let me grab my keys, walk you out."

"Thank you," Kylie said. She snuggled against Dag's side, and he tucked her beneath his arm like a tiny treasure. "And thank your sister for us. I'm really, really glad she decided to send that e-mail."

"So am I," Ash admitted.

Drum rolled his eyes. "Trust me, if we're going out to Clondrohitty tomorrow, I'm sure you'll get the chance to thank her yourself. Maeve couldn't keep her nose out of this business if we cut it off and hid it from her."

Kylie wrinkled her nose. "Ew, thanks for that image there, Mr. Keats. That's sure going to help me sleep."

"You will sleep like the dead," Dag said with no hint of concern. "You always do, though you will wake in the morning as ill-tempered as you always are."

They followed Drum to the door of the flat and then down the stairs into the darkened pub. Ash went along so that Drum would not be making the return trip alone, as short as it might be. At least, that was what she told herself.

"Oh, speaking of the morning, I wanted to ask you guys something really important," Kylie said just as Drum unlocked the entry door to let them outside where the taxi waited beside the curb.

"What's that, then?"

She smiled up at them. "Do you know of anywhere in Dublin where a girl can get a decent bagel?"

Chapter Sixteen

Being the tallest person among his own close acquaintances, Drum had neglected to pay much attention to the notion of passenger comfort when shopping for a new car. He had been too busy considering such matters as fuel economy, environmental impact, and ease of maneuvering through Dublin's sometimes narrow streets. Of course, at the time, he had never expected to be driving one unremarkably small woman and two full-sized Guardians along the lanes toward his native village. He considered it fortunate that everyone maintained their human shape and that his newest visitors appeared to have no trouble with the idea of cuddling in the backseat during the trip.

This time his hands remained relaxed on the steering wheel except for the fact that he held two of them crossed in hopes of warding off a repeat of what had happened last time. So far, he had spotted no one who might recognize his vehicle and report back to his mother, but he continued to keep his eyes peeled. They were still a few miles from the village, but better safe than shanghaied.

Once they actually made it to the ruin, the jig would be up. Not only would they have to park near the road where any number of people could spot the car, but someone was certain to see them tromping through the fields toward the tower. Drum would be obligated to stop home before returning to the city, but that didn't mean he couldn't delay the inevitable for as long as humanly possible.

He could hear Dag and Kylie talking softly behind him, but it was Ash's voice that caught his attention. She had been very quiet last night and all of this morning. He wished he could have asked her what she was thinking.

"Do you think we'll find your sister waiting for us inside the ruins?"

The question took him by surprise for a moment. Then he snorted. "I'd not lay money against it."

If she had a response, she sucked it back down behind a sharp gasp of surprise. The car jerked hard to the left, and Drum cursed as he tried to correct their path from its new trajectory toward a large elm tree at the side of the road.

"What was that?" Kylie shouted. "Did you blow out a tire?"

"No," Drum said, clenching his teeth and wrestling the car to a stop in a clear section of road away from the elm tree and any other overhanging objects. "It's another quake."

He felt no need to elaborate, especially once the car sat stationary and yet the earth continued to move for another thirty or forty seconds. It seemed a lot longer than that. Everyone could feel it, and they all knew that it signified nothing positive.

No one spoke until the rumbles finally went quiet. Then, Kylie asked in a tone much more serious than he had heard up till now, "Have they all been like that?"

"That one was the longest, and the hardest, too. We can expect some aftershocks now."

He opened the driver's door and stepped out into an eerie silence. No birds sang, no insects whirred, no tractor engines sputtered and growled. It felt as if the world itself were in shock, unable to comprehend what had just happened. For a long moment, everything remained in a sort of suspended animation, nothing moving or sounding except for the rustles and thumps of his passengers exiting the car. The closing of the last door acted like a kind of starter's pistol, sending life racing back into the unnatural void.

Drum heard the sound of distant shouting from the nearest house and turned on instinct to rush to help. He didn't get far before a strong hand closed over his shoulder and the second lifted to point out several figures already running to offer aid. He had a lot farther to go and would never reach the problem before they did. Then the pointing hand swung around to indicate a place where he might prove even more useful.

In the distance, the ruined tower rose above the surrounding area thanks entirely to the small hill on which it stood. The remaining walls had collapsed under the strain of the moving earth, falling in on themselves and most likely covering up the opening to the cavern the Guardians and Wardens had come here to explore.

"Dammit," he heard Dag mutter. "Now we must adjust our plans."

Ash threw a look at the other Guardian. "That is clear. And the first adjustment will be to ensure that Drum's family has not been injured by this earthquake. We must go to them at once."

"Of course," Kylie said. "Is it very far?"

Drum was already sliding back behind the wheel. "Three minutes. Get in." He gunned the engine and threw the car into gear almost before the passenger doors had closed.

He steered the car down the narrow, winding lane at speeds that bypassed reckless and headed straight on to ludicrous. He saw Ash clutch at the overhead strap with one hand and braced the other against the dash to help stabilize her in the turns. No one bothered asking him to slow down or be careful, but he heard grunts and cursing come from the backseat whenever the forces of gravity sent his passengers sliding hard into the sides of the vehicle. He ignored them all and simply focused on reaching his mother's house.

When he got there and skidded to a halt in the gravel drive, he found his mother and youngest sister standing together in the front garden, well away from the old house. They had their arms wrapped around each other, and Drum yanked up on the parking brake and left the engine running as he flung himself out of the car. He cleared the low, white fence in a single leap and dragged them both into a frantic embrace. No one spoke, but he could hear Maeve crying quietly while his mother made soothing sounds. He squeezed his eyes shut and mumbled a prayer of thanks.

Nothing penetrated his circle of relief for several minutes, not the slamming of car doors or the crunching of footsteps on gravel. It wasn't until Ash pressed a hand into the center of his back that he opened his eyes and blinked at the misty sunshine.

"Was anyone hurt?" she asked, her voice containing all the calm composure that he had lost. "Maeve? Mrs. Drummond?"

Drum felt another stab of panic. "Where's Meara?"

His mother patted his arm where it crossed over her collarbone. "She caught the train back to Cork yesterday morning. She is at her flat, safe and sound. It was just Maeve and me here when the shakes started."

He sighed, the sound heavy with relief.

"And I told you already to call me Maddie, young lady," his mother continued. She pulled back from his embrace to frown at Ash. "Now tell me why you're back out here so soon, and why you couldn't be bothered to pick up a telephone to tell your own mother that you were coming."

The Guardian looked shocked, then bemused, whether by Maddie Drummond's informality or because someone had referred to her as "young lady," Drum couldn't tell, and his mother was waiting for him to answer her question. He turned his attention back to the older woman (and potentially greater threat).

"Ah, right," he said, looking up to spot Kylie and Dag hovering near the garden gate. "We, ah, we found some folks to help us with our little problem, so we brought them to have a look at the tower ruins."

Maeve pulled herself together and stepped back, using the end of her sleeve to dry her eyes. "Little problem?" she repeated, incredulous. "You call the coming of the end of the world a, quote, *little problem*? Jayus, Michael! What would you call having your throat slit? A little shaving nick?"

"Maeve! Language!"

The young woman winced. "Sorry, Ma." Her gaze drifted to the strangers standing apart from the others. She did a double take, her jaw dropping. "Oh, my G—uh, my word," she quickly corrected herself. "You're Kylie Kramer!"

The dark-haired woman by the gate grinned and lifted her hand in an abbreviated wave. "I'd better be, because this is her boyfriend, Dag Steinman, and I hear she's crazy jealous."

Maeve laughed. "Hello, then. I am Maeve Drummond, Michael's sister, and this is our mother, Madelaine." She gestured toward the woman beside her.

Maddie offered the couple a somehow formal nod of acknowledgment. "Guardian, Warden. You're both very welcome here. Please come into my home and let me offer you refreshment. I could do with a cup of tea myself right now."

Ash saw the American's eyebrows twitch, but she offered no other sign of surprise at being recognized as a member of the Guild. She smiled with real warmth and hooked her hand in her mate's elbow to tug him forward. "I hear Irish tea is in a class by itself," she said. "That sounds lovely, Mrs. Drummond. Thank you."

"Call me Maddie, dear. You're here to help my son and his Guardian. That entitles you to a few special privileges." Maddie waved a dismissive hand, and stepped toward her front door.

Ash felt an instant of surprise before she realized the woman was treating Kylie and Dag as honored guests. She made as if to follow, but Drum stepped forward to block his mother's path.

"Ma, you can't go inside," he said. "The earthquake could have damaged the structure of the house. It could still come down on our heads."

As if in response, a small aftershock vibrated through the earth beneath their feet. Maddie frowned and waited out the tremor with her hands braced on her hips. "Michael, I am not going to allow anything to drive me from my own home. I'm going inside. Now, move out of my way."

Ash could see Drum struggling with the choice between disobeying his mother and allowing her to put herself in danger. Neither would make him happy, but he managed to offer a compromise.

"I understand," he said. "Just let me take a look around first and make certain it's safe. It'll only take a few minutes, Ma. I promise. Please?"

Maddie pursed her lips and stared at her son for moment. Then she crossed her arms over her chest and offered a reluctant nod. "All right, but make it quick, boyo."

Ash spotted his sigh of relief as Drum turned to open the front door. Before he could step inside, Dag stepped up behind him. "I will help," the burly Guardian said.

The men entered the house while the others waited impatiently in the front garden. Clouds had thickened to block out the sun, and the air grew heavier as mist threatened. Maeve shivered, and Ash shrugged out of her jacket to drape it across the girl's shoulders.

"Here," she murmured. "Just understand I will want to have it back at another time."

Maeve slipped her arms into the sleeves with a grateful smile and chuckled. "Got it. Thanks, Ash. But are you certain you won't be needing it yourself?"

Ash shook her head. She didn't feel the cold. She had worn the jacket as a sort of camouflage to make her better blend in with humans.

A few minutes later, Dag pushed the front door fully open, and waved them inside. "Come. You will grow chilled. The structure is safe enough for now."

The women filed inside with Maddie in the lead and Ash bringing up the rear, but she had no trouble hearing Maeve's gasp or Maddie's swift demand. "What does that mean? 'For now.' "

They found Drum in the sitting room surrounded by the debris of the quake, pictures fallen from walls and lamps and knickknacks knocked off shelves and tables. He looked up to answer his mother's question. "There are some cracks in the plaster here and there, but they don't run into the ceilings, and I haven't found any that go into the walls themselves. It's a stroke of good fortune. I would have expected some serious damage after feeling the force of those tremors."

Kylie murmured an agreement. "For a second, I felt like I was in San Francisco instead of Ireland."

Maddie stood in the center of the room surrounded by

a lifetime of memories tossed rudely to the floor. Ash looked into her eyes and saw a flicker of pain before the woman lifted her chin, straightened her shoulders, and stepped carefully over an antique brass lamp, its cream-colored shade wildly askew.

"I've always said this family has an Angel watching over us," the woman said with a firm tone that brooked no opposition. "Michael, Maeve, if you'll straighten up enough to make sure no one hurts themselves, I'll put on the kettle and bring back a bin liner for anything that can't be saved." Then she turned and marched into her kitchen with all the dignity of a warrior queen at the head of her troops.

Her children hopped to obey without a word of protest, and Ash was happy to lend a hand. She would feel foolish just standing around, and while she didn't know where each item belonged, there were enough pieces of glass and broken bits scattered about that she could easily identify to keep her busy. Kylie and Dag must have entertained similar feelings, because they, too, joined in to clean up the mess. Maddie brought in the promised trash bag, then returned to her domain to prepare the tea tray.

When only the younger crowd remained in the room, Kylie raised her head and looked around until her gaze landed on Ash. "How did this last quake compare to the one you felt when you were at the ruin?"

Ash paused to think and dropped her handful of junk into the bag the other woman held open. "This was stronger. In fact, it is the strongest I have experienced. Why?"

The American glanced at her Guardian with a look of concern, and it was Dag who answered Ash's question. "If a weaker disturbance could rip open the earth on the last occasion, it would be logical to assume that the same could have happened this time."

"But why would anyone want to create the entrance to

some empty cave?" Maeve asked. She frowned as she set items back on the shelves of an old painted hutch. "What good does that do anyone?"

Ash considered the possibilities. None of them offered much in the way of reassurance. The least objectionable goal had to do with creating places to hide large numbers of *nocturnis* in preparation for some sort of attack or large working of dark magic. The options for disaster only grew from there.

"We cannot speculate," Dag said in his low, rough voice. "It is impossible to understand the logic of evil."

"We really won't know until we go check things out for ourselves," Kylie agreed.

"All right, then." Maeve dusted her hands together. "What are we waiting for?"

"Tea," Maddie announced as she entered carrying a large, burdened tray. "Oh, and I made some currant biscuits just yesterday. I hope you like them."

Drum lunged forward to take the heavy load from his mother's hands and set it on the low table in front of the sofa. "That wasn't necessary, Ma. We really should go take a look at things. And Maeve, when I say 'we,' your name does not appear on that list. We don't know what we might run into, and I won't have you—"

"Leaving your mother to deal with this mess all by herself," Ash finished for him. He might not have noticed the look of mutiny taking over his sister's expression, but she had.

Drum was right to put Maeve's safety first, even if he had been about to do so in the worst possible manner. They couldn't predict what they might find at the ruins, and the youngest Drummond sibling had no way of protecting herself against the things they might face. Even her untrained Warden of a brother was better prepared in a fight.

They didn't have time for an argument right now,

though, so Ash had to scramble to offer the young woman a reasonable chance to save face. She could see that Maddie caught on to her trick right away, and shot her a look of approval even as she poured tea into six cups.

"I could use a hand," the Drummond matriarch acknowledged as she handed her daughter tea laced liberally with milk and sugar. "Many hands make light work, after all."

Maeve glared at her brother but backed down at her mother's gentle prompting. "Of course, Ma. You're right. I'll stay here and help you tidy."

"Good." Maddie nodded as if that settled everything and finished distributing steaming cups. "The rest of you can leave as soon as you've finished your tea. You need something warm in your bellies after that shock and to keep away the chill."

Everyone in the room sipped obediently. Kylie's eyes sparkled over the rim of her cup, and when she set it back down in the saucer she sent Maddie a grin full of mischief. "Have you ever thought about visiting Boston, Maddie? I have a feeling my grandmother would just love to meet you."

Chapter Seventeen

Once again Drum led the way through mostly empty fields and up to the base of the tower hill. His companions remained silent even as the world around them began to recover from the shock of the quake. Birds and insects had resumed their choruses, and in the distance he could see the locals moving about to resume their lives and assess the damage. No one in the pubs tonight would be speaking about anything else, so everyone had to gather up what material they could to make their stories stand out.

Another small aftershock hit shortly after they left the house, but it had done little more than vibrate against the soles of their shoes. Still, Drum kept his eyes and ears open as they approached their destination.

Even so, the smell struck him first. He drew to a stop and looked around, brow furrowed. The air carried the scent of something sharp and rotten, bitter and earthy at the same time. The others looked to him for a moment until Kylie gagged and made a face of disgust.

"Oy, what is that *farkakte* stench? That's just nasty."

Ash inhaled and muttered a curse. She looked to Dag with a grim expression. "Brimstone."

The other Guardian nodded, though it was tough to differentiate between his grim face and his regular face. The others could only make assumptions based on Kylie's look of worry. "That's bad, isn't it?"

Drum choked back a laugh. "Brimstone? As in fire and? The literal fires of hell? That sounds pretty fecking bad to me, whatever the experts weigh in."

"I thought that all you guys said the Darkness and the Demons had nothing to do with hell or the devil, or any of that Christian religious stuff."

"They do not," Dag reassured his mate.

"It is slightly complicated from a human perspective," Ash clarified. "Your kind has always responded best to the tales to which they can most easily relate. The earlier you look back in your own history, the more important it was for a story to contain characters with recognizably human qualities. A figure called Satan or Lucifer or the devil was simpler for early humans to understand than a formless, emotionless, inhuman concept called the Darkness."

"Likewise a binary system of heaven and hell as the only other planes of existence, one in the sky and one in the center of the earth, made more sense back then than the idea of a limitless number of other planes existing alongside this one." Dag paused and shrugged. "Now there is a certain irony in the fact that those who believe in heaven and hell reject the notion of extra dimensions while your modern scientists are just beginning to understand them."

Drum sorted through the explanations in search of a few words that might actually *explain* anything. He wound up with a sharp pain above his right eye. "All right, so what you're saying is that the fires of hell don't actually come from hell? Then where do they come from?"

Ash said, "From another plane, one with many of the characteristics humans attribute to that place."

"But you're absolutely certain that it isn't."

She shrugged. "Reasonably."

"Well, that's reassuring."

Kylie interrupted with a raised hand and lifted brows. "Um, I don't mean to sound like a schlemiel here, but no one has really answered the important question. No matter where the stinky stuff may have originated, what I want to know is how it's ended up polluting the Irish country-side?"

Exactly. Drum nodded and shifted to stand shoulder to shoulder with the American. Well, shoulder to sternum. Standing next to the tiny woman made him feel like he had just been dragged under to visit the land of the pixies. If pixies flung Yiddish and subsisted entirely on bagels and Coca-Cola.

Ash and Dag shared a meaningful gaze then turned to survey the area. "We will just have to find out," the female Guardian said. "Stay behind us. If something lies in wait, we can survive a surprise attack. You Wardens can watch our backs."

Kylie wrinkled her eyebrows and dropped her gaze as they fell into formation. "Backs, butts," she murmured to Drum. "Potato, po-tah-to, is what I say."

He sputtered a laugh and followed the Guardians around the side of the hill. The woman was outrageous, but he thought he needed the laugh. Especially if they were going to run into the source of that sulfur smell.

He had a pretty good idea that Ash and Dag already knew what they were going to find and were keeping it to themselves until they could prove or disprove their theory. Part of him wanted to be offended by their refusal to share, because no one liked to walk into a potentially dangerous situation behind a blindfold. But the rest of him urged him to relax. He trusted his Guardian. He might not have any idea what feelings, if any, she had for him when it came to their untraditional relationship, but he knew in his heart and his gut that she would never willingly place him in harm's way. If he stumbled into it on his own, he also knew she would be there to get him out.

At least, she would if she were not trapped in an unbreakable prison of spellbound stone.

Drum had guessed that their slow circling of the base of the hill had something to do with reconnaissance and ensuring that nothing lurked in wait outside the pile of rubble to which the tower itself had been reduced. He felt certain nothing could possibly wait inside, given that there was no inside left worth mentioning. The stone walls had collapsed inward, converting the remains of the great round room into a quarry slag heap. Based on the depth of the piled rock, he figured that something large had locked the opening to the cavern below and prevented the debris from tumbling into the cavern.

They rounded the side of the hillock and Drum instantly spotted what the Guardians had been looking for. A ragged, black crevice split open the earth in a narrow slash, like the eye of a giant needle. It looked wide enough for a man to pass through, provided he turned sideways to accommodate his shoulders and didn't indulge too often in a traditional breakfast fry-up. Drum could only assume that it led inside the same cavern he and Ash had fallen into a few days previous. He couldn't imagine there was room for a second separate cave in that spot. It really wasn't a very big hill.

The scent of brimstone wafted out of the darkness, and Dag glanced over his shoulder at the Wardens. "Stay close," he said quietly.

Drum imagined he'd have no trouble with that suggestion. He followed the Guardians through the opening at Kylie's insistence.

"I may not be in the same class as Ella or the others when it comes to throwing magic around," she whispered, "but I've been doing this longer than you. I've learned a thing or two about defensive spells. Let me cover our backs."

He gritted his teeth and agreed, mostly because an argument seemed foolish if they needed to sneak up on something, but partly because she had a point. He hated it, though. He had grown up as the only boy in a family of girls, and as capable as they might be, his father had raised him with a wide streak of protectiveness and somewhat antiquated chivalry. Being taken care of sat uncomfortably on his shoulders; he felt much more at ease leading the charge.

Although maybe he could learn to make an exception in the case of Demons. That wouldn't reflect poorly on his masculinity, would it?

The first step through the narrow crevice plunged the group into darkness and surrounded them with the scent of sulfur. Maybe it was just his imagination running wild, but he could also have sworn that the temperature rose as they passed through into an open cavern. It was too dark to see whether it was the same one as last time, but the odds of anything else seemed astronomical. He waited for someone to activate some sort of light and shifted nervously when no one did.

"Guardians," he heard Kylie mutter from just over his right shoulder. "Just because they can see in the dark, they forget that everyone else isn't a vampire bat."

She said something else that he couldn't catch and a pale glow appeared in the darkness beside him. "Was that a spell?" he asked.

She stepped forward and grinned at him, jiggling a small flashlight. "Nope. Duracell. I always found that rabbit creepy."

Drum shook his head and turned his attention back to the Guardians. They moved forward cautiously. Kylie remained just behind his shoulder and made certain to aim the small beam of her torch to the ground just in front of his feet. He had to shorten his natural stride and shuffle a bit, but the little circle of illumination at least prevented him from falling flat on his face. Meanwhile Ash and Dag moved smoothly through the pitch-black passage, their heads turning from side to side as they scanned the cavern for anything of interest.

Or, of potential threat. At least, that's what Drum hoped they kept in mind.

It took until the two Guardians fanned slightly apart and shifted their forms, regaining their natural appearances, before Drum realized the area they had just passed through was a narrow passage into the cavern rather than the cavern itself. By now, his pupils had dilated as far as they could, and between acclimation and the small bit of light provided by Kylie's flashlight, he could begin to make out the rough corners where the passage opened into a larger space.

Well, he could make it out for a second. Then Kylie's light clicked off, and he almost jumped out of his skin.

Everyone paused, the silence of the subterranean atmosphere almost eerie in its completeness. There were no birds singing here, no crickets or buzzing bees, no sheep bleating or cows lowing. The only sounds came from them, their soft breathing and the thumping of his own heart echoing in Drum's ears.

He tried to block out his heartbeat and to concentrate on the quiet and the blackness. It took a moment of intense focus, but after a few seconds he peered around a winged form and thought he saw a dull red glow in the floor maybe twenty or thirty feet in front of their group.

"What is that?" he asked as softly as he could. "Do you see that light?"

He didn't hear a reply, but he recognized the feel of

Ash's fingertips against his chest. She pressed lightly for a moment, hovered, and then slipped away. Message received. Not graciously, but still received. He stayed in place and waited while she and Dag eased farther into the dark without making a single sound.

The almost imperceptible red glow never blinked or wavered, so he guessed that the warriors had chosen an indirect path toward the spot from which it emanated. While he understood the strategy behind the decision, he might have preferred otherwise, because it meant he couldn't keep track of their movements at all. He just had to wait there in the darkness until they either returned or didn't.

What would the cutoff time be? he wondered. Did he give them ten minutes? Twenty? A couple of hours?

Kylie shifted behind him and laid a hand on his forearm. "Don't worry," she whispered, leaning close. "They can handle this. Trust me."

It wasn't a matter of trust, he wanted to tell her. His nerves came from someplace more visceral and altogether more primal.

All humans feared the dark, whether they admitted it or not. It was why they had spent the history of their evolution creating progressively more advanced means of driving it away, first by learning to make fire, then to harness it, then to magnify it, then to replace it by newer forms of illumination that were safer, certainly, but ultimately more powerful, more stable, and longer lasting. Man had made his artificial lights so bright and so widespread that he had almost forgotten what true darkness looked like, felt like. Even in the deepest night, all a person had to do was flip a switch, or press a button, or turn a knob, and light flooded out like a divine blessing. In a large portion of the world, the lights man had made had succeeded in drowning out the stars.

It took a place like this and darkness this deep to remind humans that the blackness had not been vanquished. It had merely retreated, and it waited at the edges of civilization for its opportunity to creep forward again.

It also didn't help that they were underground. Instinct urged humanity toward open areas and defensible positions. Man wanted to see danger coming and wanted barriers between him and any outside threat to be neat and level and easily controlled. He was meant to stay on the surface of the earth, the planet's crust a barrier in the manner of human skin, not to be burrowed under except in cases of extreme need. Ants and moles could live beneath the earth, but man needed open air and wide skies as security so that he knew he would not be crushed to death in his sleep by a collapsing mantle of rock and soil.

He therefore wanted to explain to Kylie that it wasn't he, Michael Drummond, who was worried, it was the essence of humanity itself. Humanity just lacked the ability to break into a cold sweat the way he could. Of course, it didn't help his anxiety to know that the woman he thought he was falling in love with was out there where he couldn't see her, putting herself in danger, while he stood here contemplating the technological history of his species. Dammit, he ought to be helping.

Kylie squeezed his arm and stayed close, not releasing her grip as they waited for the Guardians to complete their reconnaissance of the silent cave. He tried to stay patient and to remind himself that the Guardians were experts in both warfare and the machinations of the *nocturnis*. That made them better equipped to check out the cavern than anyone else around and to do so efficiently and safely. But the next ten minutes still dragged on for a minimum of three or four weeks.

When Drum felt the first stirring of air across his face, he thought at first that he'd imagined it, but it came a second time, a little stronger. Peering into the darkness, he thought he saw something shift and was finally able to make out Ash's shape returning through the gloom. She had used her wings to create a small breeze as a warning that she and Dag were approaching.

Kylie inhaled sharply and gave his arm a final squeeze. He felt a touch of surprise at the small tells. She had seemed so calm and confident when she tried to reassure him that he hadn't stopped to think she might be feeling something similar for her own Guardian. Then she slipped past him to grab Dag in a quick, fierce hug that allowed Drum to see right through her cool, calm, and collected routine.

Lying little pixie.

"Is it safe to talk?" she asked. "What did you find?"

Ash wrapped her fingers around Drum's and shook her head. He could feel the end of her braid brush against his arm. "It is a stairway. Going down. The light shines up from below. We could see very little and hear nothing at all."

"But what's the source of the light?" Drum demanded. "Torches or something?"

"Hellfire," Dag bit off.

"Um, I'm going to assume that's not you cursing, sweetie," Kylie murmured. "So, that's the source of the light and the smell?"

"But what's down there? And how the hell did a stairway just appear in an underground cavern under an unexceptional ruin in the middle of the Kildare countryside?" Drum demanded, struggling to keep his voice low. "How does something like that even happen?"

"It does not." Ash sounded grim. "This tells us something very important, however. These caverns—this one and the one below—are important to the *nocturnis,* and have been used by them before. The stair is old. It appears to have been carved centuries ago. I believe that regaining access to this place was the reason for the earthquakes. The Order needed to find a way down here."

"And they've never bloody well heard of shovels?"

Ash squeezed his hand. "Perhaps they knew only the general area in which the caverns lay. If that knowledge had somehow been lost, if they did not have an exact map of the entrances, magic might have seemed a more expedient choice."

"Throw a few spells and get the ground to open up for you?" Kylie asked. "Lazy schmucks."

"But what makes these particular caves so important?" Drum asked, frowning into the darkness. "That's what I don't understand. Not just important enough to search for, but important enough that hundreds of years ago, some group of lunatics spent enough time in them to build a stone stairway down to a lower level?"

"The stairs do not simply lead to a lower part of the cave, human," Dag grumbled. "They lead to that level because in the chamber below us, the Order has secreted a hellmouth."

"A what?"

Drum didn't have time for a longer question. Or anything else. Before the last word cleared his lips, a horrible, shrill noise cut through the quiet, black reaches of the cave. The air around them seemed to shiver. At first, he thought he had imagined the strange effect, but then several pairs of glowing-coal eyes flicked open, and he knew this was no hallucination.

"Bloody fucking hell," he cursed, not bothering to keep his voice down anymore. "More fucking shadelings!"

"Um, I don't think that's our big problem at the moment," Kylie said. She raised her hands and he could see that one held a glowing orb of light aloft among them and the second pointed to a spot just above the entrance to the lower cavern. "Dag? Is that what I think it is?"

"Shadow!" he roared and flung himself across the room. Ash cursed in some dead language and flew after him.

Confused and angry, Drum spun to look at his only remaining companion. "What the hell is he talking about?"

"I'll tell you later," the American gasped. "Incoming!"

Chapter Eighteen

Drum spun at the sound of Kylie's shouted warning, but he was just a little too slow. A shadeling raced toward him from the shadows and threw itself against him, knocking him to the ground.

He had no idea how it happened. After all, the shadeling was a creature made of black mist, incorporeal and opaque only because of its coloring. If the thing had been white or gray, he could probably have read a newspaper through at least the lower half of its not-quite body. It should have lacked the mass to hit him, let alone knock him down, but Drum landed on his arse just the same.

Well, maybe it hadn't been the impact that sent him tumbling, but the odd sensation that accompanied it. He had to admit that the creature hadn't bounced off him, but rather passed through him, like a ghost in an old-fashioned horror movie. It felt almost like a strong, cold wind, but instead of chilling his skin and muscle, this sensation went straight to the marrow of his bones, deep into his center to deposit a layer of frost over his heart and lungs and liver and spleen. He had the thought that if he had swallowed a bucketful of ice cubes while buried to his neck in a snow-drift, he could not have possibly felt colder. He couldn't even bring himself to shiver, and wasn't that supposed to be one of the signs that hypothermia had become so advanced that death was imminent?

Fuck that. Drum had no intention of dying today, and he certainly wouldn't do it because of one puny little example of the same spook he'd kicked ass on just a few days before. And that time there had been five of them, and only one of him. This was a done deal.

You know, as soon as he managed to haul himself up off the floor.

He rolled to the side and used his arms to steady himself while he dragged his knees beneath them. All right, all fours. This was progress. He could hear a stream of words he guessed were most likely Yiddish, and judging by her tone of voice, Kylie had not engaged the other shadelings in polite conversation.

When he managed to regain his feet, he turned enough to realize that he could now see a fairly large area around him. The American Warden had illuminated the darkness by the practical method of lobbing ball after ball of bright, pale green light into the surrounding swarm of shadelings. Any time one of her balls struck, its unfortunate target would screech and explode in a shower of black particles.

She worked with an ease and efficiency that Drum couldn't hope to match, but he recognized the principle behind her strategy as the same one he had unintentionally employed during his own encounters with these entities. He might be swaying a little on his feet, but he'd be damned if he sat back and let Kylie do all the work, especially since he lost count of the pairs of shadeling eyes somewhere around two dozen. Those were not sporting odds.

It seemed equally close to cheating in his opinion when the shadeling that had passed through him rebounded from the shadows to take another pass at him. This time, though,

Drum was ready. He lifted a hand and felt a surge of energy well up from his core. He let it flow through him and pour out through his palm in an increasingly familiar blast of pale golden light. The light stream hit the shadeling's center mass and made the entity go poof.

Hey, that was almost fun, he thought as he spun to face the next attacking creature. Not that he planned to turn this into a hobby, or anything, but there was a certain satisfaction in blowing something away while having absolutely no doubt that one had chosen to do the exact right thing. Of course, he supposed there were plenty of psycho killers in the world who had the same thoughts, but they weren't the ones fighting actual monsters. That gave him a pretty big edge on the old righteous-o-meter.

"Good work!" Kylie flashed him a grin even as she launched two green missiles at two separate shadelings. Both hit and took out their intended targets. "With a little practice, I think we'll be bringing you up to the majors, kid."

Drum snorted and flung another blast of energy (he still stumbled over thinking of it as magic) that sailed past a dodging shadow with glowing red eyes. He cursed. Loudly.

"Like I said. Practice."

"And doesn't that sound like a laugh?" he muttered.

Between Kylie and himself, they managed to whittle the opposition down until Drum could finally peer through the remaining black mist and catch a glimpse of what the Guardians had gone up against. The magic flying around had generated some ambient light, but as it turned out he could have watched the whole thing by firelight, because the thing Ash and Dag were facing had set the stone floor of the cavern on fire.

Flames flickered between the Guardians and what looked almost as if a thousand shadelings had joined together to form a pool of darkness so thick the fabric of reality seemed to disappear behind it. It possessed all the mass that the smaller entities had lacked, with broad shoulders and thick, elongated limbs that gave it unnatural strides and an impossible reach. It didn't shift and shiver like its amorphous younger cousins, but its solid form seemed to dissolve around the edges. Little wisps of black mist drifted away like puffs of steam. Its eyes did not remind him of glowing coals but of deep, yawning tunnels to the molten center of hell.

Something told him that was exactly where this thing had come from. He didn't know or care if it was another plane or a religious construct, this thing made it seem very, very real.

He had to divide his attention between dispatching the remaining shadelings and keeping an eye on the bigger battle. By the time the last entity exploded, looking and sounding something like the negative image of a Roman candle, he figured that he owed his new friend from Boston something in the neighborhood of three dozen pints and the name of his firstborn child. Coming out of the situation intact but exhausted made him think he'd caught the light end of the bargain.

Placing his hands on his knees, he gave himself a minute to catch his breath and beat down the instinctive fear that tried to crawl up his throat like bile. Then he straightened his shoulders and began to cross the distance between him and the enormous, malevolent shadow.

Kylie fisted a hand in the back of his shirt and tucked him to a halt. "What, are you *meshugah*? Stay where you are, rookie. Let the first-liners handle this one."

Drum started to protest. Why the hell should they stand around and just watch when they could help their Guardians win the fight?

A sound like a barn owl caught in the throat of an angry tiger detonated in the cavern with the force of a ten-ton bomb. It shook loose a shower of dust and pebbles from the ceiling of the cave and made both humans slap their hands over their ears and wince. Kylie snapped forward at the waist as if preparing to vomit, and Drum swayed on his feet as he turned in time to see Ash swing her axe in a blow that buried the lethal blade in the middle of the Shadow's chest.

The axe hung there in the wound it had created, exposing what looked like glowing magma around the edges. It drew his attention to the fact that the Shadow no longer appeared completely black. Dozens of small injuries showed in scratches and pinpricks of orange-red light that marred the thing's surface. The two warriors had worried at it like terriers—supernatural, winged terriers—weakening it in preparation for a concerted attack.

Drum felt a surge of satisfaction, and waited to see his teammates deliver the final blow. He reminded himself that next time he might want to bring along some pretzels.

The monster flung Ash away from it, sending her a good twenty-five feet through the air before she used her wings to turn her momentum into a graceful somersault. She hovered for a moment then darted in again as if intending to retrieve her weapon for another assault.

He thought he might have shouted something, but any sound he could have made got swallowed up in the guttural fury of Dag's battle cry. The burly Guardian dropped into a crouch to avoid the Shadow's swiping claws, then thrust himself upward with all the strength in his treetrunk legs. He flew to the top of the cavern, the beat of his wings sending up a sirocco of dirt and dust into the atmosphere. Drum flung up an arm to protect his eyes, but he still managed to catch sight of the Guardian's massive hammer as it slammed down hard on the monster's skull. Or, at least, where its skull would have been had it possessed anything like a skeletal anatomy.

The blow thundered through the cave, and Drum saw a crack appear at the top of the Shadow. It sent a small chunk of darkness flying, and the crack began to snake in a crooked line down the surface of the black mass. For a second the creature looked like an inhuman version of photographs of America's Liberty Bell, but then the fissure began to widen and the resemblance disappeared in a burst of sulfurous flame.

Pieces of dark matter fell to the ground as the shape of the Shadow monster split down the center, as if someone had pulled the tab on an enormous, evil zipper. The creature costume fell away, and a geyser of hellfire spewed toward the cavern ceiling. It lit the entire chamber and made Drum grateful he had not yet lowered his arm. Getting a speck of dirt in his eye would have been painful and annoying, but losing his sight from the supernatural equivalent of staring straight into the sun would have ruined his entire day.

The conflagration lasted no more than a couple of seconds. When it died out, it took a moment for Drum to identify the metallic ringing in his ears as the sound of Ash's battle-axe clanging against the cave's stone floor. When the Shadow had fallen apart it had released the blade, which had dropped and landed on a small pile of smoldering coals.

Ash landed calmly next to the remains and scooped up her weapon. She cast her gaze over her companions and juggled her grip with alarming ease. "Was that everything?"

Drum almost choked to death when he tried to swallow a laugh and a scream on the same breath. Kylie gave him a helpful and surprisingly forceful thump between the shoulder blades with one hand, and shot the Guardian a thumbs-up sign with the other. "We took care of the shadelings, so I'm going to suggest it's a good time for us to make like it's Passover and Exodus on out of here."

"Wait a minute." Drum coughed and struggled to regain his breath. "I thought someone was going to explain to me what that thing you just killed was, and what the hell he meant when he said those stairs lead down to a hellmouth." He poked a finger in Dag's direction with what was likely somewhat excessive force.

"Um, we can totally do that," she said as she returned to her mate's side, "but maybe we want to save *Story Time: The Hellmouth Edition* for when we are not standing just a few feet from one."

"Agreed."

The nervous glance toward the stairway with which Dag, one of the most powerful beings Drum could imagine, accompanied his concurrence made Drum pause to rethink. Maybe the fellow had a point. After all, what was story time without biscuits and cocoa?

Chapter Nineteen

"Enough stalling," Drum mumbled around a mouthful of his mother's bread still warm from the oven and all but dripping with fresh country butter. "Explain to me how the twelve-ton gorilla in the cave was a shadow. I've seen shadows, and they don't usually put their fists through solid rock or burst into flame."

On the other side of the archway, Maddie sighed and shook her head as she stirred an enormous pot of stew. "Michael, please. At least make an effort not to look the complete mannerless gurrier in front of my guests."

Ash hid a smile behind her own slice of slightly sweet golden bread. The four of them had returned to the Drummond house tired, thirsty, dirty, and famished. Maddie had immediately herded them inside, set up a rotation through the shower, and begun preparing dinner. While Ash had told Drum that the angels and devils of religious teaching might not exist, his mother was making her doubt her own mind. That woman deserved a halo and a kingdom in the heavens, without a doubt.

Dag had already polished off his fourth slice of bread, so he was the one who answered the question. "Not shadow. Shadow."

Drum stared as if the Guardian had spoken in ancient Enochian.

"The second one starts with a capital *S*," Kylie clarified. "It's like a proper name, or an official title."

"Then I'm guessing it wasn't just a slightly larger version of the shadelings."

"Only if Godzilla is a slightly larger version of the paddle-tail newt."

Ash finished her bread and licked a smear of butter off her thumb. "The shadelings and the *hhissih* both are among the most minor minions of the Darkness."

"Also with the capital letter," Kylie threw in.

"They exist on a plane so close to our own that they can pass between them quite easily. As you saw in the cavern, this allows them to seemingly swarm out of nowhere with very little warning, almost as if they have been lurking here in the shadows all along."

"Not their most pleasant trait," Drum said.

"But not the worst, either. Those things are just ugly, with a capital *ug*." Kylie shuddered.

Ash continued, her gaze assessing her lover's reactions in his expressions and body language. He had done well during the fight, but he seemed tense and restless now. "They belong to an entirely different class of creature, one with barely a spark of the power possessed by one such as the Shadow. That was a Demon, one who passed through the hellmouth in order to enter this plane."

Drum's eyes widened. "A Demon? But I thought all of the Demons you were supposed to fight had names and were all, you know, somewhere else. As in, not here. Not even within shouting distance of this island."

"Not a Demon. A demon." Dag's voice rumbled, and Ash thought she saw a glint of humor in his eye.

Kylie grinned. "Lowercase *d*."

"Feck it," he growled. "I need a bloody transcriptionist

to keep track of all this shite. Can't you people think up some original terminology?"

"It is, perhaps, a bit late to think of such a thing," Dag said.

"Only by a few thousand years," Kylie said.

"We call all such creatures who come into being on the plane beyond the hellmouth, demons," Ash explained. "That place is a storehouse of immense amounts of dark energy."

Drum made a sound of frustration and slumped back in his chair while his mother carried food from the kitchen to the dining table. Kylie quickly rose to lend a hand. When they set the last dish on the table, Maddie excused herself to bring a plate to her exhausted daughter upstairs.

"All right," he said as people began to serve themselves. "I think this is where someone finally explains to me the definition of a hellmouth."

Kylie plopped a scoop of fluffy colcannon onto her plate and shot him a sideways glance. "I always thought it was kinda there in the name. Hell. Mouth. Seems pretty self-explanatory. Didn't you guys get *Buffy the Vampire Slayer* over here?"

"Please, God and Saint Peter, don't tell me we're going to have to deal with the vampires."

Dag looked disdainful, which Ash had to assume did not relate to Maddie Drummond's delicious stew. "Do not be ridiculous. Such creatures do not exist."

"Well, that's something, I suppose."

"As we have already explained, hell as a place in which human souls remain trapped in eternal torment does not exist," Ash said. "However, there is a dimension located between this plane and the planes on which the Seven have remained imprisoned. It is the source of the hellfire you witnessed earlier as well as creatures such as the Shadow against which we fought. It is controlled by the

Darkness, and the Darkness uses it as a breeding ground for its more powerful servants. The proximity it bears to the mortal world has always troubled the Guild and the Guardians alike."

"It certainly doesn't sound like the sort of neighborhood you want brushing up against your own," Drum said.

Ash understood the human's sarcasm, even empathized with the underlying anxiety that fueled it. Her own worry only increased with having to lay out the facts for another.

"It is not," she agreed, struggling to keep her voice even. Her food lay cooling on her plate, but as talented a cook as Maddie might be, Ash lacked much appetite. "That is the reason why the Guild has always monitored the borders between us and done all they could to shore up the barriers that separate our realities."

Kylie looked up from her plate and frowned. "Whoa, wait a second. That makes the fact that the Guild has pretty much ceased to exist over the last couple of years an even bigger deal than the rest of us were figuring. And we figured it was a megillah of a deal."

"It is."

Dag cursed under his breath and clenched his fist around his cutlery. "I had not considered these ramifications, but then none of us had believed the Order had regained access to one of the hellmouths."

Ash watched Drum wince.

"*One* of the hellmouths?" he repeated. "How many of the buggering things are there?"

"They have never been fully mapped," Dag said. "What knowledge we had of them was entrusted to the Guild."

Kylie grimaced. "Which means it went up in flames when the headquarters in Paris exploded."

Ash shrugged. "I am not certain how much any records would have aided us in the end. The ancient locations of the hellmouths have all been deliberately obscured to prevent their use by the Order, but rediscovering them would not be the only options available to the *nocturnis*."

"This just keeps getting better and better. What is that supposed to mean?"

"It means that with enough power available to them, the *nocturnis* could open a new hellmouth in a location of their choosing."

Drum blew out a long, unsteady breath. "But they have no reason to do something like that if they already have this one all ready and waiting for them, right?"

Ash shifted uncomfortably. "It depends on the purpose for which they plan to use the gateway."

"That seems pretty obvious, doesn't it?" Kylie asked. "If the hellmouth leads to a plane full of evil, nasty, human-eating monsters, I'm guessing that a group of warmhearted puppy lovers like the *nocturnis* want to use it to let the monsters out to play. What other reason could they have?"

Ash winced. She had really hoped not to contemplate all the myriad possibilities. Especially not the most probable one.

She felt Dag's gaze on her and met his eyes. She and her brother shared a grim and unhappy moment. Finally, he turned his gaze back to the humans and grunted out an explanation. "Ash told you that this plane accessed by the hellmouth sits between the one we occupy now and those occupied by the Seven pieces of filth. If a hellmouth is a gateway between this dimension and the next, then a gate opened in that middle plane . . ."

Drum picked up where the Guardian trailed off. "It would open a gate into one of those prisons. Dear sweet Jesus."

Kylie set down her fork, beginning to look a little green around the edges. "And then something could pass straight from those outer planes onto this one. *Got in himmel.*"

"And this mouth/gate may just be yawning open, vomiting evil into my family's fecking backyard? What's to stop a thousand more monsters like the Shadow from coming through and killing everything within twenty miles? What's to stop one of these capital *D* Demons from coming through? A No Trespassing sign? We have to *do* something!"

Dag held up a hand. "Calm yourself, human. The gate remains closed."

"How can you know that?" Drum demanded. "That Shadow thing came through, didn't it?"

The Guardian scowled. "And we destroyed it—"

"That only the Shadow attacked us is actually reassuring," Ash interrupted, leaning forward to draw the eyes of the males from their brewing confrontation. Now was not the time for arguing among themselves. "If the hellmouth were already open, we would have faced an unending horde of Dark spawn. A single creature without reinforcements is a good sign."

"And how do you figure that?"

She sighed and fumbled for the words to explain the situation for a man so new to the realities of magic. She only hoped she could draw an adequate picture that would reassure Drum for the moment without downplaying the serious and precarious nature of the situation.

"Imagine an open field between two villages," she began. "The far village represents the outer planes, the prisons holding the Seven. The near village is the mortal plane, where we are now. The open field is the hellmouth."

Ash watched Drum carefully. She could see that he was listening, but that he struggled against fear and impatience. She could understand that, but she needed him to pay attention.

She continued. "When the hellmouth is closed, it is as if that open field between the villages is seeded with land mines. Their locations are not marked, and no one possesses a map to guarantee safe passage. If an inhabitant from one village seeks to cross over to the other village, he risks stepping on the land mine and exploding. It is possible that by sheer chance an individual could cross the field safely, but the odds stand against it and make it almost impossible for groups of any size. Does that make sense?"

Drum nodded, and Kylie echoed the motion. Even Dag appeared to be paying attention.

"This explains how the Shadow came to be in the cave," Ash said. "It crossed the field without stepping on a mine through plain dumb luck. Now, if the hellmouth is open, the situation changes drastically. Open the hellmouth and you remove the land mines. With the mines gone, anyone can cross the field in safety. In fact, higher armies could move from one village to the other with ease. It would not be a matter of a single Shadow entering that cave. An endless stream of Dark spawn would already be charging through. To tell the truth, if the hellmouth were open we would not be speaking now. This battle would already be lost."

She fell silent, along with the rest of the group. Everyone needed a moment to digest her analogy, or maybe just the bottom line. They could feel relief that the gate to the plane of Darkness remained closed, but they knew, all of them knew, that if the Order had its way, it would not remain closed for long.

"And on that happy note . . ." Kylie broke the silence and pushed away her half-eaten dinner. "Don't you think—"

Three sharp, imperious raps on the front door took them all by surprise. Ash frowned and looked at Drum. "Is your mother expecting company?"

He shook his head. "She didn't mention anything. Besides, none of the locals would bother with the front door. Everyone who knows Ma knows to go around to the kitchen."

"Door-to-door vacuum cleaner salesman?" Kylie asked, her humor sounding a little too close to fear for anyone to laugh.

"Not out here."

Ash did not even need to glance in Dag's direction. He had already risen from his chair and stepped around the table to her side. She didn't need to have heard Drum's assessment to know that whoever stood outside had not come for a friendly visit.

The Guardians placed themselves between the front of the house and the more vulnerable human occupants. Ash itched to shift into her natural form, but the confined space inside the house could not accommodate her wearing wings, let alone another like her if Dag should feel the same urge. It put them at a disadvantage, something she disliked on a deep, deep level. And that made her cranky.

Her mood failed to improve when the visitor decided to forgo knocking a second time. Instead, someone lobbed a dark burning fireball straight through Maddie Drummond's front window.

Forget cranky. Now Ash was pissed. In case anyone wondered, they could tell by the way she threw herself out of the shattered window and changed in midair.

By the time she soared up to the level of the roof, she had called her battle-axe to hand and was screaming her rage into the night sky. Also, Dag had joined her, wrenching open the front door and shifting almost before he finished crossing the threshold. He swung his war hammer in great circles around his head, generating a fierce momentum that he carried with him as he threw himself into an approaching band of shambling, human-shaped figures.

Ash paused only long enough to shout for the Wardens to guard Drum's family. Then she tucked her wings against her sides and swooped down on the hooded figure gathering his Dark magic for a second strike. As far as she was concerned, this attack on the sanctuary of the Drummonds' home amounted to a declaration of all-out war.

As she believed modern humans would say, they could bring it. Ash was more than happy to grant their wish. If the Order wanted war, war they would get. She would carry it to them on the blades of her axe.

And the Darkness take any who stood in her way.

Chapter Twenty

Drum listened to Ash explain what sounded to him like the end of the world and contemplated how irredeemably bolloxed his life had become in a handful of days. In less than a week, he had gone from life as a respectable Dublin publican to someone who had dinner table discussions about the gates between alternate dimensions and the Demonically inspired lunatics who wanted to tear them down. He had been attacked not once but several times by the forces of evil—*the literal Forces. Of. Evil*—and had begun practicing how to hurl streams of magic at the equivalent of demon ghosts. And worst of all, it was all beginning to seem just a little too close to normal.

Luckily, someone chose that moment to knock at the front door and nipped that thought in the bud.

Ash frowned and looked at Drum. "Is your mother expecting company?"

He shook his head, already wondering what could possibly happen next. "She didn't mention anything. Besides, none of the locals would bother with the front door. Everyone who knows Ma knows to go around to the kitchen."

"Door-to-door vacuum cleaner salesman?" Kylie asked, her words light but her tone worried.

"Not out here," Drum growled. The Guardians rose from their chairs and moved into new positions, forming a kind of two-person shield wall between the front of the house and the dining table behind them.

Something bad was about to happen, he thought. Imagine his satisfaction when the visitor chose that moment to lob a ball of fire into his mother's living room. There was always a certain amount of satisfaction to be had in being right, even when being right sucked.

Someone shouted. Actually, more than one someone, and Drum thought he might be one of them. The mayhem lasted for maybe two seconds before it descended into utter chaos.

The window glass barely finished cracking before Ash launched herself through the opening, enlarging it by a significant margin as she shifted on the fly. Dag followed swiftly after, though he elected to use the door and slammed it shut behind him. "Throw the locks," he bellowed.

Kylie grabbed the pitcher of water from the dining table and rushed forward to dash the contents over the fire smoldering in his mother's carpet. They should count themselves lucky that the fireball had hit nothing else on the way through and had landed in an empty space, otherwise the entire room could have gone up in flames.

Drum was stomping on a few scattered embers when Ash's warning shook the walls around them. "Maeve and Maddie!" the Guardian roared. "Keep them safe!"

His heart plummeted into his stomach and then kept going. Without even pausing for breath, Drum flew past the startled American and raced for the stairs to the second floor. Later, he would not be able to say whether he took the steps two at a time or leaped them all in a single bound. He only knew that terror and panic lent him speed he could never have imagined.

And for all that, he still arrived seconds too late.

He froze in the door to the room Maeve and Meara had shared all throughout their childhood. He took in the scene with a single glance and felt his breath strangle in his throat. His mother lay draped across the foot of a narrow bed, her fingers curled into a fist as if she could maintain a desperate hold on her youngest daughter's ankle. Maeve was halfway outside, something black and sinister clutching her beneath the arms as it hovered outside the open window.

Drum saw it all in less time than it took to blink and raised his hand on a rush of adrenaline and instinct. He didn't stop to think or to strategize, or even to wonder what he thought he was doing. He simply aimed his palm at the nightmare outside and let the magic rush through him.

Once again the energy emerged in a burst of pale golden light that had almost started to feel familiar. It was the same attack he had used on both sets of shadelings with satisfying success, but this time when he released the power, nothing happened. The thing outside leaned to the left so fast that the bolt of magic missed it completely and sailed harmlessly into the night.

Drum bared his teeth in a furious snarl and threw another blast. This one grazed the shape, he would have sworn it, but the creature did not so much as blink. It just yanked his screaming sister out through her bedroom window and flew away on a shriek of triumph.

Maddie screamed as well and slammed her fist onto the mattress. "Michael, something took my baby girl!" She choked on a sob and buried her face in the disheveled blankets.

He took the words in his gut and doubled over in pain. He had caused this. At the very least, he had let it happen. He had allowed himself, had allowed his family, to become caught up in matters no human had a right to meddle with. It didn't matter what gifts a person might possess. He had just seen the evidence of that in living color with fine detail. Human beings shouldn't be messing around with magic, and because he had ignored his conscience in this matter, his family was paying the price.

Feeling numb and helpless, Drum stumbled across the space between them and put a comforting arm around his mother's shoulders. She leaned against him, her sobs quieting though her tears continued to fall. Then he just sat there and stared at nothing.

Footsteps pounded up the stairs a moment before Kylie appeared in the doorway, her expression strained. "Michael, we need to get out of here, and we have to do it without using the stairs. The *nocturni* out there has gone flame happy, and he set the house on fire. I'm sorry. I just couldn't keep up," she said. She paused, frowning, and glanced around the room. "Where's Maeve? We kinda need to get moving."

"Gone," he said, trying to shake himself out of the strange lethargy that despair had woven around him. Honestly, he couldn't think of a reason to put up much of a fight. "They took her. It's over."

"Over?" Her voice rang with incredulity, but it sounded almost muffled somehow. "You *putz,* what the hell are you talking about? Nothing's over. This *farkakte* conversation isn't even over, so get your stupid Irish ass in gear, and let's go!"

Drum just shook his head and looked down, his shoulders slumping. His mother continued to cry softly beside him.

"Maddie? Mrs. Drummond?" Kylie softened her tone, sounding confused. "Come on. Help me talk some sense into your kid, here. You can see the smoke already filling up the air in here. We need to get outside someplace safe.

I promise, we'll go after Maeve just as soon as we get everything here secured. Please."

Maddie trembled and wept. "Michael is right. It's too late. They have my baby, and there's nothing we can do."

"Nothing we can do? What kind of *meshugas* is that? Is the smoke messing with your heads? You two sound ins—" Kylie broke off and jerked back as if someone had slapped her. Her eyes narrowed as she looked between Drum and his mother. "Oh, I get it. This isn't coming from the two of you, and it's not the smoke, but something is definitely messing with your heads. Wynn told me the Order likes this trick. Now, what did she say I should do if they tried it around me?"

Her voice trailed off and she appeared to be deep in thought for several seconds. Drum felt a sluggish trickle of relief now that her American accent had stopped hammering at his aching head. He wished that she would just go away, but he couldn't muster up the energy to tell her to leave. It didn't really matter. Nothing mattered much anymore . . .

Two sharp slaps cut through the air and sent sparks of pale green magic darting through the smoke. One struck his mother, and the second landed on his cheek, the quick bite dispelling his cocoon of apathy like a switch turning off.

"Snap out of it!" Kylie yelled in an accent slightly different than the one with which she normally spoke. Then she stepped back and giggled. "Sorry, but I have always wanted to do that."

Drum rubbed his cheek and looked around. His first deep breath made him cough. "No worries. But what happened? I honestly felt as if I just wanted to lie down and die."

"Black magic. A spell that meddles with your mind. Nasty stuff."

"Good Lord," Maddie murmured, drying her eyes and getting unsteadily to her feet. She, too, coughed as she began to notice the smoke drifting up from the ground floor. "That was terrifying. I could see and hear everything going on around me, but it was like I had no control over my own emotions. I've never felt depression like that in all my days. And I hope I never do again." She closed her eyes on a shudder, and when they opened they held a world of resolve. "Now, tell me how we're going to get my daughter back."

Kylie gave her a smile and a brisk nod. "That's the reaction I was hoping for. But we'll have to figure it out after we get outside. In case you hadn't noticed, it's getting a little warm in here."

"Of course. Stephen always made certain to keep a rope ladder in each of the children's closets. For emergencies." She moved toward the door in the left-hand wall.

"This way will be faster."

Drum spun toward the sound of Ash's voice. She leaned in through the window, her expression anxious and her braid disheveled. He thought he saw a glimmer of relief when her dark gaze landed on him, but the thickening smoke was making it increasingly difficult to see.

"They have Maeve," he said. "They took her."

"We know," Ash said, her mouth thinning into a straight line even as her voice went grim. "We will get her back."

He heard Dag's voice boom from outside. "Out now. Flames are spreading. Human authorities will be on the way."

Drum nodded and snapped into action. "Ma and Kylie first. One of you can come back for me."

Ash had already taken Maddie's hands to help her through the window when they heard Dag snickering. She looked at him, and he thought he saw the corner of her mouth twitch. "We will only need one trip."

The male Guardian took hold of Maddie with one beefy arm and encouraged her to crawl her hands around his neck. "Your mother is small, and my mate is tiny. I think she weighs less than my war hammer," Dag said. The rumble in his voice sounded a lot like suppressed laughter. "I could carry two of each female and not notice the burden."

Ash met his gaze. "You will travel with me."

Drum hesitated. What was it he had thought only a few nights earlier? *Wherever this woman went, he would follow.* With the last of the black magic gone from his mind, he realized the words still held true.

He waited while Kylie settled into her mate's embrace, then stepped forward and reached out a hand to his own. He watched the fire flickering behind her dark eyes, the comforting flames so different from those eating away at his childhood home. The light that burned within Ash was one he could trust, not only with his life, but with his family and with his future.

"Whenever you're ready, *mo chaomhnóir*," he murmured. "Let's fly."

And she lifted him out into the night.

Chapter Twenty-one

They flew west and north into County Offaly to a farm a few miles outside of Clonygowan. It was late, but lights still burned in the kitchen when the Guardians touched down behind a hedge and the small group trudged toward the house on foot. Drum spotted movement in the window a moment before his sister Sorcha threw open the door to stare at them in shock.

"Ma, Drum! What on earth are you doing here and at this time of night? Why didn't you phone? Is something wrong?"

Maddie immediately folded her daughter into an embrace and murmured reassurances. He couldn't be certain what his mother was saying, but he hoped Sorcha was braced for a shock.

He hated coming here, hated the idea of dragging another member of his family into this mess of evil and madness. He simply hadn't been able to think of anywhere else to go. This was closer to his mother's home than Dublin, but he hadn't liked the idea of leaving her alone in his flat anyway. He had already been attacked there, so the Order knew that if they wanted to find him, they could look for him there. To have them come after him and hurt his mother instead would have been more than he could bear. He needed her to be safe, and here John and Sorcha would be able to keep an eye on her. Also, he had no reason to think the *nocturnis* were even aware of this place. For the moment it was as secure a hiding spot as they were likely to find. Too bad Drum himself couldn't stay.

He brushed off his sister's questions, deferring them to their mother. Right now he, his fellow Warden, and their Guardians needed to decide exactly how and when they were going to rescue his sister from the clutches of those Demon-worshipping cultists. Hopefully, getting Maddie settled into a spare bed and getting a few basic answers would be better for Sorcha than diving right into the deep end of the insanity.

She could trust him on this; the water was not even close to fine.

The others dropped into seats around Sorcha's roughly hewn kitchen table. They all looked a little tired, a little shocked, and a little worse for wear under random streaks of soot. For a moment no one spoke, so Drum took charge in the tradition of many a valiant Irishman before him— he filled the electric kettle, brewed tea, and finished each cup with a liberal splash from his brother-in-law's bottle of whiskey. John had always invited him to feel at home.

He finally slid into a chair and took a bracing swallow from his mug. Then he leaned his elbows on the table and wrapped his hands across his face, as if he could wash away the events he had just seen.

"I watched them take her," he said, his voice matching the quiet of the house. Thankfully the children had gone to bed well before he had brought this ragged group to their doorstep. "Tried to stop them, even used magic, but the thing just dragged her away, kicking and screaming."

"You could not have stopped them," Dag said. He spoke bluntly, but his voice held a note of kindness. "It was ghouls. A band of them. Without training, you had little chance. Even experienced Wardens prefer to avoid ghouls."

"Oy, Drum, you can't feel bad." Kylie winced. "It's no wonder your magic didn't stop that. You've only had to use one attack so far, and that type of magic isn't much good against ghouls. Not from what I hear. And I doubt I could have done any better. Wynn and her uncle say ghouls are real pains in the ass."

Drum just swallowed more whiskey-laced tea and shook his head. "What the feck is a ghoul?"

Dag growled. "Cannon fodder."

Ash did not disagree. "A ghoul is a human who has been corrupted by the Darkness and is under the control of a *nocturni* sorcerer. Their minds have been taken over. Completely. They have no personality, no memories, and no will of their own. They can only obey simple, direct orders from their masters, most of which involve standing between the *nocturnis* and anyone they believe could do them harm. They lack even the awareness to recognize when they have been injured, but will continue to fight with terrible wounds, massive bleeding, even missing limbs."

Drum pictured that and felt a wave of sickness. "Jaysus. Sounds like zombies."

His Guardian nodded. "There are similarities."

"Are they still people, though?" Kylie asked. "I mean, with zombies the convention says that they're not human anymore. They don't have personalities or emotions, and they won't stop trying to kill you until you kill them. I like to think I'll be okay when the zombie apocalypse hits, because I could knock off one of those stinky *behaimeh*, no problem, but I don't know if I could kill a person who was only coming after me because the Order had messed with his mind. I'd rather just end the influence spell, like I had to do with Drum and his mom."

The Guardians looked confused until their Wardens explained the spell of despair that had taken over Drum and Maddie until Kylie had sensed the magic and ended it.

Ash muttered something under her breath before she gritted her teeth and tried to explain. "A ghoul is entirely different from that sort of influence spell. With these creatures, the *nocturni* does not seek to simply steer behavior along a desired path. He seizes complete control. No, worse than that. He destroys the ghoul's mind. A human under influence will be freed if the sorcerer dies, because the spell no longer possesses a source of energy to power it. But a ghoul remains a ghoul. Its brain functions only to keep it alive and moving, but the taint of the Darkness that corrupted it takes over the direction of its actions. It continues to attack and kill humans without discrimination. Like those true zombies."

"Ech." Kylie frowned into her tea. "I was really hoping you weren't going to say that."

"That's terrible enough, but it doesn't sound like what I saw outside of Maeve's window." He thought back. "The thing that took her didn't really look human. I mean, it had a face and two arms and maybe legs, but it was black as a shadeling, and it had to be flying to have hovered outside the window like that."

Dag grunted. "Means it is an old one."

Ash nodded. "The longer the ghoul is under the influence of the Darkness, the blacker it becomes. Usually they are destroyed before they reach much more than a medium gray. They also lose their hair, but their nails grow into claws. And because they have no fear, they can climb up a straight sheer surface without hesitation. I imagine that is what they did in order to take your sister."

She dropped her gaze and flattened her hands. Drum thought he could actually see a slight tremble.

"I am sorry," she said after a moment, her voice very

quiet. "I should have considered that the frontal assault might be a ploy to distract us. Once we had guessed at the existence of the hellmouth, I should have conjectured that the Order might attempt to take your sister. I cannot ask you to forgive me, but I swear to you I will do all in my power to bring her back."

Drum could hear her sincerity and see the pain in her expression, but her words concerned him most. "Why should you have expected this? What could the Order possibly want with Maeve?"

Ash's chair made a terrible grating sound as she jumped to her feet and sent it scraping backward across the slate-tiled floor. She spun around without a word and stalked away to stand beside the window at the far end of the room. Drum watched her go, worry and confusion creasing his brow.

"Kylie?" he prompted. "Dag?"

Kylie looked almost as confused as he did, but her mate watched Ash with concern in his eyes. He sighed and turned to Drum.

"Ash told you what happens if the hellmouth is opened," Dag said, "but we both hoped you would never have to learn how one is opened. I had thought we discovered it in time to intercept the *nocturnis* before they could act."

Drum listened and found himself feeling increasingly ill. His heart began to beat too fast and off rhythm. He heard a ringing in his ears, and he felt dizzy and off balance. His stomach lurched and knotted, and he thought he could feel himself break out into a cold sweat. When he spoke, his lips felt thick and numb. "Human sacrifice."

"*Khas vesholem!*" Kylie whispered on a breath of horror.

"It is how they have managed to release those of the Seven they have already freed," Dag said. "It is the act from which the Darkness gains its greatest power. Likely it is the only way for them to get around the measures by which the Guild has kept the hellmouths closed and hidden for the past centuries. Your sister has the qualities of a very potent sacrifice."

Drum abandoned his tea and went straight for the bottle of whiskey. Then, he listened to Dag's assessment and found himself plagued by a terrible desire to laugh.

"A curse on your house for making me think about this, let alone say it out loud," he spluttered, "but I doubt my baby sister, at twenty-four, still qualifies as a virgin, Dag."

Kylie winced. "Um, not the qualities he was referring to, Drum. He meant that Maeve is a woman of power."

The whiskey bottle dangled from his nerveless fingers. "You mean this is about the fact that she has the Sight? Are you fecking having me on?"

Dag scowled. "I would never make light of so serious a situation as your sister has found herself in. Power is the only currency of any value to the members of the Order. Everything they do is an attempt to gain power for themselves or their Masters."

"It's true," Kylie said softly, her gaze darting across the room to where Ash still stood, facing into the darkness beyond the window, silent and trembling. "The potency of a sacrifice comes from the amount of potential in the blood. Virgins, young ones, have a tremendous amount of potential because their fertility is untapped, allowing them the potential to create life. Children are nothing but potential, because their futures are still waiting to be written. And people with gifts such as precognition, like your sister, or clairvoyance, like you, or digimancy, like me, we have more potential than other humans, because we can do things that other humans can't. We have the ability and the potential to work magic."

"Then what the fuck are we sitting around for?" he roared, slamming the bottle of whiskey down onto the table so hard, he felt an offhand hint of surprise that it didn't shatter under his hand. "Why aren't we out there rescuing my sister before they put a knife through her throat!"

"Because they won't do it tonight."

Ash finally turned back to face the others. Her skin looked as pale and gray as if she wore her natural skin, and the black of her pupils and irises had almost disappeared behind the leaping flames that blazed in her eyes. When she spoke, her fangs flashed between her lips, and if he looked at her hands, he could see the claws that had taken the place of her human fingernails. She looked half turned and fully ready for battle.

"To make the sacrifice tonight would be a waste," she continued, her voice hard and cold. It reminded him of the way she had sounded the first time they had met, when he had still thought of her more as a statue than as a woman. "The moon is waning. In three more days, it will go fully dark. The new moon. Performing the ritual then, as the point in the cycle when the Light is at its weakest, will generate the greatest surge of Dark energy. And at this time of year, when the barrier between the worlds is at its weakest, the dark of the moon offers an even better chance at opening the hellmouth with a single sacrifice."

"Wait, what does the time of year have to do with it?" Kylie spoke up, though she still sounded subdued. "Wynn has told me about this, but she said it was part of Celtic legend and history, so maybe you've heard it before. According to pre-Christian calendars, the holiday we now call Halloween actually marked a time when people thought that what they called the veil between our world and the world of spirits and monsters and faeries— basically all the things that go bump in the night—was weakest. That's why they thought that ghosts and all those other scary things stalked around on earth on that particular night. They believed that because of the thin veil, it was easy for them to get to us."

Ash nodded stiffly. "Correct. Timing the sacrifice of a woman of power to the night of the new moon, as close as possible to the time when the veil between the worlds is thinnest, will not only guarantee the opening of the hell-mouth, but it could generate enough energy to land a large blow on the gate to one of the Seven prisons, as well. Were I an agent of the Darkness, it is the plan I would follow."

Drum took in her predatory features (the fangs and claws), her stony expression, and the roaring inferno of her eyes and had a moment to give thanks that this Guardian was not, in fact, an agent of the Darkness. He knew without question that Ash existed solely in service to the Light. Not because her race had first been brought forth for that purpose, but because the need to protect and defend the world against those who would destroy it filled up her bones like marrow. She could no more leave a vulnerable human to the mercy of the Order of Eternal Darkness than she could join forces with them herself. Her breath and sinew forbade it.

She would get Maeve back for him, or destroy the world trying.

The certainty of it flowed into Drum as if it were a drug injected directly into his veins. He felt his rage cooling and the haze of violent hatred clearing from his vision. Oh, he still hated that his sister had been taken by the Order, still hated what they had planned for her, but he no longer hated every other living thing on the planet for not delivering her back to him like a sacred offering before an angry god. His reason had returned and, with it, his faith.

Or maybe his faith had never deserted him. He'd been shocked when Ash had fled from the table. It had confused him. His instincts had told him that someone was about to tell him something he very much did not want to hear, and he had not understood why she would not sit beside him while he listened. He had assumed he would have her strength to lean on while he faced whatever terrible truth was coming for him. When she had left to let Dag break the news, he had felt deserted, as if she had abandoned him without a care.

Now, he thought he understood. She had left because she cared too much. He might have met Ash less than a week before, but didn't some old adage say that facing combat together forged bonds that could never be broken? Drum felt that.

He trusted Ash implicitly, and he felt like he knew her better than members of his own family. He knew she was stronger than anyone he had ever met, and the strength he referred to went far beyond the physical. He knew she was loyal and dedicated to her cause, that she viewed her duty not as a job but as a sacred trust between herself and the powers of the Light. He knew she was brave and focused and sexier than the raunchiest corners of his imagination.

And he knew he loved her.

He also believed—no, dammit, he *knew* that she loved him right back, and because she did, she would do whatever it took to get his sister back safe and sound.

Drum drew in a deep breath, held it for a moment, then slowly released it as he went back to his chair, took his seat, and returned his gaze to Ash's face. This time he looked at her with sanity, resolve, and trust.

"Okay, then," he said, his voice even once more. "That's their plan. What's ours?"

Chapter Twenty-two

As it turned out, their plan consisted of something more like a preplan plan, as opposed to an actual plan plan. The first thing to do, Ash, Dag, and Kylie all agreed, was to muster the troops. The first glitch came about due to the highly inconvenient existence of time zones. What might be just before midnight in Ireland was just before six in the evening in Chicago, and while this made a perfect window for telecommunications, it made travel considerations a good deal stickier.

Telling someone in Chicago to drop everything and catch the next available plane to Dublin would result in a minimum nine to ten hours of travel time. In a situation like this the loss of those hours could prove not just annoying but deadly. This was one of the items Kylie had noted on her plan planning meeting agenda. Ash had widened her eyes as she had seen the document take shape.

The Guardians and Wardens had officially commandeered the kitchen of Drum's sister's home for their temporary headquarters. Drum insisted that after tonight they would need to find an alternate location, one that did not expose his family to any further danger; but for now Sorcha and John had graciously provided them with shelter, refreshments, and a laptop computer at which Kylie obviously struggled not to sneer in disdain.

"If I'm going to be expected to do anything useful around here," the American Warden said, "we're going to have to find a way for me to grab my own gear from our hotel. Seriously, did you guys hear this thing boot up? I think the hamster in there actually cursed us out before he jumped on his little wheel."

Dag placed his hand on his mate's shoulder and patted gently. "Now, now, little human, remember. Through adversity, we grow in strength."

Kylie sneered and set to work, lifting one hand from the computer's keyboard long enough to give her Guardian the finger. Then she completed her objective of initiating an international video chat with a woman Ash had heard referred to only as Wynn. She knew little else about the second American Warden, and two thirds of it could be summed up by those very words. Other than that, she knew the woman was also a witch, but that encompassed the sum total of her knowledge. Somehow none of this prepared her for the first words that sounded from the computer speaker.

"Goddess alive, Kylie," a voice nearly shouted. "I've been trying to get a hold of you forever. Where on earth have you been?"

Kylie looked almost as surprised as everyone else. "Um, Ireland?"

"Ky—"

"Wynneleh, I told you I had to catch a plane to Dublin immediately. Didn't you read my e-mail?"

"Yeah, but you obviously didn't read mine. You also haven't answered it, or your phone, or any chat requests in, like, two days."

The light from the computer screen flickered across Kylie's face, illuminating her nonplussed expression. It was the first time Ash could recall seeing the Warden at a loss for words, as temporary as it turned out to be. "Oh, um, yeah. I guess I have been AFK for a while, haven't I?"

AFK? Ash puzzled over the unfamiliar term.

"Away from keyboard?" Wynn sounded exasperated. "Kylie, this isn't *World of Warcraft*. This is an actual war." Her voice dropped. "We were starting to get afraid that the Order had taken you out. Fil was getting ready to launch a full-scale assault on the state of Massachusetts."

Kylie looked chagrined. "I'm sorry, Wynn. I didn't mean to scare you guys, but things over here have been a little crazy."

The computer made a snorting sound. Or rather, Wynn made it but it issued from the laptop's speaker. From Ash's viewpoint looking at the backside of the screen, the difference seemed moot.

"Yeah, we haven't actually earned the old 'of sound mind' rating over here, either. That's why I've been trying to get a hold of you. I think you need to finish up whatever it is you're doing in Ireland and take a hop, a skip, a jump, or a ferry over to England. Or maybe a plane. You know, your choice."

Kylie stiffened. "Why? What's going on in England?"

Ash experienced a conflict of urges. On the one hand, she wanted to bark at Kylie to maintain her focus on assembling the team they would need to rescue Drum's sister. On the other hand, her instincts as a Guardian urged her to listen closely. After all, Wynn was a Warden as well, and if more trouble was brewing somewhere else, then the Guardians needed to know about it. If it was close to her, then Ash needed to know in particular.

"Ella turned up a strong lead on another stone stud muffin," Wynn said with excitement coloring her voice. "Fil was going to offer to check it out, but the idea made Spar a little cranky. Sheesh, these guys can get so possessive sometimes."

Kylie's gaze lifted and settled on Ash, who sat opposite her across the table. The human's cheeks turned pink when Ash lifted an eyebrow at her. "Um, yeah, about that stud muffin comment—"

Wynn continued as if she hadn't heard. "But that's not all. Someone tawt they taw a Hierophant sneaking around London. We figured since you're most of the way there, you could give Road Runner a break and go after a puddy-tat instead."

That news certainly drew a reaction. Kylie muttered under her breath in Yiddish, Dag swore, and even Ash felt her mouth firm into a straight line of displeasure. Only Drum still looked confused.

When Kylie noticed, she immediately took pity on him. "The Hierophant. I told you about him, remember? He's the one who set up that whole disaster in Boston, the one who's been hosting Nazgahchuhl in the big ol' guest room that is his noggin. Right where his soul used to hang out. If he's in London, then that means something very bad is likely to happen over there. Soon."

Drum clenched his fists and his jaw. "Something bad is definitely happening here. In fact, part of it already did. Remember?"

Instead of looking embarrassed or angry, Kylie looked sympathetic. She nodded at the man and focused back on the computer. "Dag and I will take a look as soon as we finish up here. Trust me, right now you want us exactly where we are. In fact, you want you here, too. And Knox and the others, as well."

Wynn's voice came out noticeably sharper. "Why? What have you found in Dublin?"

"Not in it, but not far away. First off, we found another recruit. Well, a pair of them, really."

"Ooh! Guardian jackpot! Wait until I tell Fil, especially if I get to see him first," the witch crowed. "Tell me, how hot is he? Like Dag hot, or like my Knox-your-sox-off hot?"

Kylie smirked. "Here. See for yourself." Then she turned the computer around until the camera lens landed on Ash.

The Guardian got her first look at the witch. As it turned out, she had neither green skin nor a pointy, wart-bedecked nose. In fact her nose appeared perfectly normal for a human female and graced a perfectly normal, pretty face. Wynn had long, dark, curly hair, fair skin, and attractive hazel eyes that currently held a great deal of confusion.

"Um, I hate to break this to you, Koyote," the image on the screen said, "but either your aim sucks or your camera does. I'm looking at a chick. Let me see the Guardian."

"I did."

So did Ash. It smarted a little, since her wings got crushed against the back of her chair for a second before they burst free, and the chair itself let out an unnerving groan of stressed wood at her increased mass, but the look on Wynn's face was worth it. Ash grinned, flashing fang, and Kylie immediately snatched the laptop back. "Wait! I gotta see her face!"

"Kylie . . ." Wynn drew out the name for a good three, tense seconds.

"Yes, Wynnie the Pooh?"

"Uh, I'm not sure if you noticed something odd about your new friend, but that Guardian has boobs."

"*Bubbeleh,* you know I don't swing that way."

"Kylie!" the witch snapped. "That is a *female* Guardian."

"I'm sure she'd be thrilled you noticed, but she's kinda already in a relationship. Hey, aren't you in one, too? Does Knox have those clichéd threesome fantasies? Is that what this is about?"

"Kylie! There are no female Guardians!"

"Guess again, snookie."

"How is this even possible?" Wynn mumbled. "This is not supposed to be possible."

"Possible, shmossible. It's done," Kylie dismissed. "Dag isn't sure how. Heck, even Ash isn't sure how, from what I can tell, but I suppose you can ask your guy if it means that much to you. Hey, where is he anyway?"

"He'll be here in a minute. He ran out to pick up Chinese."

"Mmm, I have had some yummy food while I've been here, but I could totally go for pot stickers right about now."

"Wiley, would you focus, please, and tell me what the heck is going on?"

"You mean other than that we've got a new girl on the boys' varsity team?"

Wynn sighed. "Yes. Aside from that."

Kylie nodded, her expression turning serious. "I'd rather tell you guys—all of you guys—in person."

"Wow, that does not sound good, so I'm guessing this won't, either. We can't come."

That seemed to rock Kylie back in her seat. "What? What do you mean, you can't come? None of you?"

"Ella is grounded. No travel for at least two weeks. She went down to Seattle to disband a recruiting center near the university. She got shot. Missed her organs, but broke three ribs," Wynn said, her voice grim and her words clipped. "And while she's out of commission, she had to send Fil to chase down the other lead she dug up, only this one is not quite so pretty as a possible Guardian. Fil is currently in Alberta—so, basically, the middle of nowhere—trying to decide exactly how many *nocturnis* are in the area and planning to turn one of the most sacred First Nations sites in Canada into a gigantic, Demon-empowering slaughterhouse."

"*Oy, gevalt,*" Kylie breathed.

"You said it, *bisseleh*. Which leaves me the only one available to respond if another threat pops up on this side of the pond, as they say."

"When did things get this bad? I mean, I know we've all dealt with some pretty epic battles, but when did the accumulated small skirmishes get this out of hand?"

"When the Order stopped trying to guess how they were going to release the Seven and started actually doing it," Wynn said. "I'm guessing having one of them back in control and munching on the brains and soul of their head honcho might also be playing a factor. Things were bad enough when the Hierophant was in charge of the chessboard, but now that Nazgahchuhl is using him as its own personal sock puppet, it's all just getting worse."

"Yeah, and your optimism is contagious." Kylie sighed and leaned into the camera. "Wynn, we really need some help here. We think the Order has located a hellmouth, and they're planning to open it the night of the new moon."

A string of creative expletives poured from the laptop's speakers, some of them in a language Ash recognized but had never heard. The witch cursed in Welsh. "That's going to require an awful lot of juice, even at this time of year."

"They're going to have it." Kylie looked up and waved at Drum to join her in front of the camera. "This is Ash's Warden, Michael Drummond. He's clairvoyant. His mother and two of his sisters are gifted healers. Another sister is empathic. The youngest, Maeve, is a precog. She's the one they've taken."

Ash could see that Drum recognized Kylie's ploy, and that he wasn't too proud to take his part in it. Bright Light, but she knew he thought that if it would save his sister, the man would offer himself in her place. If he weren't older and his talent less filled with potential, she figured he would already have snuck out of the house to try that idiotic move.

She also knew, based on what Kylie had told them that first night, that Wynn would know what Drum was feeling. *Exactly* what he was feeling. After all, she had already lost a sibling to the Darkness. Her brother Bran had been possessed by the Demon Uhlthor. Wynn had discovered the fact too late, and in exorcising the entity from her brother's body, she had essentially killed him. It might sound like a completely different situation, but Ash could see that each of the Wardens felt the full weight of responsibility for their family member's fate.

Silence stretched across the Atlantic for a long, long moment before Wynn managed to speak again. "That's a low, low blow, Kylie."

"I'm sorry," Kylie said, her voice sympathetic, but firm. "I know it still hurts, Wynn. Trust me, I know. Bran was my brother, too, in every way that I can count, but we need to back up. You're the one who told me about hellmouths. We all know that getting Maeve back would be just as important if she didn't have a relative alive on earth. We can't let them take that kind of step."

"And what if this is another one of their distractions?" Wynn asked. "What if I race over there to help you out, and it turns out they rip open another hellmouth in Idaho, or something?"

Kylie nodded. "Yeah, it's a possibility, but it's like five hundred miles between Idaho and anything that doesn't taste better with sour cream and chives. Dublin is fifty miles from here and has a population of almost two million. That's a hell of a lot of mouths to feed. On."

"I don't know . . ."

"Wynn." Kylie waited a beat, probably to ensure she caught her friend's gaze. "If we're not going to have each other's backs, the Order won't even have to try to finish us off."

Ash heard a disembodied sigh. "You're right, but I need to talk to Ella and Fil first. Fil is scheduled to check in with me before ten, my time. They need to know I'm going to be gone, and I need to make sure it's for as short a time as possible."

Kylie broke out into a beaming smile. "I can charter a plane for you. It's not the Concord, but that ship has sailed. Or, that bird don't fly no more. Whatever. It will be quicker than commercial air. By the time Fil calls you, I can have everything arranged for you and Knox to fly over here."

"Whoa, hold on, Daddy Warbucks. I said I can't be gone long. That means hours, not days. You might have more money than most small Central American countries, but I can still arrange my own transportation faster than you can. I'll come by portal a couple of hours before we hit."

Kylie made a face. "First off, don't say things like 'before we hit.' You sound like you're trying to go all Capone, and you're eighty years too late for that. Second, cast yourself as an orphan again, and I'm telling your mom. But finally, and in my opinion most important, you and Ella said that portal casting takes skill on both ends, and you know my spell work still sucks compared to the rest of you. Do you honestly want my end to collapse while you're somewhere out over the North Atlantic?"

"Why should you worry? I'm the one who'd be swimming with the fishes."

"And I'm the one who's half Jewish! Like I don't have enough guilt to deal with?"

"Hey, you sounded just like Esther when you said that!"

"Wynn."

"Don't worry, Kyle E. Woyote," the witch said. "You've

got plenty of skill, and what you lack, you make up for in raw power. I'm not real worried. Besides, I'll walk you through it right until I step inside. You'll be fine."

Kylie grimaced. "I'm not the one I'm worried about."

"Chill, before I drop an anvil on your head," Wynn chided. "Now, go back to the beginning of this story and tell me exactly what kind of situation we're in. You said the Order found a hellmouth, and they want it open. Where is it, and how many *nocturnis* are we talking about?"

Ash listened with half an ear while Kylie began to outline the events of the past week. The Warden did a bit of skimming over what she only knew secondhand from Ash and Drum, but added more detail on the events she and Dag had witnessed for themselves. While she spoke, Drum stepped away from the computer to allow Dag to contribute to the conversation. When he headed straight to her side, Ash felt a stirring of satisfaction.

Well, that was what she decided to call it. It was a lot more complicated than that one word conveyed, but only if she attempted to examine it up close. Poking and pulling might have unraveled some threads that looked a lot like love, attraction, caring, admiration, pride, respect, or affection, and seeing those all picked apart and labeled would have backed Ash into a corner she couldn't fight her way out of. A Guardian wasn't supposed to feel those human emotions, and for a Guardian not included in the legacy set forth by the first collection of (all male) Guardians, it wouldn't do for her to risk it.

There was no woman of power for Ash, no end to her duties. Unlike her brothers with their talented mates, Ash would return to her statue form and sleep until the next time the Seven threatened the mortal world, and she would do it alone. Completely alone, because even if she ever got another chance to work with her brothers, it would be a new set of them, replacements called to take up the spots relinquished by their mated predecessors. Even the relationship among friends she might form here would be lost to her while she slept.

Didn't she just have a lot to look forward to?

She could have let the thought depress her. It would be easy. The easiest thing in the world, actually. She knew where she stood, to the precise millimeter between her and the cliff's edge. The easy, the safe, the sensible thing to do would be to drag her talons through the sand and say she would not step beyond this point. In fact, even better would be to step back a few yards before she drew that line. She might still have the chance to withdraw, to gather the stone from which she was made and stack it around her heart, cutting herself off from Kylie and Dag, from Wynn and Knox, from Maeve and Maddie and Drum. She might still be able to ensure that she ended the same way the first Wardens had intended her to begin—alone.

But what if it was already too late?

The precipice under her feet was so close, she thought she could feel the way her talons curled over the edge. It wouldn't take more than a startle reflex, someone shouting "Boo!" for her to shift her balance and go tumbling over. And then what?

And then, something inside her whispered, something that sounded suspiciously like her heart. *And then you fly. Isn't that why the Light gave you wings?*

Ash trembled, her breath catching in her throat, her mind all of a sudden blank, like the first page of an empty book. Every thought fled, but maybe that was what it took for her to finally feel.

In that moment she realized that thoughts provided the static that obscured the pictures her emotions had tried to paint all along. Thoughts didn't help to bring things clear, they just hung like fog over the truth. She wasn't standing on the edge of a cliff; she hadn't been for a while now. For days. She had already made her jump and had been riding the currents all this time.

She loved him.

Ash loved Michael Drummond. It was why she had returned his kisses, why she had shared her body with him and let him teach her the pleasures of mortal flesh. It was why she had felt crippled by the guilt of allowing his sister to be taken, and why she was willing to sink this island into the sea if it meant getting her back to him safely. It was why when he looked at her, when he took the seat beside her, when he curled his fingers around hers and tugged her hand to rest atop his thigh, it was why her heart expanded and her world narrowed and everything in between settled neatly into place.

It was love.

Ash had realized it too late to back away, and now that she knew, she would be damned if she'd take such a coward's way out. Their time together would be limited by her mission, but by the Light she would wring from it every last measure of joy and wrap it around her to protect her against the chill of her stone prison. Just see if she wouldn't, and the Guild and their traditions be damned.

When the time came, she certainly would be.

Chapter Twenty-three

By the time Kylie ended the video chat with Wynn Powe and her Guardian, Knox, it was nearing three o'clock in the morning. Drum might be the only one who found that significant, but he felt quite certain the others would understand in just a few hours. Seven-thirty might not sound outrageously early for sunrise, but when accompanied by the crowing of the cock on a working farm the volume would increase substantially. Especially on only four and a half hours of sleep.

At least he could see that they had spent the time constructively. The working outlines of a plan had been sketched out in electronic form with Kylie at the keyboard. The pencil and paper Drum had offered to fetch her had only offended her digital sensibilities. Besides, she reminded him, once she got it all down in a computer file, she could whip off extra copies for the troops.

The troops. Drum scoffed. The way he understood it, their attacking army consisted of him, Ash, Kylie, Dag, and a single additional Guardian/Warden pair against an unknown number of *nocturni* sorcerers, shadelings, Shadows, *hhissih,* ghouls, and worse, as well as any other

Demon-worshipping cultists. Oh, and if they really hit the jackpot, potentially some Demons themselves.

Good times.

Long, cool fingers squeezed his hand, and Drum glanced over to see Ash still seated beside him. Dag and Kylie had just stumbled into the living room to collapse on the makeshift pallets of quilts and blankets that Sorcha had laid out for them. The house was quiet, even quieter than it had been, and only a single light remained burning above the kitchen sink.

He could feel exhaustion lurking in the background, knew he ought to be ready for nothing more than a flat surface and a down pillow, but somehow the idea of sleep felt alien. Anxiety and impatience itched beneath his skin, and now that he didn't have the distraction of several voices bouncing ideas and friendly insults off each other, his mind wouldn't stop spinning. What if they were wrong about what they would find in the cave? What if they mistook the timing? What if something went wrong?

Beside him, Ash rose to her feet and tugged him gently after her. "Come. You look as if you could use a breath of fresh air before you will sleep. Walk with me."

They slipped out of the back door together.

The night carried a distinct chill and the scents of early autumn. Green grass, ripe crops, and decaying leaves perfumed the air with an odor that smelled somehow rich with life, even as the year began to die around them. Barely a sliver of moon appeared in the sky, and Drum felt the dread of the approaching new moon like a weight on his shoulders.

"I think I could count a million stars in this sky."

Ash's murmur caught him by surprise and made him turn his eyes toward the canopy of twinkling lights. He hadn't even noticed how bright they appeared. Without the moon's glow obscuring them, the stars did indeed appear unusually bright and numerous. Drum had been so focused on what the lack of moonlight meant that he hadn't bothered to think of the other opportunities it presented.

Maybe he could learn something from that.

A stirring of the breeze made him shiver, and he turned his eyes back to the ground, searching for a well-worn path in the clipped grass. When he spotted it, he pulled Ash toward it. "Follow me," he murmured, and set off along the narrow trail.

The path didn't go far, just across the garden and a little way into the field beyond. It cut through a stand of birch trees that spread out to the left of a single, squat hawthorn and ended at the remains of a disused cattle shed. The tiny barn was constructed of native stone, joined with lime and sand mortar, and topped with a roof of thatched turf. Only two and a half walls remained standing, and part of the roof had caved in over the open side, but it provided decent shelter from the wind. As Drum had expected, John still used it to store extra bits of straw and hay, the most exposed bits of which had been covered by heavy canvas tarps.

He could have picked a more romantic trysting spot, but not one that offered him room to breathe and the chance to look up at that blanket of stars. Now that Ash had pointed them out, he felt as if he had to keep his eye on them, or they might disappear as quickly and easily as Maeve.

Maybe, just maybe, his current behavior had crossed a line from rational to superstitious Irish nonsense. Definitely, most definitely, he didn't think he cared.

Drum chose a spot where a bale of hay had fallen free of its ties and collapsed into a pile of sweetly scented bedding. He settled onto it, leaning back against a stack of intact bales, and pulled Ash down after him. Spreading his legs, he tugged her into the lee so that her back pressed against his chest, and his arms wrapped around her to share his warmth. Not that the cold ever seemed to bother her, but the gesture gave him comfort, as did the feel of her in his arms.

Somehow, in the last few days full of chaos and fear and danger, this inhuman woman had become Michael Drummond's true north. Whenever he looked around, his compass pointed straight at her. She had become an object of strength and faith, a place he could lean when he grew weary, and a power he could trust to always protect him and the ones he loved. She had told him she would get Maeve back, bring her home safe and sound, and he knew that when Ash gave her word, she would kill or die to keep it. That knowledge filled him with both awe and peace.

And it made him wonder what she could possibly get from him in return. He already knew how he felt about his Guardian, but what if she felt no such love in return? She had been created to fight battles. Could he really compare to the rush of power and adrenaline such duties provided?

With a sigh, Drum forced such thoughts from his mind. He had come out here to forget his worries for a few minutes, not to add to them. He felt her weight fall back against him, and in response he dropped his chin to rest on her shoulder until he felt wrapped around her like a blanket. She didn't try to turn to look at him, just rubbed her cheek against the bristle of his late-night stubble and gazed out and up at the twinkling stars.

For several minutes they just sat there, breathing in the night air and the scent of good, clean hay while the sounds of the country buzzed quietly in the background. Finally, it was Ash who spoke. "I told you we would get her back, Drum. And we will. That's a promise."

His arms tightened around her. Then Drum gave his head a very small shake. "I don't want to talk about it. We've been talking about it all night. I'm talked out."

She seemed to tense for a moment, then her muscles softened and she slid a little bit to the side so that she could see him if she turned just an inch or two toward him. "What do you want, then?" she asked quietly. "Tell me what you need."

Drum shook his head. He couldn't. But he could show her.

His lips claimed hers in a kiss he had intended to be hot and possessive, something to force both of them to forget the problems they faced and simply feel. His mouth, though, hadn't gotten the memo. Instead of attacking, it surrendered, giving her everything before a single demand could be made. He sank into the soft, sweet flavor of her, the warmth that provided such a decadent contrast to the chill in the air, and Ash gave him everything right back.

Her hand came up, reaching back to cup his cheek in her palm as they sipped from each other. He felt himself tremble at her touch and then marveled when she echoed his show of weakness with a shiver of her own. He might have wondered if the cold had touched her for the first time if the motion hadn't been echoed in a soft, throaty moan, the kind that expressed decadent pleasure and changed the fit of his jeans in an instant.

Drum figured she noticed. The first clue came when her lips curved against him, and the moan turned into a purr without minimizing its effect. In fact, the problem in his pants only seemed to increase, no pun intended. The second clue expressed her appreciation for his dilemma when she shifted her hips to rub against the sensitive ridge of his erection. He might even have thought she wanted to drive him crazy.

She certainly didn't want him to think. If she had, she wouldn't have tried to encourage all of the blood in his body to flow out of his brain and pool somewhere significantly lower. Somewhere that throbbed painfully when she slid her free hand down and closed it around him.

Shite. Maybe crazy wouldn't be so bad?

Ash seized her moment.

Greed welled up inside her, to touch, to take, to possess. To store up every sensation, every sound, every breath against the centuries of cold sleep to come. She wanted to take Drum inside her, not just in her body, but inside whatever animating spirit she contained that passed for a soul. If she made him a part of her, then she could never lose him. Not until she lost herself.

Her hand stroked up his straining length, squeezing to tease and entice. Based on the way his hips thrust up beneath her and his lips crushed over hers, she thought she might be on to something.

She shifted her weight and turned until she could change her position to straddle his lap. Her hands reached for his sweater, tugging it up and over his head before dropping it onto the hay-strewn floor. Her fingers immediately slid across his chest, drawn to the warm, bare skin like iron filings to a magnet. To touch this man made her feel more alive than breathing, than moving, than wielding her axe in battle. To share this connection with Drum was to live, and she would live with enthusiasm for every moment fate granted her. She knew there would be far too few of them.

Curving her lips into a smile, Ash brushed her lips lightly across his mouth, then dragged them along the curve of his jaw. His prickly stubble made her skin tingle, as if the tiny bristles were waking it up from a long nap. She wanted to strop against him like a cat, but for every inch of him she explored, her greedy inner voice urged her to search out another, and another, and another one after that.

She trailed kisses down the side of his neck and across his collarbone, triumph rushing through her when she made him shiver or groan in a deep, need-roughened voice. The adrenaline went to her head faster than a combat victory and spurred her on to chart further territories with lips and hands.

The tip of her tongue darted out to play in the hollow of his throat, followed by the edge of her teeth scraping gently across his Adam's apple. That time, she felt the growling noise he made vibrate against her lips and it made her mouth water.

Little nips of her teeth stung the broad expanse of his shoulders, but she followed the tiny insults with tender attention from the flat of her tongue, savoring the taste of his skin. His flavor tasted rich and earthy, of salt and soil and woodsy musk.

But it was his heat that continued to seduce her. He felt like solid, living embers against her cool skin and she pressed closer, wanting to feel that warmth surrounding her.

His arms wrapped obligingly around her, his hands slipping up beneath her jacket and shirt to scuff across the skin on either side of her spine. His hands were lightly callused, not like someone who labored on the land, but like a man who didn't fear hard work or getting the job done for himself. His touch urged her closer, but the layers of fabric between them frustrated her. Snarling, she lifted her hands from his flesh long enough to grasp her own collar and tear her top open all the way to the hem. With an impatient shrug, she sent both garments slithering away behind her.

In the darkness, Drum's eyes sparked with a sharp uptick of desire. "That is so fecking hot," he growled, wrapping his arms around her again and yanking her bare torso against his.

Ash smiled and rubbed her breasts up close, the hard points of her nipples scraping across already sensitized nerve endings. Shivers sent them burrowing even further into each other. Unable to resist the driving instinct, she leaned down and caught the thick muscle running across the top of his shoulder between her teeth. Her jaw exerted pressure, not enough to break the skin, but enough to draw the blood to the surface and leave the impressions of her teeth in the smooth, hot skin.

He answered with a muffled roar and mirrored the action. She felt him clamp down on the curve where her neck met her shoulder and felt a rush of primitive emotion. They were marking each other, like animals holding their mates in place and leaving evidence of their claims on each other's skin. The idea appealed to her. She wanted anyone who looked at this man to know that he belonged to her, and that as long as she remained awake and aware on the mortal plane, she would surrender him to no one.

Drum tugged at the waist of her jeans, fumbling with the button as he tried to strip off the heavy denim. Her mind scrambled over ways to remove the obstacle without separating them and came up empty. They would have to break apart to strip, and if they were going to do that, Ash was going to make it fast.

She rose in a blur of movement, using her Guardian's speed for a cause even more worthy than the destruction of evil, she decided. In the space of a single heartbeat (and her heart was racing) she ripped her jeans open at the seams and then crouched to deal with Drum's. He shifted his weight to help her, and she made a throaty noise of satisfaction when she tugged them away and cast them aside.

"So, so hot," he muttered, reaching for her again.

Ash had no issues with letting herself be caught.

She tumbled into his lap and let him continue the momentum until she lay on her back in the thick bed of straw with her man hovering over her, blocking out not just the starlight, but the entire world beyond their cozy, private nest.

The prickly stalks of hay scratched at the thinner skin of her human form, but she didn't care. She could block it out. By the Light, she was pretty sure she could block out tornados, forest fires, and plagues of locusts at this point, so long as Drum never stopped touching her.

Her entire body seemed to vibrate to the rapid beat of her heart. She could hear it in her ears, feel it in her fingertips. Then Drum settled his weight atop her and her awareness dissolved into nothing but the pleasure of his body over hers and the aching need at her core. She wanted him inside her with a fierce longing.

She issued the invitation with a deliberate spreading of her thighs and a long, slow caress of her hands over the smoothly flexing muscles beside his spine. Her knees came up to bracket his hips, clamping him in place, and her nails bit into his flesh to urge him onward.

He rumbled out a sound that began low in his belly and made her shiver even before it spilled into the cool night air. She stiffened a moment when he reached around behind him to capture her wrists in his hands and move them around to rest against the hay on either side of her head. It took less than an instant to relax, to sink into the scratchy bedding and let him stretch and shift above her like a big cat contemplating its pounce. It appeared clear he intended to pounce on her, so how could she lose?

She couldn't. She could only gain, gain the hot, hard pressure of his lower belly against hers, the kind that made her nerves tingle and butterflies dance in her stomach. His gaze held hers, pinned her in place, somehow looked *into* her, even as his hips pressed forward and he sank his cock into the welcoming heat of her pussy.

Ash's mouth fell open and her neck arched as she

struggled to remember how to breathe in the wake of the shattering pleasure. Every nerve in her body seemed concentrated between her legs, in the desperately gripping muscles of her center, parting in welcome and then clenching with the instinct to trip, to hold, to never lose the perfect sense of fullness and completion that came from being joined to this man.

Her mate.

The cry burst from her throat through no act of will on her part. She felt torn open, not in her body, but in her heart. Realization, bright and blinding, lit up behind her eyes and made her dizzy, weak, and unable to think. Drum was her mate. He wasn't just the man she had fallen reluctantly, desperately, and hopelessly in love with. He was the man that fate and the Light had created to be her perfect Warden and partner. The missing half of her inner being.

Her cry caught in her throat, choked off in the flood of disbelief, wonder, and joy cascading through her. She trembled and began to struggle, trying to free her arms so she could touch him, could reassure herself of his solid presence, not just inside her, but above her, around her. *With* her. She felt as if all her inhuman strength had deserted her, leaving her vulnerable in a way she had never experienced, only it wasn't her body that she had left open and unguarded. It was her heart.

Drum groaned, his hips pressing and thrusting against her, and he shifted his grip, sliding his hands up until his fingers twined with hers. Ash gripped him back, her nails digging into the back of his hands as she rose up to meet him on every deep penetration. She took him inside her, inside all of her, and every time she felt the completeness of their joining, she felt a sense of resonating peace she had always imagined existed only in mortal fairy tales.

Their bodies moved together, muscles straining, skin slicked with sweat. Bits of hay stuck to the moisture, and now and then a cool hint of the breeze would sneak past the remaining walls of stone to tease against heated flesh. Neither of them noticed. They remained lost in each other, lost in their moment, lost in the knowledge of the perfection of their mating.

And when the end rushed toward them, breaking over them like a massive wave against a rugged coast, they remained pressed together, one in body, mind, and spirit. They dove into ecstasy together, their mouths forming the identical prayer.

"I love you."

Chapter Twenty-four

A mist settled over the eastern part of the country the next morning. At least, that was how Drum thought of it. Kylie seemed convinced she'd been caught in some kind of rainstorm. He had to work to resist the urge to pat the top of her head and tell her how adorable she sounded.

John had driven the four of them back to Clondrohitty just after breakfast, dropping them and some camping supplies off at the ruins of the Drummond house. The cinderblock structure of the outer walls remained, but a quick glance made it clear that the interior had been thoroughly gutted. Drum just gritted his teeth and turned away to get to work.

While he, Ash, Kylie, and Dag began setting up an impromptu camp inside the undamaged garage, his brother-in-law remained long enough to fend off the influx of locals who stopped by to offer sympathy and help to the Drummonds. John assured everyone of the family's well-being, and that Maddie would be staying with him and her daughter for a few days while she collected herself and began making arrangements with her insurance agents to rebuild her home. He assured them all that he would convey to her their offers and good wishes, and then sent them away to spread word down at the pub, the post office, and from door to door. That was the way village life worked.

By the time John left, Drum had inspected his car to be certain it still ran, stacked up the food and supplies Sorcha had sent along, and unpacked the camping gear his mother had stored in the former barn's loft. Combined with John's contributions, he thought they had enough to get them through the next thirty-six hours or so until the new moon.

"I know it's not cozy," he said, standing beside Ash while the others looked around the cavernous space, "but it's got four walls and a roof to keep out the weather, plus there's a bathroom in that corner." He pointed to a walled-off area the size of a walk-in closet. "Toilet, stall shower, sink. Ma liked for Da to wash off the grease and grit before he tracked it into her kitchen. If the temperature gets uncomfortable, we can plug in a space heater and keep close to it. It won't warm the whole area, but it should throw out a bit to help."

Kylie grinned. "Hey, we've got food and air mattresses. And John even lent us the laptop and a router. He said your neighbor would let us piggyback on his Wi-Fi. I think we'll be fine."

"We will," Ash said, her tone expressing no room for disagreement. "We should set up everything we think we will need, then. After that, Kylie can contact the others, and we will finalize our plans to bring Maeve home."

No one bothered to comment; they all just snapped into action. Kylie began sorting through the piles of supplies, pulling out linens and pillows while Ash grabbed a broom and began expelling dust from the floors like a bad-tempered school principal. Meanwhile, Drum and Dag assembled some old camping beds, then topped the frames with a couple of inflatable mattresses. It wouldn't be as comfortable as a decent hotel, but it was better than the

concrete floor and it let them stay close enough to
the ruins to monitor any activity and to get in quickly.
Priorities.

Drum also unearthed a camp stove and the old alumi-
num cookware that went with it, so he set that up on an
old table built into the wall beside the big utility sink.
While the rest of them similarly puttered around, trying
to pass the time as much as to make the space as comfortable as possible, Kylie commandeered a second workbench
for the laptop and Internet router, tinkering and occasionally cursing until she had everything working to her satisfaction. Then there was more time to kill until the clock
moved to a reasonable position for calling the middle of
America. You know, given that it was never a good idea
to antagonize a witch. Especially not the kind who could
throw fireballs when provoked.

Wynn answered the call, looking not so much like
she had just woken up as like she had never been to
sleep. "Houston, we have a problem," she said in lieu of a
greeting.

"We're not in Houston. We're in Clon-dohickie, according to my phone apps."

"Ky, I'm serious. Ella and I spent all night on this.
Something bigger is happening over there than just
opening a hellmouth."

Drum scowled. "'Just opening a hellmouth?' The way
Dag and Kylie made that particular activity sound, it's the
supernatural equivalent of 'just' dropping a nuclear warhead."

"Right. So imagine dropping a nuclear warhead on top
of a plutonium mine."

Dag winced. "I would prefer not to do so."

"A sentiment I think we can all get behind," Kylie muttered. "Okay, then, Pooh Bear. Lay it on me. What did you
guys find?"

"Misery and mayhem, what else?" Wynn sighed. "Ella and I dug up some information from people who spend a little too much time investigating the paranormal side of local legends around the world. It turns out that the Guild and the Order aren't the only ones who got into the idea of hellmouths. According to what we read, there are locations all over the world that supposedly function as gates into hell, the underworld, the spirit plane, or whatever the locals in that particular area want to call it. They've got a couple in Greece, of course, and scattered across the old Roman Empire, but we found mentions of ones in Iceland, China, Japan, New Orleans, and even rural Pennsylvania."

"Right, because who doesn't want to spend their vacation touring the bowels of the earth?" Kylie asked, rolling her eyes. "Like plain old caving isn't weird and creepy enough. Let's go hang out in caves that might be full of ghosts and demons and ancient gods while we're at it?"

"Sing it, sister," Wynn said. "I think some of them can be written off, since they've been turned into big tourist attractions over the years, like the ones in Italy and Greece. Even if they were gates at one time, all these centuries of human energy have likely sealed them tightly enough to make the Order think twice about going there, even if they could manage to get a group inside without winding up all over the news."

Dag crossed his arms over his massive chest and frowned into the camera over Kylie's head. "Why do I dislike the fact that you have used the word 'some,' Wynn?"

The witch sighed. "Probably because you're smarter than you look, big guy. The places you can Google are not where the Order is going to strike first, but I think we can assume that if they manage to get one of the hellmouths open, they're not going to stop there, so Ella and I did some digging. As it turns out, that site you've been monitoring on the dark web turned up a few interesting tidbits."

"Like?"

"Like . . . a rumor that says there was a gate in Ireland before the time of Saint Patrick that didn't just lead into the middle dimensions. It lined up directly to the outer planes. Specifically to a plane where something very, very old and very, very scary was being held prisoner behind heavy-duty magical wards."

Drum felt Ash stiffen beside him. Then she leaned toward the camera. "Which?" she demanded.

He saw Wynn grimace. "The Unquiet."

"In the end it matters not," Dag grumbled, though he had reacted first with a noise like an earth-moving machine cutting into rocky ground. "Whichever of the Seven they seek now, we can no longer deny that they will not stop until all the creatures have been released."

"Actually, I think it does matter, at least a little," Wynn protested. "Dhuhlzek was always said to have a particular taste for individuals with precognitive talents. The stories make it sound like 'Unquiet' is what you call a super-powerful Demonic monster to keep it from eating you for using the term 'batshit crazy.' And that the reason it's crazy is because it consumed so many humans with visions of the future, it became overwhelmed by the endless possible outcomes. Of course, it also became powerful enough to destroy half of Europe before the Guardians and the Guild were able to send it into that prison plane to begin with."

Blood of the Blessed Virgin. Drum felt his knees threaten to buckle, and it was only Ash's quick action that provided the support he needed to keep standing. His sister's life could end up not just opening a gate into hell, but letting the Devil out to play, all in one fell swoop.

He felt the eyes of the others on him and sensed mostly sympathy for his feelings, but it didn't stop Wynn's quiet voice from asking the question.

"Drum, I'm so sorry," she said, and he could hear her sincerity, "but we need to know. How powerful is your sister's talent?"

"I can't answer that. I'm not inside her head." He swallowed, his throat so tight the action felt like he'd taken a knife through it. "The things she shares are mostly small, little tricks that make us laugh or drive us batty, like telling us who's calling before the telephone rings or spoiling the outcome of the football game we've got on telly. When it comes to the big things, she usually clams up. I think they scare her. She might ask us to avoid going out on a certain night, though, and we always listen. Ma says she makes our gran look like a tosser, and there were those about the village who called her a witch when she wasn't about to hear them." He paused. "No offense intended, Wynn."

"None taken, Drum." She forced a smile. "It's fine. But I think we have to assume the worst, then, that Maeve had enough power to fuel the worst-case scenario version of the Order's ritual. That means we can't take any chances when it comes to stopping them. When we hit, we have to hit hard."

Kylie let out a little gargle of frustration. "How are we supposed to do that, though? You and I will be throwing away energy on the portal spell just before you get here, Ella can't make the trip, and you said Fil can't leave her current assignment in Alberta. Do you have the Avengers on standby to come racing to our rescue, by any chance?"

"No, but I do have a slight change in plans. You and I are going to do the portal spell tonight. That will get Knox and me there early enough that I'll have tomorrow during the day to recharge and be ready to go. I'm also going to bring Ella and Fil with me."

"But you said Ella can't travel and Fil can't be spared."

"Maybe not in body, but I can drag them along in spirit, and that's where the magic happens."

Drum listened and struggled to wrap his mind around the plan that Wynn put forth. He'd already had to accept that he wasn't ever going to grasp how magic would apparently allow the witch and her Guardian to travel from Chicago to them in the space of a few seconds. The idea of Wynn channeling extra energy from the other Wardens while they remained on the western end of the North American continent just threatened to send him over the edge. If he thought about it too hard, brain matter might start leaking out of his ear.

For a few minutes, he wished very, very hard that they had decided to have this meeting in Dublin. At his pub. Where there was Guinness. Lots and lots of Guinness.

"I'll also spend a few hours in the morning giving Drum the kind of lessons you had in the spring," Wynn continued, once the discussion stopped treating physics like paper to be torn up into tiny little pieces of confetti. "Only these will have to be even quicker and dirtier."

"Yeesh." Kylie made a face. "In that case, at least bring the boy some lube."

Everyone shared a laugh at that, but Drum found himself very much afraid that the sentiment held more than a grain of truth. The sum total of his experience in the sort of conflict he was about to walk right into consisted of putting an instinctive kind of smackdown on what the others seemed to view as the Lollipop Guild of supernatural monsters.

What the bollocks had he gotten himself into?

Then his rational mind kicked back in, and he remembered. He hadn't gotten himself into anything, not really. Maeve was the one in trouble, and it didn't matter to him how he and this band of merry monsters managed to get her free again. He would do whatever it took.

Looking around, he took stock of his allies. At his side stood Ash, tall and straight and fierce, almost as formidable in her human disguise as she was in her tunic and belt, beating her wings against the air currents and swinging her massive battle-axe above her head. He might not have known Kylie for long, but he had already fought beside her and knew her to be more than capable of taking care of herself in a tricky situation. And her Guardian? Well, anyone, human or not, who looked at Dag and decided he'd be a good choice to pick a fight with had a serious lack of mental development going for him. In either of his forms, Dag looked like one big pile of muscle, and only a fool would take him on out of choice.

As for Wynn, Knox, and the others, Ash trusted them, and Drum had already admitted to himself that where she went, so went his nation. If she felt that this group of impossible people—impossible to believe, impossible to shake, impossible not to respect—were going to rescue Maeve from the clutches of the evil villains, then that was good enough for him.

If only he didn't have to worry whether or not he was good enough for her.

After all, what could he do? So far, he had managed one spell, mostly by accident and with a complete lack of control or finesse. Sure, Wynn had offered to teach him a few things, but how much could he learn in five or six hours? Enough to keep himself alive in the kind of battle that brought out nerves even in the people who were committed to the Warden/Guardian/Demon/*nocturni* paradigm on a level Drum wasn't certain he would ever reach? And it wasn't like he had the physical abilities to make up for his lack of experience. The most fighting he had ever done was boxing, the closely monitored kind in a ring, for exercise, with safety equipment and trained monitors watching so that no one got badly hurt and no one pulled a move that could be considered illegal or unethical. Somehow he doubted the Order of Eternal Darkness paid much attention to rules or referees.

What could she possibly see in him?

Ash spoke, standing close beside him. "I lack the ability to do magic, of course, but I can also help to talk him through some exercises he might find useful. If he spends today gaining a better understanding of the flow and control of magical energy, your lessons tomorrow should prove that much more useful."

Wynn nodded and appeared supportive of the idea, but Dag and Kylie shared smirks it would have been tough to miss. Not that anyone tried.

Drum found himself frowning. "What?"

"Maybe I should supervise." Kylie grinned, looking almost ready to burst into giggles. "That way practice won't end with the two of you spending a couple of hours picking bits of hay out of your hair and, um, other more sensitive places."

What was that supposed to—

Oh. Drum felt heat crawl up his neck and into his cheeks. Apparently he and Ash hadn't gone unnoticed when they disappeared in the middle of the night. Or, at least, they hadn't gone unnoticed after sneaking back into the house just minutes after sunrise. His shower that morning had left a few sprigs of dried alfalfa swirling around his sister's drain.

He cleared his throat. Ash just scowled and attempted to make everyone burst into flames from the intensity of her glare. To be honest, he found it kind of cute.

Wynn laughed into the camera on her computer. "Oh, lay off them, Kylie. Or did you forget the compromising position Knox found you in the first time we came to visit you in Boston?"

That brought a surge of color to Kylie's cheeks, which

make Drum feel better, even if Ash continued to look kind of grumpy. Was she upset that the others knew about them sleeping together? He had thought everyone already knew, had in fact assumed that all the others were working on their own assumptions regarding the nature of their relationship. He knew so little about the traditional way the bond between a Warden and a Guardian worked, only what Ash had told him. Most of that made it sound like a complex and slightly adversarial working relationship, but everything he had heard about the current crop of Guardians who had woken to face the latest threat from the Order indicated that they had each mated with the Warden who was present at their awakening. Why should he and Ash be any different? And why should it matter that they weren't?

Unless Ash harbored some regrets about what had happened last night. Specifically at the end of last night.

They had both collapsed into heaps of boneless, quivering flesh immediately after the climax that had shaken them in its teeth like disobedient lion cubs. He'd been asleep almost before his own words had stopped echoing in his ears. Had he imagined hers?

He knew what his heart held, what threatened to overflow it anytime his thoughts lingered on her, but what about hers? He knew she cared for him, at least enough to share her body with him and to want to protect him and his family from harm, but he wasn't sure how much stock to put in such things. After all, victory in battle had always been considered a powerful aphrodisiac, and Ash had said many times that the purpose of her existence lay in protecting mortals' lives from the evil of the Order and their Demonic masters.

The confusion of it all threatened to make his head pound, and he had matters of literal life and death to worry about. Maybe he should focus on those for a while. You know, at least until they got his sister back.

"I'm certain I could use all the help you can give," he said, trying to steer the group, and himself, back to topic. "Most of the magic I've managed so far has been more accidental than anything. I doubt that's going to cut the mustard when we start trying to save the world."

"No, it won't." Wynn schooled her face into more serious lines. "Work on it while you have the chance. Ash and Dag can explain the basics, and Kylie should be able to demonstrate so you can see what they're talking about a little easier. Tomorrow night will be the big leagues."

"The World Cup," he said, mustering a smile. "Remember, you'll be in Ireland this time, not America. We respond better to football metaphors."

"As long as you respond, that's what matters." The witch paused to draw a deep breath, then stared into the camera with serious hazel eyes. "You all ready for this?"

Drum winced. "Does the answer to that really matter?"

"No," Dag said, his frown almost as deep as his voice. "Ready or not, the battle approaches."

Ash nodded and reached out to squeeze Drum's hand. The move surprised him, but it pleased him more. He squeezed back.

"Then," she said, firmly, "we will simply have to win."

Chapter Twenty-five

As nightfall approached, Ash wondered whether a colony of native bats had taken up residence inside her lower abdomen. She had heard of the human expression regarding butterflies in one's stomach, but these felt much too big for such delicate insects. Bats felt much more appropriate.

The sensation proved distracting for two reasons: first, because she was a Guardian, created for battle, and endowed with the speed, strength, and abilities of her race for the sole purpose of defeating her enemies, and therefore had no business allowing nerves to beset her before a conflict; and second, because the source of her internal fluttering crouched at her side behind a thicket of bushes that provided a view of the opening to the underground caverns, preparing to enter combat at her side.

The very thought of it made her bats flip and flop around like circus trapeze artists working without a net. She knew there couldn't be a net, because one of them dove so low, she almost looked at her feet to see if it was hopping around below her now. The thought of Drum in danger tightened her chest and made her hand itch for the feel of the haft of her axe against her palm. She had to be patient, though. The narrow crevice into the cavern restricted the Guardians from assuming their natural forms until they passed through into the darkness.

Into the Darkness.

Maybe she should rephrase that?

"We can see nothing from here," Dag said, and even at barely above a whisper, his voice rumbled through the air. "We will have no choice but to approach in the open and assume the enemy will attack to prevent us from entering the cavern. The best way to avoid projectile fire is to take a nonlineal path to the entrance."

"Duck and weave," Drum muttered. "Sounds like the best way to avoid a soaking while doing the washing up with my sisters."

"I might be able to throw up a shield between us and them, but I can't be certain how long it would last until I see exactly what we're up against. You've mentioned *hhis-sih* and shadelings, which make sense for mindless guards at an entrance point, but we can't be sure that's all they would throw at us." Wynn rummaged through a giant tote bag she had brought with her through the portal from Chicago. "Knowing the details always helps."

Ash could not be certain what the witch carried, but she could smell dried herbs, exotic spices, and a host of other, less pleasant, things wafting from within. Obviously, the Midwestern Warden believed in being prepared for anything, from minion attacks to barbecue season.

Knox shook his head and placed a hand atop his mate's. "Save your energy, little witch. While we will be vulnerable on our approach, the narrowness of the entry limits the number of attackers who may take us on without exposing themselves by exiting the cave entirely. If we go hard and fast, we may be able to push through them and be inside before they can do us much damage."

"Ooh, in that case, I think I can help," Kylie said, almost bouncing in place. "Over the last few months, I've worked out tweaks to a couple of the spells you guys taught me. I think I have the perfect one for this occasion. Can I try it out? Pretty please with babka on top?"

Dag frowned down at her. "What do you have planned?"

"Just watch. Cover me while I throw it, then run in through the entry as soon as you see my arm go up. Got it? Trust me. You'll love it." Kylie grinned even wider and gathered her legs underneath her. "I call it bowling for bad guys."

"Huh?"

The petite Warden didn't answer. She just rose to her full height (which was barely higher than the top of the bushes) and stepped to the side until she had a clear view of the narrow crevice. Then she drew her hand back at her side as if she really were preparing to throw a bowling ball, only instead of a chunk of polyurethane and resin, she tossed a perfectly round, pale green orb of glowing energy. It traveled a straight path an inch or two above the ground directly toward the cavern entrance. When it hit the darkness inside, it exploded in a blinding shock of light and concussive power and raised a chorus of unholy screeching from whatever lurked inside.

"Strike!" Kylie crowed, throwing her hands above her head and doing a victory spin even as the Guardians launched into action. They flew across the space to the cave and flung themselves in after the spell, the forward charge of their little army.

Ash burst into the cavern after Knox and before Dag, squinting against the light of Kylie's magic still radiating around them. She shifted before she even drew breath, and had a split second to be grateful when a set of razor-sharp claws tried to slice her head from her shoulders. Her thick, stony hide kept the strike from cutting too deep, and her axe hand came up to bury the pointed shaft in the chest of her attacker.

Had the entrance been guarded again by shadelings, she would have cut straight through a layer of mist, but instead, the metal spear tip lodged in flesh as a ghoul shrieked in pain and anger. Quickly, Ash turned to face the things and shoved forward, clearing the entrance to allow the others room to maneuver. Once clear, she yanked her weapon free and spun the haft to bring the larger of the two blades around, cleanly beheading the creature.

What goes around comes around, she thought. Sometimes quite literally.

She took a quick look about the upper cavern and noticed immediately that a dull, red glow illuminated the entire area just enough that she thought the humans might be able to function inside without accidentally taking aim at each other. That was the good news. The bad news was that the glow came from the opening of the stairwell down to the second cave, which seemed to pulse with bright crimson magical energy and the flickering of roaring fires. Something very big was going on in the lower chamber, and she didn't need three guesses to figure out what that was. Maeve would be down there, and about a hundred assorted ghouls and at least two *nocturnis* currently blocked the path to her.

Time to get to work.

Three ghouls charged her together, but Ash didn't wait for them to strike. She sprang forward and met them halfway, her axe swinging in a wide, deadly arc that cleaved the first one in half like a rotten apple. It wouldn't have surprised her in the least to find a worm wriggling away inside. The force of her blow embedded her blade in the rib cage of ghoul number two, and she planted a foot against its hip for leverage to yank free.

Ghoul number three seized the opportunity to leap on her back, clawed hands scrabbling at her throat. Reaching behind with her free hand, Ash closed her fingers around the back of its neck, digging her talons into flesh, and drove her spiked axe handle into the thing's abdomen. Then, she took advantage of the way pain briefly loosened its grip to flip it off over her head into the ranks of its fellow creatures.

She raised her weapon to face another attack, and another, and another. Every time she thought she was about to fight free of the advancing hoard, more ghouls would charge out at her. It almost seemed as if they possessed an infinite supply of reinforcements.

Well, duh.

"Dag!" she shouted, razing a couple of ghouls who stood in her path. "They are summoners!"

She saw the Guardian's eyes widen and turn on the two dark-robed figures standing on either side of the stairwell opening. Both had their hands raised, and a low chant issued from the space beneath their hoods. Any humans with magical talent who joined the Order of Eternal Darkness immediately received training in the use of Dark magic, but only the most powerful and advanced of these learned the black art of summoning servants to do their bidding.

Most cells of *nocturnis* only had one or two of the specially trained sorcerers in their ranks, but this one seemed to have enough that it could put two on guard at the entrance to the big dance below. That didn't bode well for the next stage of battle.

But they could worry about that later. First, they had to finish round one, and that meant cutting off the enemy's supply train.

"Per lucem!" Ash shouted, raising her axe high before she plunged relentlessly through the mass of screeching, clawing, biting ghouls to reach the cowards behind.

"Per lucem!" her brothers echoed, and she knew they had fallen into a formation that allowed at least one of them to guard her back as she sought out the bigger foe.

Another voice joined the call, one lighter but equally masculine. She heard Drum roar out the battle cry and watched the cavern light up around a particularly charged bolt of golden energy. She didn't stop to see how many of the ghouls he had taken down, but she smiled fiercely as she closed in on her targets.

They knew she was coming. Between her shout and the path she blazed among the mass of attacking ghouls, she would have been hard to miss. So she wasn't surprised when one of the pair ceased his chant and turned to face her, pointing his palm in her direction.

"Zulmaht q'uhn!" The sorcerer shrieked, and a narrow razor of rusty crimson magic sliced through the air in front of her throat.

Really? Was this one new? Because any half-trained *nocturni* should understand that a large portion of the Guardians' power against the Darkness came from their ability to resist magic. It sort of counted as one of their calling cards. The sorcerer should know his spell attack would be useless.

Still, instinct and reflex had her moving, raising her axe to deflect the beam of energy into the back of a nearby ghoul. The *nocturni* hissed and cast again, and Ash would have rolled her eyes if she hadn't seen his hand shift at the last moment and the stream of Dark energy he channeled skip past her to target an opponent at her back. Assuming the twit stupid enough to try his useless gambit against Dag or Knox, she continued her forward assault and brought her axe down on the cultist's head. Only the Demon worshipper had erected a shield of energy around himself that deflected the blade at the last minute, and she growled her displeasure even as a voice behind her shouted in pain.

A very familiar voice.

Ash half spun in time to see Drum fall to the floor, one hand clutching his opposite shoulder, the same shoulder that had been recently burned by another *nocturni*'s spell fire. Her Warden landed hard on his knees, and the ghouls closed in around him, scenting weakened prey. She cried out, ready to leap after him, ready to cut through anything standing in her way, but before she could move, something large and fierce flew across the cavern to hover above the fallen combatant and tear into the things that threatened him. He swung his double-ended blade through the air with ruthless precision, keeping the slavering ghouls well back from Ash's mate.

She would find a way to thank him later. Right now, she needed to focus on the sorcerer.

The *nocturni*'s defensive magic had turned away her weapon, but it should not be able to turn away a Guardian itself. Perhaps this situation called for a more personal touch.

Slinging her axe into a harness at her back, Ash freed her hands and flashed her fangs a split second before she launched herself at the hooded figure.

She caught him off guard. Guardians moved fast, their reflexes and speed far greater than that of a human, but when you added the tailwind generated by a hard beat of enormous wings, the warrior could appear as little more than a blur to even the most observant of eyes. In other words, Ash had crossed the cultist's magical defensive wall and wrapped her hands around his head before his brain received notice of the incoming attack. She stared into the eyes beneath the hood for a single instant before a single wrenching movement snapped his evil neck. He collapsed to the floor and remained unmoving.

One down, one to go.

The battle continued to rage around her. Kylie and

Wynn threw spells in blasts of pale, untainted magic, while Dag swung his hammer through wave after wave of attacking ghouls. Knox remained resolutely on guard above Drum's kneeling figure.

Ash turned her gaze to the second summoner. He had seen his comrade fall, and just as she had expected, he ceased his bid to reinforce the diminishing numbers of ghouls in favor of protecting his own life.

He appeared marginally smarter than the first sorcerer in that he didn't bother to try to hurt her with magic. Instead, he went straight for the Guardians' most vulnerable spot and turned on the Wardens.

Ash expected another cry of pain to echo through the chamber, but she and the cultist were both due for a surprise, it seemed. Her gaze followed the figure's magical strike just in time to see it bounce off a sheet of pale green energy between the *nocturni* and where Kylie stood a few feet ahead of Wynn. The magic seemed to quiver and ripple like a curtain of moving water or burning flame.

"Boo-yah!" Kylie shouted from behind the barrier. "If there's one thing a computer geek can do better than anyone, you schmuck, it's put up a firewall! So bite me!"

Fangs flashing in a savage grin, Ash leaped forward.

She saw the sorcerer stumble backward, his hands waving in motions she guessed would summon another defensive force, either more ghouls or something even worse. She had no intention of allowing him to finish.

Her axe flew, a single straight blow that shot the weapon forward to the end of its shaft and brought the edge of her blade within slashing distance of the muttering figure. It took a moment for each of them to realize she had hit. Ash blinked into the dimness, peering at the *nocturni*'s chest before she saw the center of his robe begin to glisten. The black cloth was absorbing a wash of thick liquid blood in a long, uninterrupted line between its wearer's left shoulder and right hip. Her cut had struck so cleanly that the tear in the cloth had barely parted, but she had hit deep. A quick whiff of offal told her his intestines had begun to spill forth. He dropped like a stone, his hands still waving before him.

It didn't matter. The magic had blinked out, and whatever the sorcerer had intended to summon remained firmly locked in its current location. Satisfied, Ash turned to dispatch the closest of the remaining ghouls, fighting her way to Drum's side.

Their band of Wardens and warriors made short work of the enemy. In only minutes, the cavern descended into silence. Immediately, she crouched at Drum's side, pushing away the bloodied hand that cradled his injured arm. "How bad?"

Drum grimaced as she poked at a deep cut along his biceps. It wasn't life threatening, but for a human it was serious, and obviously very painful. His ability to fight and cast spells would be compromised, though by how much she could only guess.

"'Tis only a flesh wound," he muttered, his brogue thicker than she had ever heard it. "Had worse."

"Liar," she growled, tearing the sleeve off his shirt and pressing it hard against the bleeding wound.

"Let me." Wynn pushed forward and gently urged Ash out of the way. She examined the wound with a practiced efficiency and pursed her lips. "He'll need stitches, but in the meantime I can bandage it to keep it protected."

She dug around in her bag for a moment, then withdrew a bundle of clean white gauze, a couple of thick pads of absorbent cotton, a bottle of mysterious liquid, and a small jar of ointment. The others stared in disbelief. It took a few seconds for her to notice.

"What?" she asked when she finally looked up and noticed their attention. "Like you thought we were all gonna get through this without a scratch? You're just lucky I came prepared."

"Nah," Kylie said, shaking her head and smiling. "We're just all trying to figure out when you mugged Hermione Granger and stole her handbag. You got a tent and a wood-burning stove in there?"

"Smart-ass," Wynn muttered, dousing one of the pads with the bottle of liquid. Ash had expected a disinfectant with the bite of alcohol, but instead the fluid had a sharp but not unpleasant aroma of herbs. The witch followed up by smearing the wound with the ointment in the jar, which had an unappealing greenish-brown color. By now the bleeding had slowed to a sluggish trickle, so she placed the second pad over the injury and bound it in place with several layers of gauze.

"There." Wynn replaced her supplies into her bag, slung it back across her chest, and pushed to her feet. "That should keep it clean, at least, and the ointment will help dull the pain. It's not Vicodin, or anything, but it does help. But we will need to get you to a doctor for those stitches just as soon as we're out of here. I can't believe I forgot to bring sutures."

Kylie giggled.

Her friend scowled. "You guys suck."

Drum flexed his arm, wincing only slightly. "And you, Wynn, dear, are a love. Thank you." He got to his feet, Ash hovering close, ready to catch him if he so much as swayed. He surprised her by standing with steadiness, his face pale but wearing a mask of resolve. "I'm sorry I ruined our chance at surprising them down below. It's been too long since the *nocturnis* went down. By now, they'll know we're coming."

Knox snorted and wiped the blood from the blades of his unusual weapon with a scrap of cloth. "They knew we were coming before we stepped through that crevice.

There was no chance at surprise, and so no need for an apology. We were lucky the foes they set upon us were not more difficult to manage. They might as well have guarded this entrance with *hhissih* and Chihuahuas."

"Chihuahuas?" Wynn repeated, frowning at her mate.

The large male shuddered. "Yappy beasts. Creatures of Darkness if I ever saw one."

Dag snickered.

Ash, however, thought about that, her brow furrowing. "Knox is right. Even with summoners standing by to re-plenish the fallen, there should have been tougher defenses guarding this cavern. If the enemy wishes to keep us up here and away from the hellmouth below, why did they not have a more formidable challenge in place to stop us?"

The group quieted, catching on to the significance of her words. "You think they deliberately made it easy for us?" Kylie asked. "That they want us to get below and take a real shot at them?"

"I think that they want to get us below; and that when we do, they believe we will not have the chance to take a shot at them."

"An ambush?" Dag mulled over the possibilities. "They have set a trap and expect to catch us in it. This would not be uncharacteristic of the treacherous filth."

"Have we a new plan, then?" Drum asked, arching an eyebrow. "Or are we looking to get ourselves killed, because I need to be letting you know I've not arranged my shifts at the Bones to be covered beyond the weekend."

"Of course not," Knox said, swinging his double-bladed staff as casually as flicking a twig at a hedgerow. "Just because the enemy knows we are coming does not mean they are ready to face us."

Drum glanced down at his arm. "Really? Looked pretty ready to me."

"You still breathe, do you not, Warden?"

Ash saw the debate end in the rage that sparked in Drum's eyes an instant later, the same instant that a long, high-pitched scream rent the air around them.

Maeve.

The Order had just reminded them all why they were here and why it mattered not a bit if they stumbled straight into an ambush. Some traps were just worth springing.

Chapter Twenty-six

Drum didn't remember sprinting toward the open stairwell, but awareness rushed back when a good three hundred pounds of Guardian tackled him a few feet short of it and crushed him against the cavern's stone floor.

"Stop and think, Warden," Dag growled into his ear. "We know the enemy means to trap us, but we need not make it easy for them. Take a moment and breathe. You do your sister no good if you get yourself killed before we can rescue her."

As soon as he could remember his own name instead of just the instant of impact, Drum nodded and sucked in air. Sweet, sweet oxygen. How quickly a body started to miss it.

"I get it," he gasped. "Sorry."

"Do not apologize." The Guardian climbed to his feet and held out a beefy hand. "Think. It will get you further."

Drum nodded and brushed the worst patches of dirt from the front of his trousers. He cast a surreptitious glance at Ash. She stood with her axe handle braced on the floor, her fingers curving over the top of the haft. She didn't look at him, probably because she was embarrassed by his stupidity. God knew Drum was.

He cleared his throat. "So, um, I think I asked this before, but what's the plan, then? We send Kylie bowling again?"

Wynn shook her head. "No trick works as well the second time you play it. The fact is, we know where they are, and they know where we are. Our best bet is just to close the distance in the fastest, cleanest way we can manage, and then let the chips fall where they may."

"The Church says gambling is a sin," Drum muttered. "Of course, so is Demon worship, so . . ."

"So, let's start with a roll of the dice." The witch flashed him a grin, then turned to her mate. "Fast is where you guys come in. The stairs make us into sitting ducks if we go down that way. How do the Guardians feel about playing parachutes?"

Knox bared his teeth in an answering smile. "Perfect."

At a nod from him, the Guardians shifted to stand behind their Wardens. Drum felt Ash wrap her arms around his waist then kick off from the ground like a diver from a springboard. Up they rose into the air above the stairwell opening, then they dove into the lower cavern in what felt to him unnervingly like a death spiral. He gritted his teeth to keep from screaming.

Someone else did it for him.

The stranger, though, didn't scream in fear, but in rage. It echoed around the brightly lit cave, bouncing off the hard stone ceiling and pinging off the walls like a squash ball. Oddly, someone wasn't happy to see them.

Ash landed and immediately stepped away from him to give herself room to maneuver. He assumed the other pairs did something similar, but he was too busy looking around him to check. A man didn't get to see the inside of hell every day, after all. At least, not if he was lucky.

Torches illuminated the egg-shaped chamber, attached to the walls in heavy, iron sconces. At first his gaze skipped over them, but something about the flickering flames made him look again. The fire wasn't natural. It might have the right color, dance and sway in the right manner, but it burned too brightly and produced no smoke. If it had, the room would have been filled with it and so would the chamber above. The *nocturnis* had to be using magic, but from what Wynn and Kylie had taught him, maintaining that many lights with magical energy could sap the strength of a practitioner in mere minutes, yet none of the robed figures in the chamber looked the least bit fatigued. This did not bode well.

The cave appeared smaller than the upper chamber, but despite the brighter illumination, thick shadows seemed to lurk at either end of the oblong space. Nerves and recent events had him peering intently into the darkness, trying to discern whether any sets of glowing-ember eyes gazed back. Not at the moment, anyway.

Drum tried to orient himself to the cavern entrance and the landscape above them, but all he could tell was that the length of the chamber stretched on a roughly east-west axis with the darkest corner pointing somewhere in the vicinity of Fionn mac Cumhaill's field. He reflected briefly that the big, bad-tempered bull would have made a bloody brilliant distraction at the moment if he'd been present. Too bad this lot hadn't decided to hold their Convention of Evil outside in the fresh air. Might have done them some good.

The cave held seven of the cultists, and when Drum counted off the final digit inside his head, an icy tingle darted down his spine. Try to tell him the number wasn't significant. Go ahead. He dared you.

They stood around a flat-topped boulder, behind which a slice of air seemed to shimmer in the light of the torches that outlined it. The shape was clearly meant to suggest an arched doorway, and it didn't take a genius to guess where it led. This was the hellmouth the Order intended to open.

On top of the boulder, less than five feet from the doorway, his sister reclined, bound hand and foot like a lamb for slaughter. She wore a familiar pair of men's-style flannel pajamas, though they looked dirty, torn, and badly rumpled. Her feet were bare and equally smudged with dirt, though Drum clenched his fists when he spotted some dark smudges on the soles that looked like blood, both dried and fresh. It took all of his control not to charge into the crowd of evil fuckers and snatch his sister away before they could so much as blink.

Well, all his control, plus a mental reminder that it likely wouldn't go quite that way. The cultists would fall on him like a pack of wild hyenas and tear him and his sister to pieces before the Guardians could even twitch. That did nothing to temper the urge, but it did keep his feet on the ground. Barely.

"Ah, our guests have arrived," purred a silky-smooth voice coming from the hooded figure at the far side of the makeshift altar stone. He sounded like a politician, all kind words and unkind intentions. "So glad you could join us, my friends. I have missed you these last few months, and I so feared you wouldn't be able to make our little gathering tonight."

The figure reached up a pale, thin hand and pushed the robe back to reveal the face of a handsome human man somewhere in his fifties. To Drum, he looked vaguely familiar, but nearby he heard Kylie and Wynn cursing in at least three languages. He didn't understand most of it, but two words definitely caught his attention.

"The Hierophant."

He heard Ash moving behind him, then her voice drifted forward in a low snarl. "Not anymore. The skin he wears might belong to the one who led the Order to free him, but nothing remains of human essence inside of it now. That is the Corruptor. Nazgahchuhl in human's clothing."

The figure's eyes flicked over them, and that was when Drum first noticed. He should never have mistaken this thing for human. It had eyes like a snake, no white visible, flat and iridescent, with a vertical slit for a pupil. Dark copper, the color reminded him of old, dried blood, and they stared with the cold, unblinking regard of a reptile.

What Drum wouldn't give to lay a little Rikki-tikki-tavi action on his ass.

Then something odd happened. The Demon swept its gaze to Ash, and what looked like a second eyelid blinked rapidly across its pupil. A forked tongue darted from between its lips, and it hissed, sounding almost nervous. "What is this thing that pretends to stand with the doomed warriors against us?"

The Guardian stepped forward, her axe held in two hands, one gripping the middle of the shaft, the other just below the double-bladed head. "I am a Guardian, foul beast, and the only doom you foresee is your own."

"Kill them!" the demon screeched, raising a hand with a black, glinting knife above the altar, and everything in the universe happened at once.

The figures in hoods sprang forward. Two immediately raised their hands to the roof of the cavern and set the earth to shaking. The rock groaned in protest before a crack sounded, like thunder directly overhead, and dust and debris hit the floor of the upper chamber, sending stray rocks bouncing down the stairs. The cultists must have used magic to seal off the exit from the upper chamber. They were all trapped in the same space, six murderous, black-magic-wielding cultists, three Guardians, three Wardens (one of whom only had one arm to work with), one battered human woman, and one of the most powerful Demons ever created, who currently looked like the star of a men's hair-coloring commercial.

Now they were suckin' diesel.

Drum held up a hand to deflect a blast of magic one of the remaining *nocturnis* sent his way. The bastard probably expected him to back off, or at least dig his heels in at his current position and start exchanging spell for spell in a useless waste of magic and energy. But Drum had other ideas. Instead of the obvious choices, he put his shoulders down and rushed the enemy like a Gaelic footballer looking to make the tackle.

The sorcerer was ready for him, raising his hands to hold a shield before him, but Drum was ready for him to be ready. So to speak. Instead of hitting the man or his shield, Drum swerved aside at the last minute and threw himself in between the altar and the Demon. He knew in his gut the act might spell his death, but it might also save his sister, and that was the only thing that mattered.

He felt the knife pierce his shoulder through the back and the Demon brought it down with a scream. Drum gave a pretty good cry of his own, because fuck, that hurt, but he continued his momentum, hoping to knock the monster to the floor. All did not go as planned.

The Demon stayed put, absorbing the force of the hit and deflecting it to send Drum hurtling into the stone wall behind him. Only decent reflexes and the few games of *caid* under his belt allowed him to change his orientation and spread the blow over the surface area of his entire back. If he hadn't, he almost certainly would have broken a number of bones. As it was, he just had the opportunity to wonder if that could really have hurt any worse. He honestly wasn't sure.

Luckily, he had prevented the knife from striking at his sister again by the genius move of keeping it buried in his shoulder, and it bit deeper when he hit the wall. The enemy never expected that kind of long-term strategic thinking. Ha!

And also, ow.

"Ow" turned into an embarrassingly high-pitched scream when he reached back and yanked the blade free. It probably wasn't the brightest thing he could have done, first because he could very well have done more damage to himself taking the knife out than the Demon had done to him sticking it in. Still, the idea of walking around a battlefield with a weapon sticking out of his back like a handle or an invitation just didn't sit right.

The second reason he should have left the bloody thing alone was because the pain nearly made him pass out, and it did make him vomit. He just leaned over to the side, opened his mouth, and gawked.

As he waited for the pain-induced stars to stop floating before his eyes, Drum could hear the sounds of battle raging anew all around him. Steel clanged against steel and rock, energy sizzled, and voices shouted to be heard above the din. The sound that mattered to him the most, however, was that of a Demon howling its rage as its prey escaped.

He blinked his eyes clear just in time to see Ash snatch Maeve up in her raptorlike talons, lifting her from the altar and swooping over the heads of the *nocturnis* to deposit her well away from the fighting. Relief almost brought him to his knees. If it had, he never would have gotten up.

Nazgahchuhl turned on him, eyes glittering with the heat of rage, and raised a hand. A bolt of lightning as black as peat sparked through the air toward him, casting shadow around it the way actual lightning illuminated the surrounding area. Drum sprang to the side, avoiding the hit, but catching the flak from a spray of rock that burst from the wall of the cave and spread out like shrapnel from a pipe bomb. He felt shards slice through his skin and lifted a hand to wipe the sweat from his eyes. His fingers came away red. Blood.

The Demon focused on him, forked tongue flicking out to scent the air. He knew he was hurt, knew he bled from a whole bunch of places at this point, and the monster with the human face was beginning to look at him in the same way a ten-foot boa constrictor looked at a juicy rabbit. Flattered, he was not.

Unfortunately, what he was, was cornered.

Nazgahchuhl gave a serpentine smile and began to stalk forward, obviously taking its time. Since Drum had nowhere to go the only reason for such behavior was to provoke fear. It wanted him to be terrified, for reasons Drum couldn't quite grasp. He'd read somewhere that when a prey animal died in fear, the adrenaline pumping through its blood gave the meat a bitter flavor. Humans preferred to avoid it, but evil snake-Demons might well consider it a delicacy. No accounting for taste, was there? Though he'd much prefer not to be on the menu.

He racked his brain for a way to escape. He didn't need to take the Corruptor in a fight, he just needed to survive long enough for the Guardians to break through the surrounding *nocturnis* and ride to his rescue. Or fly to his rescue. He didn't plan to quibble over details.

Everyone had warned him not to bother using magic against one of the Seven. It would be useless, they assured him, and likely only focus the Evil One's attention in his direction. Given his present circumstances, it looked like Drum no longer had anything to lose.

Still, he wasn't stupid, and his goal was not to piss off something that already planned to rip out his heart and bathe in his blood, so he refrained from attacking the monster directly. Instead, he cupped his free hand in front of him, calling up a ball of pure, white-gold light, and threw it straight up into the air between them with a little twist Kylie had showed him—a time delay. A single second ticked by, not enough time to hit the Demon with something more powerful, and not enough time for his opponent to guess his intention, but just enough for Drum to turn his back and close his eyes.

The sphere of light bobbed in the air for a moment, then detonated like a pyrotechnic device, doing nothing but making a loud noise and exploding in a burst of bright light. Blinding light. Drum had protected himself from the blast, but the Demon failed to react in time, and it shrieked with disoriented hatred.

Not waiting around for a more up-close-and-personal reaction from the fiend, he sprinted away from the altar area and toward his sister. On the way, the glare from his trick cast a revealing light on the end of the cave that had previously been shrouded in darkness. The end closest to Billy Evers's property. The end that appeared to lead to a narrow passageway cut through the surrounding rock and soil.

No wonder the *nocturnis* had left this area in shadow. They had sealed off the main entrance and exit to these caverns, but another possible escape path lurked here at the far end of the cave. And now the good guys knew about it.

Instantly, Drum made his move. Pouring on a burst of speed, he raced to Maeve's side and yanked his sister unceremoniously to her feet. "Come on!" he urged in a low, insistent tone. "Through here. Go! The tunnel has to lead somewhere, or the fuckers wouldn't have tried to hide it. Get out if you can. If you run into something unexpected, turn around and get your arse back here double-quick. Understand?"

"Ye-yes," Maeve stuttered, shivering from what was likely shock. It was warm down here next to the hellmouth, after all.

Drum didn't hesitate. He shoved his sister into the darkness and sped back into the center of the cavern, hoping no one had noticed his detour.

Still clutching the dagger, he cast his gaze around the room and felt a new surge of adrenaline. One *nocturni* lay dead on the floor a few feet away from his head, and another crouched behind a couple of small boulders. He seemed cornered by Kylie's relentless blasts of magic, which somehow managed to make it out through her second, smaller firewall while nothing the sorcerer threw at her could penetrate the shield.

Wynn stood with her feet spread and her arms outstretched, maintaining the power to a huge floating bubble a few feet off the ground. Inside, behind a shimmering layer of magic, two more *nocturnis* appeared to rail against her, though the bubble seemed to muffle the sound quite effectively. It took a second for Drum to notice that instead of facing her palms toward the bubble (she had taught him that palms most easily allowed the outward flow of energy, followed by fingertips for spells with narrower focus), she directed energy out of the backs of her knuckles while she held her middle fingers extended toward the trapped pair.

He would have laughed if he weren't still fearing for his life.

Two *nocturnis* remained, clearly the most experienced of this cell of the sect. He came to that conclusion after seeing the way they managed to dance out of the way of Dag's and Knox's flashing weapons, even as they continued hurling magic. They didn't target the Guardians themselves, but the environment around them, attempting to bring rocks down on their heads, or to soften the ground beneath them, or to trip them with invisible wires strung between stones.

In their hooded black robes, the quick-moving cultists looked like dark dervishes, one half of an elaborately choreographed ballet with the Guardians as their partners. Following one spinning leap that Knox met in midair, catching the cultist's quickly drawn knife against the central staff of his weapon, Drum caught another movement out of the corner of his eye.

Ash had once again charged to his rescue, attacking the Demon while Drum attempted to send his sister to safety. She had driven the creature away from his altar and back toward the narrow end of the cave, the same direction in which Maeve had fled. And if that weren't bad enough, he could see that she had taken a beating at the hands of Nazgahchuhl. Her tough, stony hide had been sliced through with dozens of tiny cuts, and Drum watched in horror as more appeared with a flick of the Demon's fingers.

The fiend held no weapon and never touched Ash with tooth or claw, but apparently the immunity a Guardian possessed to the black magic of *nocturni* sorcerers did not extend to the power inherent within one of the Seven. Another flick, and another thin line appeared on Ash's gray skin, blood welling to the surface, as red and dark as Drum's own.

She didn't react, not with a flinch, not with a sound. Ash simply darted forward and completed the swing of her axe, bringing the blade in line with the Demon's throat. Nazgahchuhl raised a hand and caught the blow on its forearm, an act that would have shattered the bones of a human, but that didn't even make the monster hesitate. It brought its free arm up and grasped Ash around the throat, lifting and squeezing until the Guardian began to struggle violently.

"You think you can defeat me, Guardian," the creature hissed, its lips drawing back and parting to reveal long, slender fangs that dropped from the roof of its mouth like a viper's. Above its forked tongue, Drum could see the extended glottal opening of a snake, and the entire picture became so unnaturally *wrong* that he felt bile climb into his throat. "You think you and your pathetic group of friends and Wardens can defeat *me,* let alone stand against our united Darkness? Foolish creature. I thought your sex to be a sign of your evolution over your useless brothers, but I see now I need not have worried. You are even weaker than the rest of them. I shall enjoy watching you die."

The Demon squeezed harder until Drum could see its fingers digging grooves into the flesh of Ash's throat. She fought hard to get away, her feet lifting to rake her rear talons across the adversary's abdomen, but Nazgahchuhl appeared not to even notice. He just continued to apply pressure until he got what he wanted.

Ash didn't die. She still continued her violent struggles, but the Demon stopped noticing, because Maeve reappeared behind him at the opening of the black tunnel, still shivering and now even dirtier than before.

" 'Tis a dead end," she rasped out, her hoarse voice nearly rendered inaudible by the chattering of her teeth. They needed to get her somewhere safe and warm before her shock became life threatening. "Michael, what do we do?"

Nazgahchuhl released Ash, who dropped choking and gasping to the floor. "Why, child," the Demon purred, fixing its unblinking stare on the bleeding, trembling young woman. "You die, of course."

The Demon's pride and desire to have the last word gave Drum the opening he needed. Before it could step forward and close the distance between it and Maeve, he lunged, fist clutched around the hilt of a sacrificial dagger still stained with his own blood. Just as the fiend had done to him, Drum plunged the blade into the creature's back, but unlike the monster, he hadn't originally aimed at something else. He hit his mark.

The knife plunged into the human flesh encasing the

Demonic force and pierced the heart of the man who had once been Richard Foye-Carver. The creature threw its head back and shrieked, a high-pitched, ear-piercing noise that contained notes of agony, rage, and triumph. It was the triumph that set Drum to cursing.

Before his lips could form around anything appropriately obscene, there was a loud clapping sound and a giant release of pressure in the air, almost like a miniature sonic boom. At once, a bright light flashed and the torch-framed door of the hellmouth released a shock wave of light and sound that made Drum's earlier spell look like a tenpenny firecracker. His heart lurched and for a moment, he thought the gate had been thrown open.

This was it, a very detached voice inside his head noted while his eyes tried to readjust to the dimness of the chamber compared to the light that had briefly exploded from the hellmouth. He, his sister, his new friends, and the woman he loved were all about to die, and it looked a lot like he had somehow been the one to cause it all.

Unintentionally, of course, but it was probably a good thing that the road to hell stood so close by. He wouldn't have to go far to start his journey.

Then the glare of the light faded and Drum realized two things: no one appeared dead, and the space between the torches still shimmered faintly with no open doorway to the fiery pit marring the view of the cave wall beyond. The hellmouth remained closed.

That was the good news. The second realization conveyed the bad news. The body containing Nazgahchuhl might have died, but the Demon itself looked very much alive as it peeled away the shell of the Hierophant's corpse and assumed its true physical form.

Maeve screamed when she saw it, and frankly, Drum couldn't blame her. What he could do was lurch forward to grab her hand and yank her back into the opening of the dead-end tunnel while their friends scrambled to get to their sides and defend them against the most horrible nightmare vision he had ever set eyes on.

The Corruptor grew out of the *nocturni*'s corpse like a toxic vine from a pile of dung. It rose and rose, expanding as if it would fill all the space in the cave before it was done. It didn't, of course, but it easily loomed twelve feet high, a giant inhuman beast that wore the shape of a hooded cobra tapering into a squat, truncated body with eight pairs of arms and no legs at all. Its scaly hide was the color of blood mixed with water, just a few shades lighter than its reptilian eyes. It radiated an aura of terror and disease like heat from desert sands that clouded the mind, and Drum had to struggle to push it away before it brought him to his knees in a wave of crushing despair.

That was the Demon's influence, he realized, and he dug deep for the strength to shrug it off. He might have done it a fair sight easier if he weren't already wrung out with exhaustion and struggling to stay vertical long enough to save his sister's life. It was all in the details.

"By the pure, blessed Light," he heard Knox breathe, the horror in his voice unmistakable, "it is risen. The Corruptor walks among us."

"Fools." A new voice rose over the threatening hiss of the snake Demon who loomed before them. The entire group watched as a robed figure stepped forward, one of the remaining *nocturnis* that Dag and Knox had driven back near the altar and then abandoned as they realized Nazgahchuhl was ascending from the Hierophant's corpse.

"Stupid mortal fools." The cultist laughed and drew back his hood to reveal a human man with stunningly ordinary brown hair, brown eyes, and lightly bronzed skin. "We do not need to defeat you to claim this world for our own. We need only stand back while you defeat yourselves."

Kylie staggered against her mate's side, nearly planting face-first into the rocky ground. "Demon. He's a demon."

"Well." The man's face twisted into a smile of cruel madness. "Maybe not all of you are quite as stupid as you look. What is your name, little girl? Would you like to know mine? I could tell you. I could tell you so many, many things."

And in that moment, Drum realized the true consequences of his actions. In attempting to kill the Demon threatening his sister, he had unknowingly completed the sacrifice for which she had been taken. He had killed a human, or what little remained of one, and while the power generated had not been enough to open the hellmouth permanently and weaken the gate to the next Demon's prison, it had done those things for the space of a clap of thunder, and that had been enough for something to come through. It had also set Nazgahchuhl free of its mortal shell, and now the Corruptor had regained its full strength and stared down at them like those rabbits it intended to gobble up for dinner.

Dear Merciful Mother of God, what had he done?

"Dhuhlzek," Dag growled, spitting the name out like something foul. Which, of course, it was. "Think you the Guardians of the Light will be defeated by the likes of you? You barely had the strength to pass through the gate. I can see the weakness of the hold you have over your human slave. Why not surrender now and return to your prison before we *put* you there."

"Insolent puppy!" The Demon within the sorcerer raised its hand and unleashed a bolt of black energy not at Dag, but at the center of the gathered Wardens and Guardians. Ash's axe flashed up, deflecting the stream so that it missed the good guys and instead sliced across the snake-Demon's exposed flank.

Immediately, Drum felt hands tugging at his back.

"Come on!" Maeve shouted, waving her arms frantically. "Everyone into the tunnel!"

Drum let his sister drag him into the dark passage, utterly confused. No one else seemed to have heard her report on what she had learned about it on her first trip through. They crowded in after him, following the young woman's instructions. "But Mae, you said it was a dead end. We'll be trapped."

"Trust me, Michael. I can see this working." Maeve turned and fixed her blue eyes on the other Wardens. "Kylie, and you, sorry, other Warden lady. Blow the cavern. Bring down as much rock as you can! Hurry!"

The two Americans exchanged glances, then turned, and urged their Guardians deeper into the passage, and faced the entrance with grim expressions.

"I really hope this chick knows what she's doing," Wynn shouted as the Demons in the cavern howled with frustrated fury.

"What have we got to lose?" Kylie yelled back. "You want to go back out there?"

"Good point!"

Visibly straightening their shoulders, the two women stood side by side as they released a concussive blast aimed at the cavern ceiling. The earth gave a shudder like the ones the *nocturnis* had created to tear the caverns open, but this one pulled the roof down on top of it. An avalanche of soil and stone rained down into the cave just outside the passage entry, sealing it off into a lightless space that felt distressingly like a tomb.

Drum tried to fight back the instinctive human fear of dark, enclosed spaces, but he had to admit he wasn't certain he would have won if one of the other Wardens hadn't conjured a small ball of light to brighten the narrow area.

"Oh, good." Maeve sighed just before she collapsed into

a heap on top of Drum's boots. He immediately bent to scoop her up and cradle her against his chest.

"Thank you, Drum." She spoke again, her voice thick with fatigue. "Now if you don't mind, lead the way to the end of the tunnel. I think I could use a drink."

Chapter Twenty-seven

Fifteen minutes later, Drum understood exactly what his sister had meant by the last word she spoke before passing out in his arms. Wynn had to cast one last spell before it became clear, but once the dead end of the tunnel exploded in another burst of magical force, it all became apparent.

It turned out that he had been right when he estimated that the passage in the corner of the cave ran in the direction of Fionn mac Cumhaill's field. In fact, it ended right below the abandoned one-room cottage nestled in the corner of that very paddock, the one Fionn's owner, Billy Evers, had always claimed was cared for by the Little Folk. Billy had been counting on his wild stories and his bad-tempered bull to keep anyone from discovering that beneath the cottage was a secret basement concealing his very well hidden and very illegal *poitín* distilling operation.

Given its illicit nature, Drum didn't feel all that guilty about blowing a hole in the basement wall, or about helping himself and the rest of their battered company to a dram. Or seven.

Knox made sure they didn't linger. After taking the unconscious Maeve away from her wounded brother, the eldest of the three Guardians—in terms of how long they had each been awake on this current mission—led the way up through the cottage's trapdoor and out into the gray mist of predawn Ireland.

At which point, they came face-to-face with the great hero himself.

Drum, one arm draped over Ash's shoulder the only thing keeping him upright, closed his eyes on a groan. "Don't move. Not a one of you. That beast is as vicious as he is ugly. Try to run for it, and you'll get his horns in your backside followed by an ugly trampling death. Just let me think for a minute."

"About what?" Wynn asked, sounding tired but inexplicably cheery.

"About how to get ourselves out of this mess," Drum said. "I told you that—"

He opened his eyes in time to be struck dumb. The American witch stood in front of the shaggy, infamous bull, scratching the base of his horns like he was some kind of pussycat. And damn Drum if the beast didn't look ready to purr like one. He blinked at Wynn with adoration in his dark bovine eyes, his jaw working as he calmly chewed his cud. Everyone else just stood around looking exhausted. And a little bit baffled.

Drum turned his gaze on the Warden and tried to close his mouth before a fly rushed in.

"What?" she asked, shrugging self-consciously. "Animals like me."

And thank Saint Paddy himself for that. It made the rest of their escape infinitely less dangerous, though Drum kept looking over his shoulder, expecting to see an army of Demons chasing after them. In the case of the Seven, he could now swear to a jury that two felt like more than enough to call an army.

"What is it?" Ash asked him, as she helped him over the fence and out of Fionn's pasture. As soon as they were clear, Wynn gave the animal a last friendly pat and scampered after them. The bull stared after her looking almost forlorn.

Drum shook his head. "I feel like we should still be running. What if those things come after us?"

He hooked his arm over her shoulder again and leaned heavily on her strength. His supposed masculine pride should have been nagging at him to stand up straight and look tough in front of his woman, but he was too sore and too injured to bother. Besides, when he'd first resisted her help down in the basement of the cottage, she'd punched him lightly in the stomach. He'd almost hurled again. Pride be damned.

Ash helped him across the uneven ground, but they still managed to fall behind the others on the trip back to his mother's barn. "No. Dag was right that Dhuhlzek lacks the strength to pursue us. It barely made it through the hellmouth on the energy provided by the Hierophant's death. Nazgahchuhl had occupied that shell too long for much that was human to remain."

"Yeah, well, that one certainly looked strong enough to chase after us."

"Not from beneath several tons of fallen stone." Ash grunted when he tripped in a furrow and braced herself against his side to steady him. "Your sister's plan was clever. She found us a route of escape and trapped the Demons at the same time. We all owe her a debt. The cave-in would have crushed Nazgahchuhl's form. It could not kill him, but it would cause enough physical damage to force him to abandon that shape until he can gather more energy to re-form. It buys us time to decide on our next move."

Drum grimaced. "Yes, our next move against five

bloody Demons now, instead of Seven. And it's my fault the fifth one got loose."

"What nonsense is that?" Ash demanded, stopping in the middle of the field behind the converted barn where there were beds and food and a shower. He nearly groaned at the pain of denial. "Why do you speak so, Michael Drummond?"

Drum forced his mind and his gaze back on his Guardian. "You know exactly why I said it, Ash. If I hadn't taken that knife to the Hierophant, there would have been no sacrifice. The hellmouth wouldn't have blinked open, even for a second. Dhuhlzek wouldn't have come through onto our plane, and Nazgahchuhl would not have gained the strength to shed his human host and take his natural form. This is all my fault."

She dropped the hand that held his in place across her shoulder and used it to smack him, right in the middle of his forehead. It stung. A lot.

"Ow! What the bloody hell was that for?"

"For your stupidity," she spat, glaring at him. "Do you also wish to take credit for the existence of the Darkness? For the destruction of the Guardian I replaced? For humanity's greed and lust for power that allows them to be corrupted by the Order?"

"It's not the same thing. I'm only trying to take responsibility for my own actions. I'm the one who—"

"Who saved his sister's life! Who prevented the Demon from making a sacrifice a hundred times more powerful than the death of its mortal shell. Had your sister died tonight instead of the Hierophant, or what remained of him, the hellmouth would even now be pouring forth wave after wave of servants to the Darkness. The whole countryside would be overrun with creatures out of humanity's darkest nightmares. Your neighbors would be dying, and there would be little we few could do to stop it. Dhuhlzek would have returned with ten times the power it did, would be able to command those legions of evil and turn them into an army that would take over this entire island within days. Hear me, Michael Stephen Drummond, when I tell you that your actions tonight have prevented disaster!"

She continued to glare at him for a long time after she finished her speech. Drum said nothing. He couldn't; he was too busy being stunned. He had never stopped to consider what alternative he'd had or hadn't had back there in the cavern. He had been operating on pure instinct, and yet somehow he had still managed to do the right thing.

Maybe he shouldn't tell anyone it had been an accident, though. They might not find that news reassuring.

Making a low, grumbling sound of frustration, Ash took his arm and slung it back over her shoulder before turning and dragging him back into motion. She stomped several yards closer to the barn while he struggled to keep up and to figure out how he could respond to her tirade without making her angry all over again.

"Ash, I—"

"Shut up," she snarled at him. "Sometimes, Michael Drummond, we are both better off when you simply do not speak."

Well, he couldn't really argue with that.

Drum held his tongue for the rest of the slow and painful trip back to the barn. By the time Ash half carried him through the door, Dag and Kylie lay sprawled side by side across one of the cots, with Maeve curled up under a huge mound of blankets on the other. Meanwhile, Knox helped a clearly exhausted Wynn reset the circle of candles and the mirror they had used for the portal spell that had brought them here.

"Wynn, you're killing me here," Kylie groaned without raising her head. "I haven't got the energy to cast aspersions, let alone cast another spell, and if you try to tell me you do, I'll smack your face and call you a liar. I'm begging you, just get a couple of hours of sleep and then we can send you home faster than you can think."

"Don't worry about it, Koyote," Wynn said, stifling a yawn. "You don't have to get up. Uncle Griffin is doing the heavy lifting on this one. I deliberately had you build this end of the portal with a whole bunch of redundancy. I don't have to do much more than snap my fingers and let Grif pull us back home. It's all good."

Drum frowned at the pair lighting candles in a circle. "You're leaving already? But—I haven't even gotten a chance to thank you, and I'm too fucking knackered to think of how now. You have to stay at least until I can get my brain working right again."

Knox straightened and looked at him, the corner of his mouth tightening in something that might have been a smile on a more expressive face. "No thanks are necessary, Warden. In fact, if any are owed, it is ours to you. Your actions prevented a great evil tonight. You should take pride in having done your duty with honor."

Wynn did smile, though it held more than a hint of sleepiness. "He's right, Drum. You did good." She stepped out of the incomplete circle to hug him, then repeated the gesture with Ash, who seemed surprised, then returned it fiercely. "I'm glad we found the two of you. Or, I suppose it's more accurate to say I'm glad you two found us. I'm very much afraid we're going to need your help again before too long."

Knox nodded a grim agreement.

His mate stepped back to his side and bent to light the final candle. When she rose, she sent Drum a stern frown. "In the meantime, get thee to a doctor, mister. You need stitches in that arm, not to mention what needs to be done to treat the stab wound. Now, shoo!"

Then the figures turned to face the mirror and linked hands. Wynn muttered a few words, raised her hand, and a shimmering curtain of light seemed to appear in the air in front of them. It parted to let them step through, then fell shut behind them and winked out of existence, leaving nothing but an empty circle of flickering candlelight.

Kylie heaved a loud sigh from her position on the bed. "Great, now someone has to blow out those candles before we burn this place down, too. Not it."

"Not it," Dag echoed quickly.

Ash shot them a glare, but she quickly settled Drum into a folding canvas chair and took care of the tiny flames. When she returned to his side, she reached for his hands as if to tug him to his feet. "Come. You heard Wynn. We must bring you to a doctor and have your wounds tended to. You will tell me where to go, and I will drive your car. I admit I have been very curious about the operation of such a large machine."

Drum let Ash grasp his hands, but instead of rising, he used the grip to pull her down into his lap. He almost regretted it when his battered body screamed at him, but the pain faded quickly (after all, his legs had sustained the least injuries of just about anywhere on his frame), allowing the feel of strong, supple woman to register with his fractious nerves.

Ah, that was better.

He wrapped his uninjured arm around her and urged her closer, rolling his eyes when a long, loud, and obviously fake snore rose from the camp bed a few yards away. The giggle Kylie added didn't do much for the mood he wanted to create here, either.

Ash didn't seem to notice, though. She twisted her upper body to face him, taking obvious care not to jostle any of his visible injuries. "Did you not hear me, Drum? You must visit a doctor. Wynn said it is important."

"I heard you, *mo chaomhnóir.*" He sighed, squeezing her hip. "I heard Wynn when she said the same thing, and I'm not arguing the necessity, just the timing. I think we can wait a few minutes while we settle something more important."

"More important than your health?" she demanded, her eyes narrowing. "What about your sister, then? What about her health? She had many wounds, as well. Did you not wish for her to be examined by a physician?"

He narrowed his eyes. "Nice try, but that trick won't work on me. Maeve is safe and warm now, and none of her cuts or scrapes were very serious. As soon as we get a few things straight, I'll pick up the phone and call Dr. O'Fallon. He's retired, but he lives just on the other side of the village and he doesn't mind coming out now and then for emergencies."

"Very well." Ash crossed her arms over her chest and raised her stubborn chin. "What do you believe needs to be straightened and settled more importantly than your health?"

"You."

She met his revelation with stunned silence. Dag and Kylie added the sound effects. Drum just tried to tune them out.

Not Ash, the others.

"Me?" Her jaw fell open in an expression of mortal offense. "What precisely do you believe is wrong with me, human?"

He had to wrestle back his grin like an invading Fomorian. "Absolutely nothing."

"What?"

The grin won. She was adorable when she was confused.

"Aw, he's so sweet! I just want to pinch his cheeks," Kylie whispered loudly enough to be heard in Dublin.

"You'd better mean the ones of his face," Dag rumbled in response.

Drum gritted his teeth and tried to refocus. "I mean just what I said, Ash of the Guardians of the Light. There's nothing wrong with you. In fact, I think you're perfect. Fucking brilliant. Except for one, tiny, miniscule, microscopic little thing."

She just blinked at him.

"You've never told me you love me."

She sputtered. "I have so! The other night, in your sister's husband's half-demolished barn! I told you then!"

Kylie burst into giggles, then slapped her hand over her mouth to muffle them. Dag chuckled and didn't even try to disguise the sound.

Drum ignored them. "Did you? Hm. Does it count when you say it—" He broke off to glare at the pair on the nearby cot, daring them to interrupt. "Er, when you say it in the heat of the moment like that?"

More giggles. Another chuckle poorly disguised behind a cough.

"That's the only time you said it, either!" Ash snapped, thumping her fist against his chest with no force whatsoever. It still stung.

Drum winced and rubbed the spot with his fingertips. "Not true. I'm saying it right now. I love you. I love you, Ash. You're my heart, *mo chaomhnóir.*"

Ash, warrior woman, Valkyrie, the strongest woman, the strongest *person* he'd ever met, burst into tears.

Kylie repeated the Gaelic phrase, butchering it so badly that Drum winced, even as he struggled to ignore her and comfort the woman in his arms. "What does that mean?"

"The way you said it?" Dag asked dryly. "Nothing. When he said it, it meant 'my guardian.'"

"Aw, that's adorable. So why is she crying?"

"You stupid human!" Ash cried out, lifting her head

from Drum's chest to glare at the American through a veil of tears. "I am crying because I am forced to stand apart from my brethren. Our legends tell the story of our kind finding the mates of their hearts, the partners designed for them by the hand of fate, and yet I am left with nothing."

Kylie sat up on the camp bed to frown at the weeping Guardian. "I know, *bubbeleh*. The seven women of power who freed the Guardians from their duty to return to stone and set them free to live as mortals, while new Guardians were summoned to take their places. I thought that story was supposed to make you happy."

"Perhaps it would if I cared anything for a *woman* of power, you fool." Ash swiped a hand across her cheek, brushing away tears that were quickly replaced. "But perhaps you failed to notice that a female Guardian fits nowhere into that story of love and freedom."

Oh.

The light dawned for Drum in a quiet rush, explaining his mate's reticence, her passion, and her tears all in one neat package. No wonder he had felt she tried to hold herself back from him. She had believed their relationship doomed, that when the Seven were defeated and she no longer needed to fight to save humanity from the threat, she would be forced back into her statue form and trapped in magical sleep. Hell, the idea would have tied him into knots, too.

He opened his mouth to soothe her, but Dag beat him to it.

"Silly female," the other Guardian rumbled, his tone softer than Drum had heard it when speaking to anyone but his mate. "You know the story and yet you remain ignorant of its meaning."

Ash scowled. "Call me silly again, brother, I will test the silliness of my axe against your skull."

Dag just grinned. "I merely speak as I find, sister. Tell

me, do you believe it benefits the Light to divide from each other those whom love has brought together?"

"What do you mean?"

"He means," Kylie said softly, "that love is the greatest weapon the Light has against the Darkness. Love is a source of happiness, of joy, of contentment. It's a source of *life,* because people who love each other build lives together. They build families together. The Light doesn't care who's male and who's female and which one carries the sword in the family. The Light just wants us to love."

Drum listened to the little Warden and agreed with every single word she said. How could he not? He might be a Catholic, and the Church may have gotten a hell of a lot of things wrong over the years, but the one thing he had always figured they had right was when they said God is Love. Whether you called it God or the Light, he didn't think the details really mattered.

In his arms, Ash shifted, her head bowing. He tried to peer under her concealing fringe to read the expression on her face. He didn't have to try for long. After a couple of deep, shuddering breaths, she looked up again, and the smile on her face could have lit up hell single-handed.

"By the Light," she whispered, lifting her hand to cup Drum's cheek and turning that smile on him. "By the Light, I love you, Michael Drummond. And I will stay by your side until the stars themselves go dark."

Hell be damned, Drum thought, because that smile lit up his soul.

"I'll love you longer," he growled, and seized her mouth with all the passion in his heart. She returned it tenfold.

Life, suddenly, felt perfect.

A muffled thump in the background didn't even make them blink as Kylie collapsed onto the air mattress.

"Oy, finally! Now can we all get a little *farkakte* sleep?"